"Who appointed you as my psychologist?"

Krista demanded.

"It doesn't take much training to figure out what you're doing." Jess leaned forward until they were only inches apart. "You failed your sister, or at least you think you did. You feel responsible for her, probably always have, from what you've told me. So now you're putting yourself in danger because you think you put *her* in danger. Well, that's not going to bring Rosie back."

"Cheap analysis!"

"How's it going to be if Rosie goes back to Maryland looking for you and you're in a morgue in Louisiana?"

"Cut it out!"

"Not until you realize the truth. Guilt's not going to bring your sister back. Punishing yourself isn't, either. Good sense might."

"And you, of course, are going to supply the good sense?"

He leaned back, satisfied. "Yeah."

Dear Reader,

This month we're bringing you an absolutely stellar lineup of books. In fact, I hardly know where to begin. First up is *Runaway*, by Emilie Richards. She delivers exactly the kind of knockout emotional punch she's come to be known for. This is the first of two novels about sisters separated by deception and distance, and it's a book with a very different sort of subject: teen runaways, the dangers they face and the lengths they sometimes have to go in order to survive. Next month's *The Way Back Home* completes the circle. I truly believe these two books will live in your memory for a long, long time.

Theresa Weir has written for Silhouette Romance until now, and has also tried her hand at mainstream romance adventure. In *Iguana Bay* she makes her debut appearance in Silhouette Intimate Moments, and what a stunner this book is! The hero is anything but ordinary, as you'll discover the minute you meet him, and his meeting with the heroine is no less noteworthy. And lest you think that's all we have in store, the month is rounded out by two veterans of the bestseller lists and the award rosters: Heather Graham Pozzessere and Marilyn Pappano.

Later in the year, the excitement will continue with new books from favorites such as Linda Howard, Kathleen Korbel and Linda Shaw, to name only a few. The moments are never dull at Silhouette Intimate Moments, so join us for all of them.

Yours,

Leslie J. Wainger
Senior Editor and Editorial Coordinator

Runaway
EMILIE RICHARDS

Silhouette Intimate Moments
Published by Silhouette Books New York
America's Publisher of Contemporary Romance

SILHOUETTE BOOKS
300 East 42nd St., New York, N.Y. 10017

ISBN: 0-373-07337-2

First Silhouette Books printing June 1990

EMILIE RICHARDS

believes that opposites attract, and her marriage is vivid proof. "When we met," the author says, "the *only* thing my husband and I could agree on was that we were very much in love. Fortunately, we haven't changed our minds about that in all the years we've been together."

The couple lives in Ohio with their four children, who span from toddler to teenager. Emilie has put her master's degree in family development to good use—raising her own brood, working for Head Start, counseling in a mental health clinic and serving in VISTA.

Though her first book was written in snatches with an infant on her lap, Emilie now writes five hours a day and "rejoices in the opportunity to create, to grow and to have such a good time."

In memory of Amy Mihaljeuic

Chapter 1

The dimly lit French Quarter bar smelled like mildew, cheap perfume and unwashed bodies. One anemic air conditioner wheezed from a window looking out on a brick wall, but the air was still heavily dewed with heat and humidity. A box radio screeched heavy metal profanity from a shelf behind the bartender, its decibel level guaranteeing only the most perfunctory conversation. Most of the bar's patrons didn't notice the noise. No one except Jess Cantrell was at Tallulah's to converse.

At the moment Jess wasn't sure whether that was his goal, either. Without wasting words he wanted to drag the teenager sitting across from him to a shower, a doctor and a convent, in that order. He wanted to lock her up until she was twenty-one with a regiment of social workers and bodyguards and, best of all, two forgiving parents who could help her find the innocence and hope she had lost sometime in her fourteen or fifteen years.

Fourteen or fifteen years. He'd had nothing stronger than club soda to drink all night, but his stomach turned inside out. He felt sick and dispirited, far from the hard-bitten investigative reporter that his reading public believed him to be. He was a man who had never fathered a child, but the child sitting across from him could be his. She could be anyone's beloved daughter. Right now, however, she wanted to be someone's lover. For money.

"It's what's inside your head that interests me, not what you can do with your body," he said, gently, wearily, in answer to a suggestion she had just made. "It's who you are, and why, that I care about."

The girl pondered his words and cracked a wad of bubble gum. It never ceased to amaze Jess that the kids he'd met on the streets could look so deceptively young as they hustled him. He knew the truth, though. They were older than he would ever be. Teenage octogenarians.

"Wanda told me you don't like girls." Bubble gum popped in emphasis. "I know this boy—"

Jess cut her off before she could finish. "I don't like boys, either, Sally. I don't like children in my bed."

"I'm not a child. I'm eighteen."

"In about three years." Jess sighed. There was an excellent chance that he was losing his objectivity. There was an excellent chance he hadn't had any when he started this project. "Look, I like *you*, though. But just for talking."

"I don't get paid for talking."

"I know. Are you going to stay and talk to me anyway? Or will you get in trouble?"

"I made my nut tonight already. Convention's in town."

Sally's "nut" was the amount she had to bring back to her pimp or risk getting beaten that night. The amount varied from girl to girl, pimp to pimp. In Sally's case Jess made an educated guess that it was probably several hundred dollars. If he pictured her without her heavy, poorly applied makeup and tawdry clothes, she was pretty. She had strawberry-blond hair and wide green eyes that had seen it all. He made note of the small mole on the side of her snub nose. He wasn't there to find runaways, but he'd seen so many missing children flyers since he'd begun his research. Maybe Sally's parents were looking for her. Maybe he could spark a reunion.

He knew that the odds had been infinitely higher that Stanley would find Livingstone in the midst of the African jungle.

"Then you'll stay and talk?" he asked, steeling himself to hear yet one more horror story.

"Got nuthin' to say." Sally stood. "Thanks for the Coke, but next time make it a beer."

Jess didn't flinch. Sally, like most of the runaways on U.S. city streets, just wanted something to deaden the aches of loneliness and despair. She hadn't yet learned that nothing could. He stood, out of long habit. A gentleman always stood when a lady did. Despite Sally's clothes and profession, in Jess's mind she was still a young lady. "If you ever change your mind, I'm here almost every night."

For just a moment she seemed to hesitate. Then she laughed and cracked her gum one final time before she turned and slowly sauntered out the door to be swallowed by the night.

Something—Jess's stomach, his soul, his whole damned being—turned inside out again, propelled by anger and a sense of futility that was growing daily. Only conviction that the world had to know what was happening on the streets of its cities made him sit down again instead of seeking the relative normalcy of his hotel room.

"She'll come back. Sally's been out on the streets awhile. She don't trust no one."

Jess turned at the sound of the woman's voice. "I'm not sure I'm ready to hear what she has to say, anyhow." He sat down as the woman, Wanda, flopped into the chair Sally had just vacated.

"Got enough dirt?" Wanda asked.

"Enough sadness?" he corrected. "There's enough sadness here to make the Mona Lisa weep."

He watched Wanda examine him. She was in her mid-forties, but she looked twenty years older. She'd told him once that her hair had been gray for a decade. He guessed the lines around her eyes were a road map leading back to the days when she, like Sally, had cruised bars for a likely john.

"There's sadness, all right," she said, after seconds had stretched into minutes, "but maybe your book can make it go away a little, at least for a kid or two."

"I hope."

Wanda stood. She no longer cruised bars to feed herself. She worked behind the counter of a local T-shirt shop that specialized in raunchy New Orleans souvenirs. She liked to joke that her customers were pretty much the same for either job, and that their minds were definitely in the same place, even if other parts of their anatomies weren't. "I've gotta get back. Maybe someone else'll talk to you tonight." She surveyed the room, as if looking for possibilities. "You ever talk to Crystal?"

Jess followed Wanda's gaze to the shapely blonde standing in the doorway. Light from a street lamp turned her long, pale hair into a bright halo—which was a strange image, Jess thought, considering what Crystal did for a living. She was tall—although at least three inches were due to the heels on her boots—and curiously regal.

Jess had seen her before, and every time he had, something had nagged at him. "I tried to talk to her once," he told Wanda, "but she brushed me off."

"There's a story there."

"There's a story everywhere. Is hers that much different?"

"I don't know. She don't talk much. But the other girls like her."

Jess knew that was unusual. The other "girls" rarely liked anyone who represented the kind of competition that Crystal did. Particularly if they had a pimp to account to.

"Is she a runaway?" he asked. Wanda would know Crystal's status if anyone did. Wanda kept her finger on the pulse of the French Quarter. The streets were her territory, and in an odd way, the girls were her kids. She counseled them, fed them when she could, and hid them from the law or the pimps, whichever was menacing them at the time. Wanda's apartment was as close to a safe house as some of the kids would ever see. Jess didn't approve of Wanda's interference with the law, but he approved of the big, bleeding heart that inspired it. Wanda cared. And on the streets, those who admitted they cared were candidates for sainthood—or the state mental hospital.

Wanda waved at Crystal and beckoned her to the table, talking as they waited. "Crystal says she ran away a couple of years ago. Says she's eighteen now. What do you think?"

Jess hadn't thought much about Crystal's age. On the one occasion he'd been close enough to talk to her, he'd spent the time wondering how anyone with such purity of form and feature had ended up on the streets.

Now, as she slowly crossed the room, he wondered the same thing again. She was a Scandinavian beauty, and he suspected that when she'd run away, it had been from a farm or small town in the Dakotas or Minnesota. In the course of his research he'd learned just how common that was. New York City had even dubbed one of its infamous streets the Minnesota Strip after the young women of the northern plains states who haunted it, plying their trade.

Crystal belonged in a field of ripening grain, at a Lutheran church covered dish supper, on a Ferris wheel at the Iowa State Fair. She did not belong in a filthy New Orleans bar surrounded by dirty old men. But, of course, none of the other girls who wandered in and out of the bar did, either. No matter where they had come from, ghetto or mansion, they did not belong here.

Crystal stopped, just out of reach, almost as if she expected payment before coming any closer. "Wanda." She nodded stiffly to Jess.

"You know Jess Cantrell?" Wanda inclined her head. "He's looking for company. But he just wants to talk."

Crystal stared coolly at him, as if now she had heard everything.

Wanda laughed. "Honey, Jess here's a reporter. He's checking out the life, you know?"

Jess interrupted. "Actually, I'm talking to all the kids on the street, and I'm not repeating anything they tell me to the cops. I'm writing a book about what happens when kids run away."

Crystal's eyes were a deep, Great Lakes blue; they shimmered with intelligence and questions. Jess went on, convinced he had interested her. "I don't like what happens to kids out here," he said, lowering his voice to draw her closer. "I think they deserve better."

Crystal stood her ground. "I can't help you," she said, her words low and musical. She turned and started toward the bar. Disappointed, Jess watched her go, but he didn't try to stop her.

Crystal's tight skirt skimmed her thighs, just below her shapely bottom. Her spangled T-shirt hugged her slender waist, and when she'd been facing him, he hadn't failed to notice that it had hugged her ample breasts, too. She was dressed to walk the streets, but as she moved away from him, Jess noticed one thing, one perplexing, heartbreaking thing.

Crystal walked the streets, but she hadn't yet learned *the* walk, the hips-thrust-forward, rolling stroll that proclaimed her profession. Crystal, corn-fed, Midwestern fallen daughter, still walked like a high school homecoming queen. Even in cheap, imitation alligator boots.

"I saw you talking to Jess Cantrell." Perry, the bartender, handed Crystal a drink before she could even ask.

"You saw me telling Jess Cantrell I didn't *want* to talk to him." Crystal swallowed her drink in one long gulp. She'd had no reason to sip. Perry knew her tastes. The drink was plain club soda, gone flat at that. She fished the sliver of lemon from the bottom and sucked on it for something to do. She couldn't exit the bar right away. If she did, it would look peculiar, and she didn't want Jess Cantrell, of all people, to get suspicious.

A reporter, particularly one of Cantrell's abilities, was the last thing Crystal needed in her life. If he continued to camp out at Tallulah's, she was going to have to stay away.

She stifled the urge to turn and see if he was watching her. Even without looking at him again, she could still envision the rugged man with dark wavy hair and darker eyes. A reporter's eyes. Eyes that saw everything.

Perry came back from serving another customer, picking up the conversation right where they'd left it. "So Cantrell ain't your type?"

Crystal shrugged. "My *type* pays for my time."

"There's a guy in the corner who might be your type, then."

Back still turned to Jess, Crystal swiveled just far enough to see the guy that Perry pointed out. He was a hundred pounds overweight, and even from a distance she could see that his clothes were drenched with sweat. He leered at her suggestively from under the brim of a ten-gallon Stetson. She forced herself to suppress a shudder as she faced the bartender again. "Sorry, Perry, but I'm done for the night."

"Then *you* pay for that drink."

Crystal slipped her hand inside the silver purse hanging from a thin chain over her shoulder. She pushed a bill across the bar. "There's enough for both of us here. Join me."

Perry raised one bushy eyebrow. "A good night?"

"You could say that."

"I just wondered. Ain't the way I heard it."

"No?"

"One of your johns came back after you left with him. Said you scared him off."

"Some guys scare easy, Perry." Crystal dropped the lemon rind into her glass and pushed it toward Perry for a refill. She wasn't surprised that the john in question had come back to Tallulah's to blubber. She was more surprised that he was the only one so far who had.

Perry continued. "Said you told him he'd have to protect himself because you had a *problem*."

Crystal forced a laugh. "That's what I tell them all when I change my mind. And I changed my mind because I got the feeling he was the type who likes to slap his ladies around."

"If you were one of Chaz's wives, he'd stomp all over you for an excuse like that."

"That's why I don't have a pimp. I don't let myself in for trouble, and I keep the money I make."

"How'd a kid like you get so smart?"

Crystal took the new club soda and raised it to her lips. She wondered what Perry would think if she told him the truth. She'd been considering it for days. Tallulah's was a lodestone for all the runaways passing through New Orleans. Perry knew everyone and everything. If there was one person in New Orleans who could help her, it was him. But he was also in the pay of most of the slimeballs hawking their wares up and down Bourbon Street, two blocks away. Unless she could pay him more than they could, Perry couldn't be trusted. Which was a shame.

Just one more rotten shame to add to a list one year long and wide.

"Let's just say I've got street smarts." Crystal placed her empty glass on the counter. "I got them without having to spend a day in school."

"You and the rest of the kids that come in here." Perry walked off to serve another customer, but Crystal wasn't alone long.

"You've got pretty blond hair. I like blond hair," a voice drawled behind her.

Crystal smelled the man at the same time she felt the damp heat of his body. When he touched her hair the fear and revulsion inside her fought and tied for a nauseating first place. "Then buy a wig," she snapped to cover the clatter of her heart, "and leave my hair alone."

"Now that's not being very friendly." The man sat down on the stool beside hers.

Crystal had already guessed that her would-be customer was the fat man who had leered at her from the corner. She was right. "I don't have to be friendly," she said, in her most discouraging voice.

The man laid a fifty dollar bill on the bar, just to Crystal's right. "Make you friendlier, little lady?"

She wanted to run, but she knew what that would do to her credibility. "Not a whole lot, Tex," she said acidly. "Shades are drawn, and the door's bolted for the night. I don't open for business again 'til tomorrow." She stood up, flinging her purse over her shoulder.

"How about this?" The man held up a hundred dollar bill, then laid it beside the fifty. "Won't this buy me a key?"

Crystal looked up to see that Perry was watching them, his small, rodent eyes gleaming with avarice. She sighed audibly. "You going to take a cut?" she asked the bartender. "You didn't even introduce us?"

"If you wanna walk through this door again I am," he said with a grin that revealed the space where three teeth had perched before a wintertime brawl temporarily closed Tallulah's.

"Thirty," Crystal said, reaching inside her purse.

"Fifty," Perry countered.

Crystal was already counting out four tens. "Not a penny more."

Perry took the money with a grumble.

"You pay first," Crystal told the Texan, holding out her hand.

"I pay first," the man agreed, handing her the fifty. "But only some of it. You get the rest after."

Crystal slid off the stool. She didn't really care what arrangements she and the man made. Whatever was decided would change drastically in the next five minutes, anyway. "You got a room, honey?" she asked, careful not to touch him. "Or do you want me to rent one for us?"

"Oh, not mine," he said, horror washing over his face. "My wife's there."

Crystal choked down something. She wasn't sure if it was laughter or tears or nausea. She knew that, whatever it was, it was mixed with a strong dose of regret that her life had come down to negotiating tricks in a sweltering, hellhole bar. And the worst part was that she deserved it. Whatever came her way now, she deserved it.

She was halfway across the room before she caught Jess Cantrell's eye. He sat alone at his table, watching her. His clean, strong features and broad-shouldered frame contrasted so sharply with his sordid surroundings that for a moment she wanted to run to him, to touch someone decent again, to be reminded that the world was a better place than it seemed right now.

Instead she managed a brief smile, not even aware as she did how sad, how profoundly sad, the smile was.

It was Crystal's smile that brought Jess to his feet in recognition. He had sat quietly nursing his club soda for a minute after she left the bar. As he had sipped and stared at the table, something had nagged at him again, the same flash of awareness that he had felt the first time he'd seen her. Then he had realized what it was. Crystal wasn't a stranger. Sometime, somewhere, before he had come to New Orleans, he had spoken to her. Sometime, somewhere, he had seen that same, sad smile and been touched by it.

But he couldn't remember when or where. The awareness, the recognition, was there, but the memory was an elusive one. Something blocked it from surfacing.

Along with the conviction that he had spoken to her once before was the buzz a good reporter feels when he knows he's on the track of a story. Jess didn't know why his instincts were rattling to the driving beat of the radio behind the bar. They were, though, and the exhaustion he had felt earlier was gone. It was almost three a.m., but his stride as he left the bar was that of a man who'd just awakened from a refreshing night's sleep.

Outside, the April air seemed to sweat, condensing on his skin in a clammy mist that did nothing to cool him. The streets were still crowded with people, although the throngs streaming off Bourbon Street had changed subtly. Gone were most of the tourists, the conventioneers who had come for one night of gawking, drinking and souvenir hunting before returning home to tell their friends what they'd seen in the wicked city.

Some of those who had hung on were true patrons of the legitimate jazz establishments that peppered the famous strip, pouring the musical soul of New Orleans into the streets. Those who didn't care about the music were a tougher, more aggressive group, dedicated to a night of hard drinking or panting over the myriad diversions that money and a strong stomach could buy.

Still others were the flotsam and jetsam of city life, the barkers who stood outside the live sex shows and described what was happening inside, the female impersonators who paraded the sidewalks in hopes of attracting patrons for the strip shows, the proprietors of the peep shows and adult book stores, the gun-toting troublemakers.

And some were the kids, kids who weren't kids anymore and might never have had the chance to be, anyway. Kids who were kids only by virtue of the dates on their birth certificates.

Jess saw them all, but he didn't pay attention to any of them. He was looking for Crystal. There were places where girls like Crystal took their johns, places that rented space by the hour and asked no questions if you didn't have luggage. He was headed in that general direction now, watching carefully for red spangles and a bright splash of blond hair.

The streets were narrow, the buildings lining them historic. He passed under awnings and balconies, increasingly aware as one block became another that he had missed her. Right now she was probably inside some grimy rented room giving the man she had left with the thrill of his lifetime.

The thought sickened Jess. Despite everything, there was a quality about Crystal that contrasted sharply with the life she had chosen. Not quite innocence, not quite arrogance, Jess could only call it breeding. There was pride and poise in the way she held herself, intelligence in her eyes, and education in her voice.

Of course, he might be wrong. He'd been on the streets for six months talking to parents, runaways and the people who had dedicated their lives to helping them. He had lost his heart to the kids, along with his objectivity, objectivity that had stood inviolate beside him on Capitol Hill for a decade and was now in serious jeopardy. Jess knew he had begun to see heroes and villains everywhere he looked, that frequent nightmares reflected the depth of his concern, that more and more often he had to fight himself not to step in and help the kids instead of squeezing them dry until each warm-blooded, hurting child was reduced to ink on a page.

Objectivity? Jess stopped, thrusting his hands in his pockets. His objectivity and the meager contents of his wallet might just get him a cab back to his hotel. And that was exactly where he ought to be. He was a big man, but he wasn't a fool. French Quarter streets were no place to spend the early hours of the morning. Apparently Crystal had reached that conclusion, too, and his search was futile.

He had turned and was halfway down the block he had just traveled when he saw Crystal and the man from the bar standing on the opposite corner. Once again lamplight made a halo of her hair, a beacon in a relentlessly dark night.

Jess stepped into the shadows. He didn't know what he was looking for; he didn't even know why he had followed her. He had watched the man pick her up in the bar, and he knew what happened next. Something still nagged at him, though. Something reminded him that things weren't always what they seemed.

Nothing that happened in the next few minutes proved him wrong.

Chapter 2

Crystal spoke quietly to the man who had picked her up in the bar. "Stop just a minute and look casual. Someone's following us."

The man began to wheeze in fright. Crystal hoped her lie wasn't about to bring on a heart attack.

"It could be nothing. . . ." She let her voice trail off until the wheezing had calmed a little. "Or it could be a cop," she added, when he took her arm. The man began to gasp for breath in earnest.

"The laws are pretty strict, but the fines aren't too bad here," she whispered, reassuringly patting his hand. "Of course, the police'll have to call your hotel to verify your I.D., but most of the staff at our hotels are smart. They probably wouldn't even put the call through to your wife. Where are you staying?"

The man wheezed the name of a local hotel and dropped her arm.

"Oh," Crystal said, shaking her head. "That's too bad. But maybe they'd cooperate just this once."

The man put his hand over his heart. "You really think it's a cop?"

"Probably not." She added doubtfully, "Of course, in this neighborhood a cop's one of the better things it could be."

"Where the hell's this room you were talking about?"

Crystal looked around, her gaze settling on a shabby building just up the block. Four tough looking men, one dressed from head to toe in black leather, sat on the front stoop. "Just up there," she said, pointing. "Don't worry about the guys on the porch. They're a lot friendlier than they look. A *lot*," she emphasized.

Her "customer" stepped out of the lamplight into the shadow of the closest building. He turned his head frantically back and forth, scrutinizing every shadow. "I'm not going in there!"

"A big Texan like you?"

He mopped his forehead with the back of his hand. "Look, little lady, keep the money, I don't care. Forget it. I'm getting out of here."

For a moment Crystal wondered if she'd gone too far. She'd planned to scare the man, but not to death. "You're sure?" she asked.

"Sure." The man turned and started back the way they had come.

Crystal watched him for a moment. For a man who'd looked as if he were about to suffer cardiac arrest, he could really sprint. She stopped worrying and made a mental note to send the ten dollars—the difference between what the man had given her and what she'd had to pay Perry—to the local runaway shelter.

She wanted to laugh; she wanted to sob her relief. This hadn't been a close call, but she'd had close calls before. Every time she left with a man, she knew she was flirting with disaster.

Now she was doing the same by standing on a street corner at three a.m. in full view. Crystal stepped back into the shadows and made a quick investigation of the area. The four stoop-sitters were too interested in each other to represent danger. But there was a bar halfway down the block with customers spilling in and out like polluted waves on a garbage-strewn beach. She definitely could not walk by it alone, especially dressed as she was. If she did, she'd have more customers than she could weave tall tales to scare away.

She glanced across the street, then squinted painstakingly into the darkness. Tall tales? She had told her Texas "boyfriend" that they were being followed. Now she saw that there *was* someone standing in the shadows across from her. Someone who didn't want to be seen. Someone watching her.

Crystal sent a silent plea to the heavens. "I'm going to be more careful," she promised over and over in a whispered litany as she turned down the block that ran away from the bar. "If I get home safely, I'm going to be more careful from now on."

She felt, rather than saw, the presence of the man who'd been watching her. He was somewhere behind her. She was walking as quickly as she could, but she doubted it was quickly enough. She could run, but her high-heeled boots were treacherous. If she twisted an ankle, she would be at his mercy.

She hadn't been in New Orleans long, but she knew the streets in this section of the Quarter as she knew those of her hometown. She wasn't far from the apartment she was renting. She could be there in five minutes—if she was lucky enough to have that long.

She passed a deli where street kids drifted in and out during the daytime to buy milk and stale doughnuts. It was closed now, locked and barred against its best customers, who turned predator after dark and carried off everything that wasn't nailed to the floor. She hastened past a cluster of boarded-up houses. The Quarter lost its charm at almost this exact spot. There were no pastel, gingerbread-adorned cottages or plant-covered iron-lace balconies here, only houses—and occasionally shops—that had not aged gracefully. The buildings were simply forlorn, and they housed people who were forlorn, too.

There were no footsteps behind her, but she couldn't shake the feeling she was being followed. Her feet ached, but she walked faster, covering two more blocks. She turned once more and saw that the street stretching in front of her was empty. For the first time since she'd come to New Orleans, she *wanted* to see a cop. Just one cop, walking a beat, escorting a local resident to jail, breaking up a domestic quarrel.

Just one cop to scare off the man who was silently following her.

She covered several more blocks in record time. At the point right before she had to slip down an alley and duck into her own courtyard, Crystal stepped inside a doorway and steeled herself to turn and look behind her. The street seemed deserted, yet she couldn't believe she'd lost her pursuer. She waited two minutes, then five. At last, with one final prayer, she edged along the front of the building and into the narrow alleyway that led to her apartment.

She skirted the broken fountain in the courtyard, afraid, as always, that someone might be hiding or sleeping in the overgrown vegetation surrounding it. She had to kick aside two bottles and another resident's discarded table before she could climb the stairs leading to her apartment. Only when she was inside and her door was securely bolted did she rest her head in her hands and whisper a heartfelt "thank you."

Why had the man from the bar left Crystal standing in the middle of the sidewalk? And why had he suddenly taken up jogging?

As the man in the ten-gallon hat disappeared up the street, Jess had stayed hidden in the shadows across from where Crystal stood. Her expression had been hidden because she no longer stood in the lamplight, but even in the near darkness, he had seen the sudden slump of her shoulders, the hand lifted to momentarily cradle her forehead. He recognized relief, even when it was veiled by the night.

Jess felt an impotent surge of rage, rage at the man whose flight had left Crystal so shaken, rage at a world where kids like Crystal had to face situations like these. What had the man said to her? Asked of her? And what had she said to him to make him run away?

Until this moment Jess had been following a hunch. He'd seen Crystal before, although he couldn't remember where or when. It might have been in line in a grocery store; it might have been across the room at a restaurant. But his hunch told him it had been more than that, so he'd followed her tonight. Now, after watching her relief as her next meal fled down a dark

French Quarter street, he knew his hunch had been a good one. There was a story here. And he was going to get it.

He watched as Crystal straightened and looked around. He was standing in deep shadow, but she looked right at him. Stared right at him. Jess flattened himself against the brick facade at his back and stood motionless. He knew he hadn't fooled her when she turned and started quickly down the sidewalk.

Damn. He cursed softly to himself and considered calling out to her. She'd apparently had one bad fright tonight already. He didn't relish the thought of giving her another. Yet if he revealed that he'd been following her, she would be careful not to let it happen again. And he wanted her story. Wanted it badly. Badly enough, he supposed, to let her suffer a little more.

He stayed well behind her, hoping that she would think he hadn't followed, but as she picked up speed, he knew he hadn't fooled her. He wrestled with his conscience, but he kept silent, moving lithely in and out of shadows and doorways, stopping, waiting, moving again. He was no stranger to surveillance techniques. He had made his name as a reporter on the *Washington Post*, and he had stalked the dark sidewalks of the nation's capital until he could maneuver them blindfolded.

He'd rarely followed anyone, however, who was as perceptive as Crystal. She seemed to drink in the night, absorbing each sound, each changing nuance of her surroundings, then calculating its danger. Once he stumbled, his foot making only the faintest scraping sound across a broken slab of sidewalk. She hesitated for the briefest second, then moved faster.

He narrowed her lead, although not by much. Just as he reached the shelter of a storefront, Crystal stepped into a doorway and turned. Jess flattened himself against the door so hard that the welcome bell on the other side of it tinkled faintly. He held his breath and waited. Minute stretched into minute, but Crystal didn't move. Then, just as he was beginning to wonder if he'd been mistaken and she had gone inside the building, he caught a glimpse of red spangles winking in the lamplight. The spangles were suddenly eclipsed, and Crystal was gone.

Jess no longer worried about secrecy. In seconds he reached the place where Crystal had disappeared. There was a narrow alleyway between two brick houses strewn with broken glass and assorted litter. He picked his way through it with care. The courtyard just beyond the alley was no surprise. Jess knew that many French Quarter homes had courtyards, or patios, as they were sometimes called locally. The earliest settlers of New Orleans had valued their privacy. Edged around this particular one was a pair of two-story brick buildings, once slave quarters, perhaps, or a carriage house and stables. Now the buildings were obviously apartments, shabby and sinister, but apartments nonetheless.

Jess stood in the shadow of a huge magnolia and observed. The brick patio floor was in sad disrepair. Vegetation had dislodged many of the bricks; others were shattered or missing. A crumbling fountain was nearly hidden by overgrown shrubbery at the patio's edge. As Jess watched, a skin-and-bones black alley cat parted the shrubbery, victoriously displaying its newly caught mouse supper.

Apparently Crystal lived here, although Jess had no way of knowing in which apartment. She lived here, perhaps with other runaways, perhaps with a pimp. Perhaps this was just her place for the night, or for a week or month. Street kids didn't stay put for long. They developed the habit of moving on, and even if they became working girls like Crystal or involved themselves in other unsavory pursuits, as they usually did, they still moved from place to place. Sometimes because they had no choice, sometimes because they just didn't know how to stand still.

He knew where Crystal lived now, but that told him nothing about who she was or what had brought her here. It told him nothing about her life except that she was luckier than some of the kids he'd met. She had a roof over her head, such as it was.

He debated what to do next. He had learned nothing of value, and he still had a hunch that wouldn't lie down and die. He considered burying his hunch six feet under and calling it dead. The hour was very late, or very early, depending on one's orientation. The exhaustion he'd felt earlier was beginning to overwhelm him again. He wasn't so far from Esplanade Avenue that he couldn't find his way there and be in a cab on the way back to his hotel in minutes. He could forget he'd ever been curious about Crystal-whoever-she-was.

Except that he couldn't.

Jess wondered if the skinny alley cat had cleared the shrubbery of mice. He hoped so. If he was going to spend the rest of the night on the damp ground, scratched and tormented by the tangled branches of azaleas and camellias, then the last thing he needed was a lapful of mice for company.

He ended up with a lapful of cat, instead. The so-called alley cat had obviously once been someone's pet. He discovered Jess immediately, and with unerring feline instinct, knew he had found a sucker. Short of standing and hurling the purring animal to one of the four winds, Jess knew that, at least temporarily, there was nothing he could do. His lap was about to be rented by a mangy, flea-bitten tom. Jess contented himself with the thought that at least now the more intelligent rodents would stay away. He tried to make man and cat as comfortable as possible.

He was sheltered almost totally by the bushes, yet he could see his surroundings fairly well. He observed through drooping eyelids. He'd waited in worse places, and he'd waited in better. What hadn't changed was his ability to come to rapt attention when he needed to.

He didn't need to until more than an hour had passed. Then two young men came through the alleyway and into the courtyard. As Jess watched they unlocked one of the bottom apartments and entered together. Lights went on inside for a short time; then the small complex was dark once more.

Jess's whole body was cramped, but other than shifting his weight there was nothing he could do. The space he occupied was so small there was only one way to fit into it.

What was he hoping to find, anyway? Crystal surely wouldn't be up before the bright light of morning forced him from his hiding place. What did he think he would see before then? He had learned nothing of value so far, and that wasn't likely to change. But even if the chances were one in a million, he might learn something. And "might" was one of those words that thrilled a journalist's soul.

The cat's rattling purr lulled Jess into a state of semisleep. He dreamed he was back in Washington, at one of the endless cocktail parties he'd been obliged to attend. As usual, ninety percent of him was bored. Ten percent was listening to the perpetually mundane conversations of other party-goers, hoping to find just one lead that would make attending worthwhile. Then the room grew smaller; the people receded and disappeared. And Crystal, dressed in red spangles and imitation alligator boots, came walking through the door.

Except that it wasn't Crystal. Not exactly.

Jess woke with a start. The first light of dawn washed rose-tinted light across a leaf-shrouded, French Quarter patio. For a moment he wasn't sure where he was. He was filled with a curious sense of well-being. The glow of morning highlighted the once-proud architecture of the apartments and the graceful bend and sway of the magnolia at the courtyard entrance. The air was scented with ligustrum and sweet olive, and overhead a mockingbird trilled the counterfeit call of a cardinal.

Reality intruded when a door creaked, and Jess watched as an old woman in a faded blue housedress stepped out of one of the second-floor apartments onto a wide gallery and dropped an unsealed trash bag into a garbage can directly below her. Her aim was poor.

"Breakfast," Jess whispered to the cat, who was kneading his leg, claws unsheathed. "Go for it."

The cat took his suggestion and went to investigate. Without taking his eyes off the woman, Jess brushed the cat hair off his lap, preparing to abandon his hideaway. He had waited long enough. As soon as the old woman went back inside, he was going to have to leave. Otherwise someone might see him crawling out of the bushes, which might be difficult to explain.

The problem was that the woman didn't leave. She was apparently a morning person, filled with energy and the desire to set her little world to rights. Taking a broom from the gallery floor she began to sweep, singing in a hoarse, off-key alto that silenced the mockingbird's song and sent the cat back into the bushes. Jess tensed, waiting for a chance to make a break, but the old woman was determined to sweep away every particle of dust.

She finished sweeping at last, and then, broom still in hand, slowly took the stairs, shaking her head in disgust as she did. At the bottom she laboriously bent and picked up every item that hadn't made it into the trash can, along with the other assorted garbage to boot. She even set a discarded table on its three good legs and plopped a potted fern on top of it for decoration.

Jess closed his eyes in disbelief as she began to sweep the bricks running in front of the bottom apartments. She picked up the song where she had left off, sweeping in time to her own music. He wondered what the tenants thought of her serenade. He could vouch for the fact that at least some of them hadn't gotten much sleep the night before.

Finally the bricks were swept to her satisfaction. Jess watched closely as she started toward the stairs. The moment she opened her door he was going to bolt.

At the bottom step, the old lady raised her broom and began to sweep once more. Jess stifled a groan and estimated her time of arrival at the top step. He was afraid that at the rate she was going the sun would be dead overhead.

She had almost made it to her doorway; he was already wriggling forward in anticipation when the door beside hers opened. The woman who stepped out on the gallery looked as much out of place in her surroundings as Jess felt in his. She was dressed in pale blue, a linen skirt and blouse belted at the waist, but the cut of the fabric and the way it hung said the simplicity had been expertly calculated and hadn't come cheaply. Her pale blond hair was pulled back from her face in a loose knot and tendrils fell against her cheeks and neck in adornment. She wore no jewelry except silver earrings, but she was such a stunner she didn't need jewelry.

Every nerve in Jess's body was suddenly standing at attention.

Then she spoke. "At it again, Mrs. Duchamp?"

"Child, you scared me to death!"

"I'm sorry." The young woman smiled. "I'll try to warn you next time."

The voice and the smile were the last clues Jess needed. The voice was just as melodious as it had been last night; the smile was infinitely more relaxed, but the woman was the same. He mouthed her name. "Crystal."

"How's it look?" the old woman asked, gesturing to the gallery and beyond.

"Clean enough to eat from." Crystal hesitated. "You know, I think it's clean enough that you won't have to sweep it again until tomorrow."

"I tell myself that." The old woman shook her head. "I tell myself that, but then I find myself sweeping it anyway."

Crystal patted her arm in commiseration. "Well, we all appreciate how nice you keep it."

"I try. I try."

Crystal started down the stairs. Jess watched her coming closer. Her head was held high, and she walked with the graceful, easy stride that he had noticed the night before. But this morning she was wearing low heels of soft, blue leather, and he was no longer reminded of a homecoming queen. Without the garish makeup, the cheap, revealing clothes, she looked more mature. If she'd ever attended a homecoming, it had been years before. Crystal was older, not younger, than the eighteen she claimed. And if she'd run away from anyone, it had been a husband or a lover.

Jess no longer had a hunch there was a story here. He knew there was. And he was going to see that she told it to him.

Crystal passed no more than five feet from his hiding place. Jess gritted his teeth and waited for the old woman to go inside. She started to, then, as if she'd seen a speck of dust she'd missed, she began to sweep again.

Just as he was sure he was never going to be able to leave the bushes, an old man came out of her apartment and led her, protesting, back inside.

Jess was out of the bushes and through the alleyway in seconds. His feet felt as if they were on fire, and he stumbled twice before the blood began circulating normally again. At the end of the alleyway he paused, surveying the dawn-flooded street for pale blue linen and white-gold hair. He just caught a glimpse of Crystal as she turned the corner three blocks away.

They played cat and mouse for blocks as she headed toward Decatur Street, but today Crystal didn't seem to know she was a cat's prey. As they neared Jackson Square she walked through the just-wakening streets, waving once to the street cleaners whose monster machines were inhaling all signs of the night.

She crossed the street at the Square and wandered into the open-air Café du Monde. As Jess watched from the doorway of a Decatur Street bar, she disappeared, then reappeared carrying a foam cup and a small white bag. She munched on the Café's famous *beignets* as she continued down Decatur and sipped what was probably coffee from the cup.

She looked like a woman going to a society-approved job. She could be a teacher or a young executive, up early for a morning stroll before putting in a long day. Jess wondered if Crystal ever slept. He knew when she'd gone to bed last night, but she didn't seem tired, while he felt as though he'd spent the night tortured by branches and cat claws.

If there wasn't a good story here, he was going to forget all his ethics and invent one.

Crystal was almost to Canal Street before she turned again. She was lost to Jess for the minute it took him to get to the corner. When he finally reached the place where she had turned, he scanned both sides of the street, but she was nowhere to be seen.

There was a coffee shop across the street, just next to a small hotel parking garage. She could have gone inside for breakfast, but it seemed unlikely, since she had just eaten *beignets*. Perhaps it was a meeting place or a place to pick up men. But Crystal hadn't been dressed for that, and it was only six-thirty in the morning.

The rest of the street yielded no clues. She could have entered any building, any shop. Despite the way she was dressed she could have entered the hotel through the side door for an early morning rendezvous with a regular customer.

Jess realized he couldn't wait in a doorway for Crystal to reappear. If he tried, he would fall asleep standing up and end up at the local shelter for homeless men.

Since the coffee shop seemed the likeliest place to begin, he crossed the street. He stopped at the sidewalk in front of the parking garage. He could hear the sound of a car on the ramp inside and waited for it to enter the street, paying scant attention to neither car nor driver as he debated how best to find Crystal.

It was only when the car paused just in front of him and startled blue eyes looked directly into his that he realized Crystal had found him first.

Chapter 3

Although the morning rain was an effective shield, Jess raised the *Times-Picayune* a little higher to conceal his face from anyone passing on the sidewalk. The movement was just a precaution. Few people were out, and those who were couldn't have cared less about the occupant of a burgundy sedan parked in a tow-away zone across the street from a hotel parking garage.

The air was cool, and a fine drizzle washed the car's windshield as Jess turned the page, searching for something, anything, that he hadn't read. It was no use. Twice he'd scanned the paper from Sections A through E. He'd disagreed vehemently with the editors, laughed at the comics and taken Ann Landers to task for what he considered the wrong advice to a mother plagued by a bratty teen.

It was past six-thirty, and Crystal had not appeared.

The last time Jess had seen her had been yesterday morning as she'd sped out of the parking garage and run the stop sign at the end of the block. To his credit he thought he had controlled himself as well as could be expected. He knew he hadn't completely prevented a shock of recognition from crossing his face, but just after he'd locked eyes with her he had glanced down at his watch, then put it to his ear as if nonchalantly checking to see if it still ticked. By the time he'd looked up again, Crystal had almost caused an accident at the end of the block.

He *had* been quick-witted enough to get her license number. It was a Maryland tag. An extravagant tip to a hotel parking attendant had gotten him the information that the space for the car, a white Buick Regal, was paid for monthly by a K. Jensen.

After a long sleep, Jess had spent yesterday afternoon prowling the Quarter for clues. He had talked to Wanda again, but she'd had nothing new to tell him. He had walked the streets of Crystal's neighborhood, even chatted with her landlady in the guise of checking for a place to rent. That night, he had installed himself in a dark corner of Tallulah's. But there had been no sign of Crystal, and no one he had casually questioned seemed to know a thing.

So here he was, camped outside the parking garage. The same tip to the parking attendant had netted him the information that the "fox" who owned the car usually took it out right at six-thirty every morning. The attendant didn't know when she came back, because he was off duty by then, but it had to be sometime after noon.

Jess knew for a fact that the white Buick was sitting in a space on the second level of the garage right now. He had seen it himself, even wrestled with a powerful urge to pick the lock and check the glove compartment. He only hoped he would be more successful trailing Crystal if she showed up this morning.

At quarter to seven he admitted he might be wasting his time. Apparently Crystal's plans had changed. He needed to reconsider his own.

Five minutes later, sparked by the glimpse of a meter maid, he closed his paper and prepared to circle the block. When she was gone, he would return, but he wasn't going to wait much longer. The ignition key was turning in his hand when a white Buick Regal pulled out of the garage.

Crystal had apparently entered from the next street. Jess ducked low, banging his head against the steering wheel as he did. Cursing softly, he peeked through the windshield. She was driving slowly today; apparently she hadn't seen him. He waited until she had turned the corner before he pulled into the street. The traffic was light, the hour still early, and they were heading away from the business district, so there was no chance of getting stuck in the middle of rush hour.

The easy swipe of Jess's windshield wipers crooned "success" as he started after her.

Crystal paid little attention to anything except the clock on her dashboard and the gray drizzle fogging her windshield. She was late, getting later by the second, and the rain wasn't helping matters. The first time she had been late she had almost lost her job. Now, four weeks later, she had completed her trial period. Her boss knew she was a good employee, conscientious and scrupulously honest. She only hoped he would take that into account.

She had been so tired this morning. Usually, after prowling the bars and the streets until the wee hours, she went home, showered, ate and took care of any chores that needed to be done. She rarely dared to let herself sleep before going to work because she knew if she did, she might not wake up in time to get ready.

She had proved that theory correct today. Last night had been particularly tiring. There had been a party, and she had been invited at the last minute. A street kid she had met the week before had found a job. It wasn't much of one, just washing dishes and sweeping floors, but it was something. He'd celebrated in the boarded-up hovel that he and three other kids called home.

Kids had drifted in and out all evening. Crystal had stayed until everyone was falling asleep before she had given up and gone home. Kids had drifted in and out all evening, but not the right kid.

Not the right kid.

Crystal forced that thought out of her mind. If she thought too hard, too long, on her reasons for being in New Orleans she would start to cry. And that would make her even later. She had come home from the party depressed, collapsed on the bed—she had promised herself just fifteen minutes—and that had been that. Now she was paying the price for that hour of oblivion.

It didn't really matter that her body craved sleep, demanded it, took the matter out of her hands at times and forced it on her. As long as she still had any choice, she was going to keep up the pace she'd set. And if that pace felt like punishment, then so be it. She deserved it.

She paid scant attention as she crossed over the Mississippi River bridge. The rain was coming down harder now, putting an end to the summer-hot heat that had characterized the last week. She had lived in the Washington, D.C., area for enough years to be used to heat and humidity. But she wasn't used to them in April, and now even the rain seemed a blessing.

Of course, it would be no blessing for the kids who were living on the streets. For them a doorway, an awning, the shade of a live oak, were their only protection.

Crystal was glad when the familiar little plaza came into view, both because she had finally arrived at work and because now she would be too busy to think.

She pulled her car into a parking space at the side of a convenience store and turned off the engine.

Crystal drove a Buick Regal, dressed—at least during the daytime—as if she shopped exclusively at Lord and Taylors, and she worked the early morning shift at a convenience store.

Jess watched a short young man with a nasty scowl unlock the front door of the Kwick Korners from the inside. Either Crystal made a killing on her back in squalid hotel rooms to supplement what she made here, or there was something very funny going on.

Jess was sure it was the latter. Crystal had the looks and—he suspected—the brains to be a high-class call girl. She didn't have to haunt Tallulah's, soliciting the dregs of the earth. There were downtown luxury hotels where she could sit in cocktail lounges and pick and choose her clients. She could even call the extravagant sums she took away with her every morning "gifts" from her admirers.

She didn't have to haunt Tallulah's, but apparently *she* felt she did. She didn't have to work for minimum wage at a West Bank Kwick Korners, but apparently...

Jess sat in his car, parked just to the side of the brick and glass building so that with the help of the rain he wouldn't be noticed, and watched the drama unfolding inside. Crystal was getting a lecture. She was nodding her head, as if she agreed with everything the man shaking his finger at her was saying. Then, with obvious tact, she was showing him to the door.

Jess rolled his window down far enough to hear their parting words.

"Next time you're late, I'll have to report you to management," the young man threatened.

"Of course you will," Crystal agreed. "I'm just so glad you're not going to say anything this time, Tom." The rest of her words were lost in a crack of thunder.

Jess rolled his window back up as Tom dashed across the parking lot. He felt a curious sense of satisfaction as the clouds opened up and soaked the still-scowling man before he could unlock the door of his car.

Jess settled back, his arms behind his head. He'd found out one more interesting fact about Crystal, but, like everything else, he wasn't sure what it meant. He'd wasted plenty of time following her around, asking about her, thinking about her, but nothing so far had the makings of a good story. There was probably a logical explanation for everything he'd witnessed, a boring, logical explanation.

The problem was that no matter how many times he told himself to stop pursuing Crystal and concentrate on street kids who were really kids, the answer came up the same. No. Unequivocally.

So now he was faced with a decision. Either he could continue sleuthing, or he could confront her with everything he knew. Maybe then she'd break down and tell him the rest.

Perhaps. Or perhaps she would run, and he would never know what he'd missed.

Whatever he decided, he had a few minutes to think it over. The rain was slashing across his windshield. If he got out, he would get as wet as her boss. If he drove away, he would have to crawl at a snail's pace until the rain let up. He mulled over his options as the rain shrouded his car in silver sheets.

He had just about decided to go back to his hotel after the rain slowed and get some sleep when a car pulled up and parked on the other side of the store. A middle-aged man dressed in jeans and a denim jacket got out. In the seconds before he made it to the overhang, he was soaked.

Cigarettes, Jess thought idly, watching the man shake himself like a dog fresh out of a mud puddle. There was nothing that would make a man come out in this weather except cigarettes. No one got soaked for a loaf of bread or a gallon of milk. Cigarettes or baby formula.

Jess slipped down in his seat. The chance that the man in jeans would see him, go inside and mention it to Crystal was remote, but it existed. It *was* a little odd that a man would just be sitting in his car in a convenience store parking lot, particularly this early in the morning. Crystal might peek outside to see, and if he made a production of hiding his face, she might get suspicious and call the police.

Might, might, might, but not probably. Still, he knew better than to take chances. Interestingly enough, he realized as he slipped farther down that this time his wariness seemed to be paying off. The man under the overhang seemed in no hurry to go inside; he was a curious fellow.

Eyes just level with the top of the dashboard, Jess watched the man look around. He seemed more interested in the parking lot than the store. Jess's car and Crystal's weren't the only ones there. The little plaza also had a laundry, a drug store and a beauty salon. The laundry was open for business already, and employees of the other businesses were preparing for the day.

The man in jeans examined each car, as if making sure that no one was going to be in the parking lot in the next few minutes. It took Jess moments to get suspicious, then moments more to wonder why he hadn't been suspicious immediately. This guy was no ordinary customer. Ordinary customers didn't watch for movement in the parking lot before they went inside. Ordinary customers didn't flatten themselves against the brick wall and edge their way to the door once they were satisfied that no one else was around.

Jess sat up straight. The man, who had just reached the door, wasn't interested in the parking lot anymore. He was interested in what was happening inside. And right now he seemed to be concentrating on the fact that Crystal was alone, standing behind the central counter. Alone and vulnerable as bait on a hook.

The man's nod was almost imperceptible, but Jess caught it. He seemed satisfied about something, and Jess was afraid he knew what. Both Jess and the man in jeans reached for door handles at the same moment. The man slid into the relative comfort of the convenience store; Jess slid into the pouring rain.

In moments Jess was flattened against the building, his head turned to take in everything happening inside. As he watched, the man approached Crystal. She smiled politely at him, but the smile seemed to freeze before it reached completion. Her face lost its color, but she showed no other signs of fear.

The man's back was to Jess, but Jess saw him reach inside his jacket. Then his arm extended full length, and Jess could see the glitter of metal. Jess mentally assessed distances and speed, reaction times and courage—both his own and what he knew of Crystal's—as he moved toward the door.

"We've just opened," Crystal told the man holding a gun on her. "There isn't enough money here to make this worth your while."

"No?" The man gestured toward the register. "I'll be the judge of that."

Crystal tried to swallow her fear. "Please, just take what's here and go."

The man seemed to consider her words as he considered her. Crystal watched his brown eyes do a brief investigation. In every way he seemed an average customer, better looking than some, better dressed than others, certainly wetter than most. His hair was neatly trimmed; he was neither underweight nor overweight. He didn't slouch; he didn't fidget. He seemed to be a normal, middle-class white male—with a gun pointed right at her heart.

"Your mother ever tell you some jobs are just damned dangerous?"

Crystal nodded, her eyes wide and trained right on the gun.

"This is one of them, babe. Why are you working in a convenience store?"

"I'm making a living."

"You oughta find a better way." The man moved a step closer. "Open the register and hand me the cash. And no funny stuff or you won't have to worry about making a living at all."

Crystal nodded again. She moved slowly toward the register as he motioned with the gun. For a moment her mind went blank, and she couldn't remember how to open the drawer.

"Just pretend you're ringing up a sale."

Crystal did as he'd told her. The drawer slid open. She gathered the cash as quickly as her trembling hands would allow and handed it to him.

The man accepted the money without counting it, stuffing the bills in his jeans pockets and shaking his head when Crystal tried to hand him rolls of change. "Don't want to get weighed down," he said, then smiled, as if he expected her to laugh at his joke.

"Please, I won't call the police or set off the alarm until you've driven away. Just go. Please." Crystal tried to sound as if she was telling the truth, but the words fell flat.

"You've seen me," the man said, shaking his head. "And you could identify me."

"It's not my money. I don't care if they don't catch you."

He motioned with his gun toward the rear of the store. "We're going in the back room, babe." With no alternative, Crystal slipped out from behind the counter and started toward the back.

She had only gone a few feet when a voice cracked out behind them. "Police! Drop your gun!"

The man whirled, but Jess had already rocketed across the room. As the man tried to take aim, Jess threw himself forward. The gun discharged as Jess knocked it from the robber's hand, and the sound of shattering glass filled the room.

Crystal was horrified, but in her horror, she retreated, which was the best thing she could have done. Her benumbed brain had no time to ask why Jess Cantrell was rolling on the floor with the man who had robbed the store. She screamed once; then, recovering, she threw herself across the counter and felt for the alarm button that would activate the store's security system.

The two men fought with the strength and tenacity of jungle animals. The gun clattered to the floor after Jess, with a death grip on the other man's wrist, slammed it against a shelf of canned goods. Cans spilled to the floor, rolling over and between the struggling men. The man who'd robbed the store grabbed one and tried to smash it against Jess's throat. Jess ducked, and the can grazed his temple instead, but he did not release the other man's wrist.

They rolled over once more, and this time Jess was on the bottom. The other man lurched forward, feeling for his gun as he began to triumph over Jess's waning strength.

"Crystal, the gun!"

Jess's voice was no more than a grunt, but it sent the horror-stricken Crystal into action. She reached the gun and grabbed it just as the robber's long fingers were sliding over the butt. Then she raised it with trembling hands. "Stop right now. I'll use this. I swear I will."

The two men rolled over again. Jess dropped the other man's wrist and lunged for his throat. The other man hadn't been smashed in the head with a can, however, and his reflexes were still acute. He rolled away, and as Jess fell forward, he pushed him, sending him sprawling. Before Jess could fully recover, the man was on his feet, running for the door.

Crystal wanted to shoot, not to kill but to stop the man. Her index finger slid to the trigger and froze there. Moments later, when Jess took the gun from her hand, her finger was still crooked as if waiting for a signal from her brain that would never come.

"He's gone," she said, as if she couldn't quite believe it.

Jess knew shock when he saw it. As he watched, Crystal's skin turned the stark white of the blouse she wore. He could vouch for the fact that her hands were ice-cold and trembling. Whatever force normally held her together seemed to have deserted her. As she watched she began to sway.

Without a thought Jess wrapped his arms around her to keep her from falling. The top of her head came halfway up his cheekbone. He tucked it firmly on his shoulder and wished that there was just one chair somewhere in the room to sit her on. "Convenience store" was a misnomer.

"He's gone," Jess crooned. He swayed gently back and forth to calm her as he tried to ignore the soft curves of her body against the harder planes of his. "You're safe."

"I let him get away," Crystal mourned softly. "I couldn't pull the trigger."

"His robbing the store wasn't worth killing him for." Jess tentatively stroked her hair. It was as soft, as naturally blond, as dandelion fluff.

"I wasn't going to kill him. He was going to kill me!"

Jess continued to sway. Shock was definitely setting in, and he prepared to feel Crystal's whole weight slumped against him. "He wouldn't have killed you," he assured her, although he had to admit there had been a moment when he had wondered. It wouldn't have been the first time a clerk at a store like this one had died. When he had seen the man moving Crystal toward the storeroom, he'd been forced to act.

"You didn't see his eyes." She shuddered, and for a moment the room seemed to sway independently of the rhythm Jess had set. "He was enjoying this. I don't even think he cared about the money!"

Jess wanted to calm her, but he suspected nothing he could say would convince her she was wrong. "It's all right now," he said instead. "He's gone, and you're fine."

"I wouldn't be if you hadn't come flying through that door!"

Jess wondered how long it would be before she asked *why* he had. "Well, I did," he assured her. "And you're fine."

"What about you?" Crystal forced her head up to examine Jess's face. She frowned. "You're going to have a nasty bruise where he caught you with that can. You might have a concussion."

"No concussion. Bruise, yes." Jess winced as Crystal brushed his hair off his forehead to get a closer look at the injury. "Ouch!"

"You didn't even say 'ouch' when he hit you." Crystal thought what a shame it was that anyone had marred the broad expanse of his brow. It dominated his face, along with eyes the precise color of flint. Penetrating eyes. Eyes that saw everything.

Reporter's eyes.

"I was too busy for conversation." Jess watched Crystal's expression change from concerned to wary.

"Busy rescuing me."

One moment Crystal was warm and soft in Jess's arms. The next he could feel her body grow rigid. He suspected that the reason had nothing to do with the police siren that was suddenly screaming somewhere close by.

"Rescuing me," she repeated, almost too softly for him to hear.

But he did hear. "Rescuing you," he agreed. There was no point in pretending she hadn't just realized that his presence wasn't a coincidence. "And following you," he admitted. "Can you forgive the one since it led to the other?"

Crystal tried to pull away, but Jess could still feel the fine trembling that was likely to leave her in a heap on the terrazzo floor if he removed his support.

"You bastard!" Crystal placed her palms against his chest and shoved. "Who do you think you are, anyway?"

Jess reluctantly let her go, staying close by in case he had to make a grab for her. "I'd rather tell you who you are, but I can't, because I haven't got that figured out yet."

Crystal backed up against the counter and gripped it for support. The sirens were getting louder. "I'm a two-bit whore," she said, practically spitting the words at him. "And I'm a nobody. I work this job because I don't make enough on the streets. That's all I am, and that's nobody's idea of a good story, so leave me alone!"

"I don't want to upset you," he said gently. "You've already been through one ordeal today."

But Crystal was beyond upset. "Stop following me!"

"I'm not following you now. Where I'd like to be is right beside you when you tell me who you are and why you're in New Orleans." He held up his hand when she threatened to interrupt. "And how you manage to dress like a debutante on the salary of a clerk or a prostitute, much less drive a new car and park it in an expensive garage. And how you've managed to convince Wanda and who knows how many others that you're a runaway, when the only thing you've probably ever run from is a good job."

Crystal felt fear clutch her. "You've got to leave me alone. I know who you are and what you do. I can't talk to you! Please, can't you just leave me alone?"

A police car, siren blasting, screeched to a stop just outside the front door.

"If I could have before," Jess told her, "I can't now. The police are going to ask us both for identification. What's it going to be, Crystal? I'm about to hear part of the truth. Do you know what a reporter can do with half a truth?"

In the seconds left to her, Crystal tried to weigh her choices, but that was impossible. Half a truth, unlike half a loaf, was definitely not better than none. She had been backed into a corner. There were no choices to weigh. She had to tell her story to Jess Cantrell and plead for his silence.

She waited for rage to wash over her. But all she felt was relief.

Chapter 4

How do you spell that first name?" The policeman who was taking statements paused, his pencil raised over his notepad.

"Krista. K...r...i...s...t...a. Krista Jensen." Krista didn't look at Jess. "I have identification, if you'd like to see it."

"I thought Mr. Cantrell was calling you Crystal. That's why I asked." The policeman scrawled on his pad. "Your address?"

Krista hesitated, then gave him the address of her French Quarter apartment. There was no point in trying to hide it from Jess. With his skills, he could discover it on his own.

"Lived there long?" the policeman continued.

"No."

The policeman looked up. "You're not from Louisiana, are you?"

"No."

He shrugged. "Well, this looks like the usual kind of holdup. Lucky no one was hurt when that gun went off. Sometimes there's no one left to interview when these guys are through." He seemed to notice Krista's distress. "You might want to get a different job," he said kindly.

"That's what he told me."

"Who?"

The guy who robbed the store."

"I'm on his side on that one."

The door opened and Tom, Crystal's boss, came in at a near run. "I just got the message." He went straight to Krista, ignoring the policemen, and began to give her the third degree.

Jess listened quietly just as long as he could take it—which was less than thirty seconds. Then he clamped his hand down on Tom's shoulder and twisted until the young man was facing him. "Listen, friend. I saw the whole thing, and Crystal—Krista—handled herself and the situation as well as anyone could have, including you, so lay off her. Understand?"

"I'm perfectly capable of taking care of myself, Mr. Cantrell," Krista said, looking at Jess for the first time since she had given the policeman her story. "Lay off me, Tom," she said, still looking at Jess.

"You work for me—"

"Not anymore." Krista finally pulled her gaze from Jess's eyes and faced Tom. "Find someone else. I quit."

Tom didn't seem to know what to say. "Quit?"

Krista dismissed him with a regal nod of her head. "Do you need me for anything else, Officer?"

The policeman chuckled. "No. We'll get in touch with you if we do. Mr. Cantrell, will you keep us advised of where we can reach you if we need you to make an identification?"

Jess assured him that he would. Then, with a hand on Krista's shoulder, he started to guide her toward the door.

"Quit?" Tom squeaked from behind them. "You can't—"

The door severed the rest of his sentence.

"Your car or mine?" Jess asked Krista. The rain had stopped, at least temporarily, but the sky was still gray and the sidewalk slick.

"You take your car and I'll take mine. I'm sure we're not going to the same place."

"We're going out to breakfast, and I'm going to listen to you tell me everything you can." Jess pressed on before she could interrupt. "I'm not a cop, Krista. And I'm not a P.I. I'm just a man who wants a story, and I know you've got one."

"You can't *make* me tell you anything."

"We both know I'm going to keep trying."

Krista knew she was just wasting time by protesting. Jess Cantrell had enough pieces of her puzzle to help him assemble the whole sad picture, more of it than she wanted him to know. "All right," she agreed. "Breakfast. And then we're done. No more following me, no more questions. I'll tell you what I can, and then you'll leave me alone."

"If that's what you want when we're done."

Krista hesitated. She didn't want to drive, but neither did she want to admit to any feeling of weakness. Reporters were like vultures. She'd seen them close in before, and she knew that if she faltered Jess would swoop down for the kill. "We can take my car," she said finally. "I'll drop you off back here afterward."

Jess noted her continuing pallor and the trembling in the hands that were reaching for keys. "I'd rather take mine, if you don't mind. I'm low on gas. You can help me spot a station."

She considered saying no, but only for a moment. "Fine." She let him lead her to his car, noting when he opened the door of the sleek new Legend that reporting, unlike crime, must pay. She settled against the soft leather seat and shut her eyes. When they stopped at a gas station, she realized that she hadn't been any help. She apologized when Jess got back in.

He pulled back onto the street. "You're obviously dead on your feet. When do you sleep?"

"After work."

He didn't ask which job she was referring to. "For how long?"

"Not long enough."

"Obviously." Jess scanned the street as he drove, looking for a likely breakfast stop. He finally settled on a restaurant that specialized in all-you-can-eat buffets. If Krista's nutrition was as poor as her sleeping habits, this could be the first good meal she'd had in a while.

Once inside, however, Krista refused all food. "Just coffee," she told the waitress. "Strong, please."

"You're sure?" Jess asked before he rose to fill his plate.

"I lost my appetite when a man pointed a gun at me this morning."

He refrained from coaxing her because his wasn't exactly at peak, either. When he came back to the table, Krista had already finished half a cup of mud-black coffee. "There's no nutrition in that."

She looked up, and, despite herself, she smiled. Jess felt it clear down to his toenails.

"Mr. Cantrell, are you somebody's father?"

Jess shook his head. He didn't even realize he was still standing.

Krista smiled again, sadly this time. "Well, you can't be mine, either. I'm not one of the runaway kids you're so set on interviewing. I'm twenty-four, though I know I don't look it, particularly when I don't try. I had one father, and now I'm on my second one. Two is plenty for one lifetime."

Jess lowered himself to his seat. "Twenty-four?"

"And I'm not a prostitute, despite the fact that I hang around Tallulah's."

Jess let that small bombshell explode and settle before he spoke again. "Why don't you start at the beginning, Krista?" He picked up his fork and began to eat. Surprisingly and suddenly, his appetite had improved.

"In the beginning there was a girl who got very upset at her parents and ran away from home." Surprised, Krista realized that her eyes were filling with tears. She was exhausted, still in shock and—this was a revelation—bone-deep lonely. She hadn't really talked to anyone in so long that even this situation, artificial as it might be, was bringing all her feelings to a head.

Jess wanted to comfort her, but the reporter in him cautioned him to remain silent.

"That girl wasn't me," she went on, finally. "It was my sister, Rosie. She was sixteen, and she came to me before she ran. She was having problems with my mother and stepfather. Rosie was always exaggerating. I knew her well enough to realize she was doing it again. My mother's a very gentle person." Krista hesitated. Gentle wasn't exactly the right word. Weak was closer to the truth, but she couldn't make herself admit it. "My mother never knew how to put limits on Rosie. When I lived at home, I was the one who did that. I practically raised her."

Jess grunted sympathetically.

"My stepfather tried to put limits on Rosie, too. She wasn't quite eleven when he married my mother. He always treated us both like we were his own children, but Rosie resented him. She didn't want him telling her what to do. She didn't even want to be in the same room with him."

"It can't be easy to be a stepparent," Jess said.

"No. And nothing's been easy for Rosie. Not in her whole life."

"Are you angry at her, Krista?"

Krista shook her head sharply. "No!" She took a deep breath and forced herself to be calm. And honest. "I guess I was angry at first, right after she ran away. I thought she was just trying to get attention. She'd asked me if she could move in with me, and I'd told her she couldn't. After she left I thought she had just run away for a few days to prove how bad things were at home so I'd change my mind."

"But she didn't go home?"

Krista stared into her coffee cup. "That was a year ago. Fifteen months, to be exact. No one's heard anything from her in all that time."

Jess heard everything Krista hadn't said. The pain, the shame, the guilt, the fear. When a child ran, that child's family was left with nothing but feelings and questions. And the hardest question was, "What could I have done differently?"

"You feel like you're to blame." Jess lightly touched Krista's hand.

"Is that what the other families you've talked to tell you?"

"Not all. Some blame the kid instead. He's a troublemaker or an ungrateful brat or a bad seed."

"Rosie wasn't a troublemaker. She was . . . troubled."

Jess was conscious of how soft Krista's hand was, and how comfortable he was touching her. An attraction he might very well have been repressing when he still thought she was a prostitute made itself known. He schooled himself to ignore it and picked up his fork again. "Troubled?"

"Nothing was ever simple for Rosie. School, friends, life in general. Our father died just a few years after she was born. My mother didn't adjust well. She...she ignored Rosie or she smothered her. I was just nine, but I tried to help. I guess I didn't know what to do with her, either. We're very different."

"You were just a child."

Krista sipped her coffee and wondered how much more she could tell Jess. She certainly wasn't going to tell him the whole truth, but she debated what she *could* say. "Rosie seemed very bright to me, but she did terribly in school. She couldn't learn some of the simplest things. After a while she began to believe she couldn't learn anything. She turned into a behavior problem at school. One year they held her back. Another year they advised my mother to put her in a school for emotionally disturbed kids. My mother put her in therapy instead, but it didn't help."

"Was she learning disabled?"

Krista met his eyes and sent him a wry smile. "Where were you when we needed you?"

"Watching a nephew of mine go through the same thing."

"Rosie was almost thirteen before they discovered the problem. After he married my mother, my stepfather managed to get Rosie admitted to a strict private school in...in the city where they lived. She was so far behind the other kids that the school psychologist had to test her to place her in classes. That's when they found out. Rosie's IQ is sky-high, but she's got a mixture of problems that makes it hard for her to process the information she hears or sees."

"My nephew was dyslexic. The schools he attended never discovered it. They found out by chance after he ended up in an institution for juvenile offenders."

Krista made a sympathetic noise. "Were you close to him?"

"I should have been."

"I wasn't close enough to Rosie, either." Krista toyed with her coffee cup and wished she could get a refill. "After my mother remarried, I went on to college. I only went home occasionally. After they diagnosed Rosie's problems, she seemed to be doing better. She talked about schoolwork like it was something she could really do for the first time. She didn't have many friends, but she had made one or two good ones. I guess I wanted to believe all her problems were solved."

"And then?"

"Then she stopped being a little girl and became a young woman. And all her problems came back to haunt us." Krista saw, with relief, that their waitress was coming with the coffeepot. She grasped the cup like a lifeline once it was full.

Jess held up his hand to halt the waitress. "Krista, are you sure you won't have something to eat?"

Krista examined him over the rim of her cup. He seemed truly concerned. She felt a small flutter of awareness for the man, not the reporter. Jess Cantrell was every woman's idea of masculine. He wasn't handsome, not in the pretty-boy sense, anyway. His features were strong, vying for attention in a face that would always be dominated by his eyes. His hair was wavy, almost unruly, and just a bit too long. There was a sprinkling of silver strands mixed with those of darkest brown, and a network of fine lines around his eyes that placed his age at just over thirty. He was no pampered paper pusher. Krista had seen Jess rolling on the floor with an assailant who was desperate to beat him. She had seen him sustain a blow that would have knocked a weaker man senseless. Now she was seeing a different side of him. He cared about people. He was here to get her story, but he wouldn't digest it and her, then spit them both out changed and degraded. She had heard enough about him to hope he was a man of principle. Now she was almost certain of it.

Still watching Jess, she ordered an English muffin. He nodded, satisfied.

"Do you worry this much about everyone you interview?" she asked, when the waitress was gone.

"I've interviewed people who barely qualify as human. I'm careful when I choose the ones I worry about."

"Is a prostitute barely human?"

"Nothing's ever that easy to categorize. I've interviewed death row inmates who've made me worry about them. I've interviewed governors and senators and only worried about how I was going to expose them in print."

Jess noted the way Krista sat up a little straighter and dropped her eyes. He had hit a nerve. He probed a little. "That surprises you?"

She shrugged.

"All I'm really saying is that things aren't always what they seem." He waited for her response, but when she remained silent, he probed some more. "You, for instance, Krista. You say you aren't a prostitute, yet you prowl the streets and the bars of the Quarter looking like one. You pick up men. I saw you take money from one the other night. What does that make you? And what does it have to do with Rosie?"

Krista mentally skimmed through her own story, weeding out clues to the things Jess couldn't know. He was good, too good. He picked up every nuance of speech, every bit of body language. He had caught her at a time when she was most vulnerable. She would have to work hard to keep her secrets.

"Krista?"

She met his eyes again. "After Rosie ran away, my family began to discover the hard facts about finding kids who don't want to be found. The police took all the information, but after a few weeks it was clear that they weren't doing much. There are thousands of runaways every year."

"The numbers are higher than that. A million is more like it. Some estimates say at least a million are on the streets of this country at any one time."

"You don't pull any punches, do you?"

"I know this subject."

Krista accepted her muffin from the waitress and began to spread it with jelly. "I know it, too, from the inside out. I know that this expert disagrees with that one. I know that when your kid is missing, or your sister or brother, you don't much care what the experts say. You just want to see that kid's face again. And not in the morgue of some strange city."

"Go on."

"We made the classic mistake that a lot of families make. We waited too long to begin looking for Rosie in earnest. By the time we did, the trail was cold."

"You said you thought she'd come back."

"Lot of parents have thought the same thing and never seen their kids again. After two weeks my stepfather hired a private investigator. After two months the investigator told him he was wasting his money. Rosie didn't want to be found."

Jess had met very few investigators with that kind of ethics. And those few were seldom ready to call it quits so soon. "Do you know where they looked?"

"Everywhere, apparently. Rosie had just vanished."

Jess let Krista eat. So far she had concentrated on the story of her sister. Now it was time for her to talk about herself. When she finished her English muffin, he questioned her. "So why are you here, Krista?"

She sifted through her answer before she gave it. "I disagreed with my stepfather...and with my mother. I wanted them to hire another investigator. I thought the first one had given up too easily. They said they'd done what they could, and that it was up to Rosie now."

She didn't add that she had sensed a certain relief from both her mother and stepfather when the investigation had been ended. She didn't doubt that they believed Rosie should be home with them, but she did wonder if, at least on some level, they were relieved she was gone. Rosie had been a burden on a marriage that was lived in the limelight. Even if they worried about her now, life was easier without her. As far as the world knew, Rosie was in a posh Swiss boarding school. In a way, Krista's parents acted as if they almost believed it themselves.

"So what did you do, Krista?"

"I hired someone myself."

Jess knew exactly what that must have cost her. "How could you afford it?" he asked bluntly.

"I have a good job." She smiled at his expression. "I should ask you to guess what I do, but I won't. I'm a librarian, and I'd saved a little money. I also had a trust fund." She sobered. "It's gone now."

"A librarian?"

"At a university."

"In Maryland?" he asked. Krista looked startled, and he added. "Your tags. On your car."

"Oh." There was no point in denying the truth. "College Park."

"So you used up your trust fund and your savings on a detective?"

"He was highly recommended. At first he seemed to be doing a good job. He got a lead right away. Rosie's photograph was identified by the staff member of a runaway shelter in New York. She had been there a month or so before, but at least it was a lead."

"And then?"

"Then nothing. Finally he told me the same thing the other investigator had told my stepfather. He said continuing the search would be wasting my money. By then I had precious little to waste, so I began to search New York myself."

"You quit your job?"

"Not at first . . . not at all, actually. I'm on a leave of absence right now. At first, though, I just looked for her on weekends. I'd fly up to New York and stay with a college friend. Then I'd walk the streets where runaways are known to congregate. I had thousands of flyers made, and I passed them out to anyone who would take one. I talked to kids, to social workers, to cops. . . ."

Krista thought about everything she had seen. Kids lost and frightened, kids selling themselves for their next meal, kids hooked on drugs and booze and despair. Running away wasn't Huck Finn having endless adventures on a raft on the Mississippi. Running away was shivering all night on a sidewalk subway grate and searching through garbage cans in dark alleys for dinner. Running away was Times Square at midnight, destitution, degradation. Running away was the end of hope and, often, sadly, the end of a young person's life.

Jess knew what Krista had seen. He had seen it, too. He touched her hand again, then, as if they had been friends for years, clasped it in his. "Rosie may be all right," he told her, although he didn't believe it for a moment.

"The kids who survive are found and counseled and loved back into wanting to live. Their parents are called, Jess. Mine haven't been."

There was nothing else to say. Krista knew the truth, and she was facing it head-on. He didn't release her hand, though. "Why are you here, then? And what are you doing in places like Tallulah's, taking money from strangers?"

Krista felt awkward with Jess holding her hands, but she also felt comforted. Whatever else she felt was too preposterous to consider. "One of my flyers ended up in the hands of a kid who knew Rosie. She called me one night in Maryland, collect, of course, and asked me how much I'd give her if she talked. I told her I'd give her five hundred dollars if she could prove she'd seen Rosie and another thousand if I found Rosie because of a tip she'd given me."

"What kind of proof did you expect?"

"She'd mentioned right at the start that Rosie had been staying with her, and she still had some of her things. I went up to New York that weekend and met her. She was a tough kid, streetwise and hostile. Her name was Joy. She lived with a . . ." Krista's voice faltered. "A pimp."

Jess didn't say anything. There was nothing to say.

"She showed me a jacket she said Rosie had left there. I recognized it. I'd given it to Rosie on her fifteenth birthday. She said that Rosie had left New York about a month before with some other people and gone down to New Orleans. Joy said Rosie had planned to come back, but must have changed her mind. Joy never heard from her again, but she said that someone told her they'd seen Rosie in a bar in the French Quarter."

Jess released her hands and curled his around his coffee cup. "And that's why you hang out at Tallulah's?"

"Joy told me something else." With her hands free Krista felt strangely bereft. She toyed with the last half of her muffin. "She said she'd seen my flyer weeks before, but she didn't want to talk to me because it felt like she was squealing on Rosie. She said she finally called me because she needed money. I guess she felt sorry for me, though. It was funny, I wasn't even sure she had any feelings left. But when I was leaving she told me if I was going to look for Rosie, I ought to do it one of two ways. Either I should offer a big reward so someone would turn Rosie in, or I should pretend I was a street kid, too. If I didn't, then no one would talk to me."

"And you didn't have the money to offer," Jess said, thinking out loud. "What about your parents?"

Krista sidestepped the truth. "They said it could lead to extortion or even to someone holding Rosie for ransom. They wouldn't do it."

"So you came here and pretended you were a street kid? Street *walker*?"

"You don't approve, do you?"

"I saw you the other night at Tallulah's, remember? I saw you take money and leave the bar with a man."

"But you didn't see me get rid of him." Krista looked up just in time to catch a subtle change in Jess's expression. "Or did you?"

He debated whether to be honest, but he really had no choice. "Yeah."

"It was *you* following me!"

"And it wasn't easy."

"You frightened me to death!"

"Somebody ought to frighten you." Jess leaned forward, his eyes gleaming. "You're playing with fire. What ever possessed you to pretend you were a whore?"

She flinched. "I don't like that word."

"You used it yourself. If the shoe fits . . ."

"I didn't pretend I was! Not at first, anyway. But if you hang out in bars late at night by yourself, it's just assumed. And I found out that if the street kids can't figure out how you're making enough money to live, they're suspicious of you. They think you're a cop or a detective. If they know how you're earning your keep, though, and if they know you're outside the law, too, they'll talk to you. I needed them to talk, and I needed them to trust me, and I needed to be accepted into the places where Rosie might show up. Little by little this whole thing developed."

"And what about your 'customers'? How do they like it when you tell them they've made a mistake and you're really just a sweet young librarian looking for her baby sister?"

"You're angry."

Jess realized she was right. He *was* angry. Krista believed she knew what happened on the streets of America's cities, but he doubted if she knew it all, or she wouldn't be risking her body and her life night after night. He was appalled that she was innocent enough to believe she could pull this off.

He didn't answer her directly. "What do you tell the men who pick you up, Krista?"

Krista could feel her cheeks heating. The things she had done had been done for love of Rosie. But that didn't make them any easier to talk about. "Do you need that for your story, Mr. Cantrell?"

Jess leaned back in his chair and pinned her with his gaze. "After everything that's happened today, I think you can call me Jess. Don't you?"

"I'd rather not call you anything. I agreed to tell you my story so you'd leave me alone. You know it now."

"I don't like it."

"Liking it wasn't part of the deal. Whether you believe it, well, that's your business."

"Oh, I believe it. It's too terrifying to be a lie." His eyes softened just a little. "And I admire you, Krista, for caring so much. But I think you're a fool."

"You're not alone."

His voice softened, too. "Your parents?"

She didn't know why she added the next part. "And the man I was going to marry."

"Was?"

"He broke our engagement when I told him I was coming here to search." For a moment, in her bitterness, she forgot it was a reporter she was talking to. "I supposed I missed one too many parties. Scott's a very political animal."

One shaggy eyebrow lifted in interest. "Political?"

Krista's heart beat faster. "I just meant he's always trying to get ahead. Impressing people, glad-handing. I'm sure you know the type."

"You don't sound like a woman nursing a broken heart." Jess was curiously glad of that.

"I was hurt. I lost Rosie, then I lost Scott. Maybe you can put that in your book. When a child runs away, it's like a pebble being dropped in a pond. The ripples go on and on."

"What else can I put in my book, Krista?"

She thought about what she had told him. Nothing she had said would give away anyone's identity, although, of course, if Jess researched her background, he could easily find the truth. She could only hope that he wouldn't believe there was any reason to check further.

She shrugged. "You can tell the story just the way I've told it if you change names and places. I'm not proud of what I've had to do to try and find my sister. I don't want anyone connecting what you write to me or Rosie."

"You'll be more than connected if one of those men who picks you up finishes you off in some hotel room one night."

Krista exploded. "I don't go to hotel rooms with men! If I'm forced to leave a bar with one, I get rid of him outside on the street, where there are people around. I've got excuses enough to get rid of the whole damn U.S. Army if I have to! No one's going to finish me off, and I'm not going to be finished here in New Orleans until I find Rosie! You can think what you want about me, but if you write this so that I'm identifiable in any way, I'll sue!" She stood as if to leave.

Jess saw the fierce blaze of her blue eyes and the proud set of her shoulders. He stood, too, dropping a couple of bills on the table. "I'll take you back to your car."

She wanted to refuse, but she had no way back other than to call a cab, and she had no money to waste. Silently she followed Jess outside.

They were immersed in traffic before he spoke again. "I'm not writing this book to bring pain to anybody. I'm not writing it to exploit anyone or any issues. I'm writing it so that people just like you will know what's happening out here."

Strangely, she believed him. He was a man of integrity, a steel-hard man wrapped around a core of sensitivity and honor. He would spare no one and nothing in his search for the truth, but what he did with the truth when he found it would never hurt those who needed protection.

"I have to find my sister," she said finally.

Jess pulled into the parking lot of the Kwik Korners next to Krista's car. "You worked here to support yourself?"

"I couldn't look for anything in my field. I didn't know how long I'd be in town. I knew I had to work outside the Quarter so that none of the kids I'd met would see me. This job was easy to get, and I knew it would be easy to leave."

"What will you do now?"

"I'm going to sell my car. I can live on the money for a while, and that way I'll be able to look for Rosie full-time."

Jess wanted to tell her to go home. Looking for her sister was like looking for the proverbial needle in a haystack. Krista was living on hope and foolish dreams. And she was asking for trouble. He knew, though, that he had no business telling her anything. She cared desperately. Rosie didn't know it, but she was lucky to have a sister like Krista. He wondered why Rosie had run away if she was so loved. Something just didn't add up.

There was also the fact that nothing Krista had told him explained the hunch he'd had about her all along. Why had Krista looked familiar? Why did he have the feeling that she wasn't being completely honest with him?

"It will be hard to look for your sister without a car," he said, searching for a way to keep Krista there and to keep asking questions until something clicked.

"I can rent a car if I have to leave the city." Krista put her hand on the door handle. She didn't know what to say. Thank you? For saving her life, for breakfast, for listening? Somehow nothing seemed appropriate. They were no longer strangers, but certainly not friends. "I'm glad you were following me this morning...Jess," she said at last. "And I do trust you. I know you'll use what I've told you wisely. Good luck with your book." She turned to open the door, but Jess put his hand on her shoulder to stop her.

"You never showed me a picture of Rosie."

"What's the point?"

"That should be fairly obvious. I've been researching this book for most of a year. I've been to every major city, in every major shelter, to every major news event or conference. I've seen thousands of kids. I may have seen your sister."

Krista hesitated. Hope flared inside her, but she knew enough to keep it tamped down. She debated the merits of showing Jess Rosie's picture. If he had seen her, Krista could have a fresh lead. She tried to think of reasons not to show him. The obvious one seemed so improbable that even while she was still debating her decision, she was pulling out her wallet.

"This is the best photo I have. Rosie was fourteen here. I have several more recent shots, but they're not very good. I took them, and I'm not much of a photographer. This was the last school picture she gave me." Krista drew it from her wallet.

Jess saw her reluctance to part with it. He guessed that the photograph was one of the few mementos Krista had of her sister. He almost hated to take it from her for the moment he needed to look at it.

Krista watched Jess stare at the photo. His expression didn't change perceptibly, but he seemed to come to attention. Hope flared inside her, and this time would not be smothered. "Have you seen her?"

Jess continued to stare at the photograph. As in his dream, he was back in Washington, D.C., at one of the endless cocktail parties he attended to pick up information about Capitol Hill. The party was more boring than most. He was finishing his drink so that he could gracefully escape when a young teenager came through the doorway. She retreated, bored and alone, to the corner.

Curiosity piqued, he had gone to investigate. They had spent half an hour in animated conversation. He had never forgotten her.

"Roseanna," he said at last.

She cried out in joy. "You've seen her, then? You know where she is?"

Jess shook his head and watched the light die in her eyes. "I know where she *was*, Krista. At a cocktail party in Washington two years ago." He watched wariness replace light. "And I know *who* she is, too. She's Hayden Barnard's stepdaughter. And so are you."

Chapter 5

Hayden Barnard, mighty senior senator from Minnesota, chairman of this committee, influential adjunct to that. Hayden Barnard who had the ear of the president, and the potential plus—if the rumor was true—the ambition for election to that office himself.

Jess handed Roseanna's photograph back to Krista. "It seems you left out some details when you told me your story."

Denial was useless. She had traded caution for hope and lost. Big. She took her time inserting the picture back in her wallet. "Washington's not a small town," she said at last. "I can't believe you recognized her."

"Roseanna and I had a long talk at your stepfather's party. She was delightful company, the only genuine person in the whole room. I've wondered about her since."

Krista stared out the window. "Welcome to the club."

"She looks like you."

"I know."

Jess turned in his seat so he was facing her. "I've had a hunch about you since the first time I saw you. You looked familiar, but I couldn't put my finger on where I'd seen you before. It wasn't you I'd seen, though. It was Roseanna. You looked

particularly like her when your hair was down and you were
dressed as a teenager."

"Rosie's hair is a little darker, and she goes for flashier
clothes. She's smaller than I am, too." Krista drew a harsh
breath. "Of course, she may have grown."

"I guess I don't have to ask why you didn't tell me who you
were."

"I guess not."

The seconds ticked by as both of them put this new turn of
events into perspective. Krista was the first to break the silence. "Jess, please tell me you won't use my stepfather's name
if you report this in your book."

"Surely you must know how important this could be. Kids
run away all the time. The kids of senators don't, at least, not
that the public knows about. I've been looking for something
to make my point that running away isn't a class problem. It
happens in all segments of our society. You've handed me the
perfect illustration."

She faced him, and her eyes snapped with anger. "I handed
you nothing. You stalked me, playing your hunches. And
you . . . you—"

"Saved your life?"

There was nothing she could say to that.

"I probably didn't," Jess continued, "but you'll have to
admit it was fortunate I 'stalked' you. Now it seems it was fortunate for both of us."

"I don't want Hayden's career harmed. It's bad enough that
Rosie ran away, but if you report what I've been doing to try to
find her . . ."

All Jess's instincts told him that he had Krista right where he
wanted her. She had no choice but to cooperate with him. He
already knew enough to make both her life and her stepfather's miserable.

The problem was that he didn't want her to feel cornered,
and certainly not by him. She was an unusual woman. She had
sacrificed her safety, her income, her parents' good opinion,
even her fiancé, to search for her sister. She loved deeply and
completely, and she was fiercely loyal when she did.

She was an unusual woman, and, to his surprise, he realized that she already mattered more to him than the story she could tell. He wasn't a man to settle for less than he could have, however. He wanted both Krista's good opinion and her story.

And he wanted her safety. Enough to bargain. Enough to volunteer as her quasi bodyguard until she gave up her search.

"There are ways of telling a story that make it both effective and impossible to trace." Rain began to fall again, and Jess spoke as gently, as soothingly, as the soft patter of raindrops on his windshield. "I don't want to hurt you, Krista, and though I'm not really an admirer of Hayden Barnard's, I wouldn't do anything to hurt him, either, unless he deserved it. I don't sensationalize, and I don't distort."

"Then you won't use what you've learned?"

"I didn't say that."

Krista ran a hand through her hair in exasperation. "What *are* you saying, then?"

Jess watched her hair fall softly back into place below her shoulders. "I have a proposition to make." When she grimaced he wished he had used a different word. "I can stay in New Orleans another month or so. I'm scheduled to start writing after that."

Krista resisted the warmth in his voice. "So?"

"I'd like to help you look for your sister."

Krista assessed Jess. She wished that one dark curl wasn't highlighting the bruise he'd sustained on her behalf. She couldn't easily forget what he'd done for her this morning with that bruise gleaming on his forehead.

"Why?" She tried to sound angry. "So you can get all the sordid details about her life on the streets?"

Jess knew she was scared, as fiercely loyal to her stepfather, apparently, as to her sister. He tried to push down his own annoyance. "Krista, do you know how many kids I've already talked to? I'm not a voyeur."

She had the grace to look ashamed. "I'm sorry. I—"

"You're upset and worried, and you want to protect the people you love. I know. I understand that, and I admire you for it. But hear me out."

She nodded. It was the best she could do.

"I'll help you look for Rosie. I'm not without contacts or skills. We'll work out a plan to find her together. Then, if we do, you'll encourage Rosie to let me tell her story. I'll do it in such a way that no one in the world will be able to recognize her."

"Why don't you just make up something, then? If you're not going to use real names and places, why not invent the whole thing?"

"Because I don't write fiction. Changing identifying details won't invalidate the truth."

"That's all? You'll help me find Rosie in exchange for an interview with her when we find her?"

"*If* we find her."

She almost choked on her next words. "And if we don't?"

"We'll both go back home. And when I write what I *have* learned, I'll let you censor anything that worries you."

"I'm not going home until I find my sister."

Jess's eyes shone with compassion. "You've got to admit the truth to yourself. If you haven't found her yet, and you don't find her or a good lead in the next few weeks, then you're not going to. She could be anywhere. It's senseless to risk your safety in places like Tallulah's if Rosie's in San Francisco or back in New York. A lot of kids stay on the move, especially the ones who have been gone as long as Rosie has."

"Joy said—"

Jess couldn't find a way to gentle the truth. "And how credible is anything Joy told you? Joy says Rosie was staying with her. Joy lives with a pimp, so Rosie was living with a pimp, too. Now Rosie's gone. Would the pimp be happy that his 'guest' took off?" He heard Krista's soft gasp, but he went on relentlessly. "The truth is staring you in the face. Rosie didn't go off on a trip with some other people. She ran from what was probably an intolerable situation. Chances are that Joy was glad to see her go. Girls like Joy are jealous of other girls who come into their families."

"Families?" Krista felt sick. "How can you use a word like 'family' to describe what you mean?"

He touched her shoulder in comfort. "It's not my word, and I didn't invent the system."

She waved off his explanation. "You weren't there that day. Joy's a tough kid, but she knew what she was talking about when she told me Rosie was in New Orleans."

"Why would she tell you the truth? You gave her money just for showing you Rosie's jacket. Even if she was right about Rosie being here months ago, she knew you probably wouldn't find her. And if you did, you were under no written contract to pay the thousand dollars. So what would it have benefited her to tell you the truth?"

"You sound like my stepfather!" Krista opened her eyes and forced herself not to cover her ears.

"Then maybe Senator Barnard and I have at least this much in common. Apparently we both want you safe."

Krista knew that the events of the morning had finally caught up with her. She was too tired to consider anything, much less a plan with such far-reaching ramifications. She didn't want to admit to Jess that he was probably right. She could haunt New Orleans bars until she was an old lady, but it wouldn't do her any good. If she didn't come up with something in the next few weeks, her chances of ever finding Rosie were slim to none.

"I need some sleep." Krista turned to Jess. He could see the exhaustion and the despair on her face.

"Will you consider what I've said?"

She nodded.

"How about dinner tonight to finish talking this through?"

She knew there was no point in putting it off. This had to be settled immediately, or Jess would take matters, and the story, into his own hands. "Dinner," she agreed. "I know you have a general idea where I live. Do you know which apartment is mine?"

He smiled. "You live right next door to the landlady with the insatiable broom."

She wasn't even surprised. "Let me guess. You followed me out of Tallulah's that night, then hid in the courtyard until morning."

"Don't make my techniques public."

"You really did?"

"Scout's honor. I spent the night in the bushes by the fountain. With an animal on my lap."

"Animal?"

"An old black tom. Quite a mouser."

"Why?"

Even though his hunch had paid off, Jess wondered why himself. Now, in retrospect, his pursuit of Krista seemed insane. At last he shrugged. "I couldn't get you out of my mind."

Krista turned the door handle. "About six?"

"Fine."

"I don't want to be seen in the Quarter with you."

"We'll go somewhere else. Get some sleep."

Krista nodded. She stepped out into the rain; then, as Jess watched, she got into her own car and drove away.

In the hotel restroom Krista slipped on jeans and a faded T-shirt and put her hair in a high ponytail before starting back to her apartment from the parking garage. In the mornings she walked to the garage dressed for work because she knew that her chances of being spotted by any of the runaways she had befriended were small. They were night creatures, these sad-faced, weary children, and they were rarely out before noon.

She always changed for the walk back, however, just in case she was seen. She carried her work clothes and shoes in the large purse she took with her. Today she was glad she had been so careful.

"Crystal!"

Krista stopped and searched for the source of the voice calling her.

"I'm over here."

Krista recognized the voice. "Tate?"

"Over here."

Krista followed the sound of the girl's voice between buildings and into the doorway of a shop sporting a For Sale sign. A young teenager with short black hair and enormous blue eyes was waiting for her. "Why are you hiding?" Krista asked.

"That guy who runs the show next to Paddy's Oyster Bar was following me."

Krista knew just who Tate meant. "Chaz."

"Yeah."

"He's a pimp, Tate. You've got to stay away from him."

"You think I don't know? I wasn't born yesterday."

To be exact, Tate had been born fourteen years ago. She had admitted her age to Krista once while they shared a pizza in a bar and grill off Bourbon Street. Tate had cautioned Krista not to tell a soul. "I look sixteen, seventeen, maybe," she had said. "I don't want anyone to know the truth."

In truth, Tate, with her slender body, pixie hair and puppy dog eyes, looked no older than twelve. After months on the street, however, Tate was fourteen going on a hundred.

"Where are your flowers?" Krista asked.

"I sold some. I dropped the rest and took off when Chaz saw me."

Krista knew just what that meant. Tate wouldn't eat that day, not unless someone shared with her or she scavenged for food behind one of the Quarter's fine restaurants. Tate supported herself by buying past-their-prime roses from a French Quarter florist, then selling them to tourists. She had no license, so the sales were illegal, but she was faster than the French Quarter cops, and she knew every side street, every courtyard and doorway.

"I've got money," Krista told her. "Let's get something to eat."

"I'm not hungry."

Krista wondered what or who had instilled such pride in the child beside her. Tate was at least ten pounds underweight. Like most of the runaways Krista knew, her nutrition was terrible. When she ate, she ate junk food. The only chance she had to get fruits or vegetables was out of garbage cans or the rejects from the wholesale produce brokers at the nearby French Market. Her young body was growing, and she needed good food to nourish it.

"Tate," Krista admonished, "if I was hungry, you'd share, wouldn't you?"

"No."

Krista laughed. "Yes, you would. I know this cheap place with a salad bar." Tate's expression didn't change. "And pizza," Krista added. "With lots of cheese."

"I'm not hungry."

"That's too bad. I can't go by myself."

"Why?"

"Last time I was there, the guy who works behind the counter came on to me," she lied.

"So how's that different than what you do at night?"

Krista was caught in a trap of her own making. Tate wouldn't be talking to her if she didn't believe that Krista was a runaway, beyond the law just like she was. Tate was particularly wary of adults, but Krista *was* an adult, and she didn't want Tate to believe that what she was pretending to do was right. She had considered telling Tate the truth before, but she was afraid that if she did, Tate would spread the word, and no one on the street would ever talk to her again.

Krista phrased her words carefully. "Tate, what I do at night isn't right. Not for me, not for anybody. I only hang out in bars because I have to." That part, at least, was true. "But I don't let guys pick me up unless I'm forced to." That was true, too. "You know, you're still young enough, you've got a choice. There are other places where you could stay, go to school, grow up like other kids do."

"I was caught twice after the first time I ran away," Tate said caustically. "They sent me to a place like that. It was like jail."

"But not every place is."

"*You* ran away. Why're you trying to make me go someplace?"

"I don't want you to end up picking up guys in bars."

"You do."

"And I hate it!" That part was *definitely* true.

"You're old enough to get another job."

"Tate, no one can get any kind of decent job without some kind of an education."

Tate was silent for a moment. When she spoke she sounded like the child she was. "That's the one thing I miss being on the streets, you know? I liked school. I had this teacher who said I ought to think about college when I got older."

Krista cleared her throat. How would she explain tears to Tate? "What about that pizza?"

"I guess."

* * *

Four hours of sleep wasn't enough, but it helped. By the time Krista had showered and changed into a pale lemon skirt and cotton sweater, she felt almost alive again—just in time to throw herself to the lions, or the lion, as this particular situation demanded.

She still hadn't decided what to tell Jess—or rather, she hadn't admitted to herself what she was going to tell him. She really had little choice. If he was willing to help her find Rosie, she had to say yes. She just resented the way she had been trapped into it.

She was also worried. There were things she hadn't told Jess, things Rosie surely would if she were found. From the moment of Rosie's disappearance, Krista had known that everything she did to find her sister might affect her stepfather's career. Hayden Barnard had been good to her, and he had been wonderful for her mother. Unquestionably, however, her first loyalty had to be to her sister.

Outside, Krista greeted her landlady, who was washing the long narrow windows of the apartment to the east of Krista's. The apartment had been vacant for two weeks, and the sparkling glass only emphasized the shambles the last tenant had left it in. Both Mrs. Duchamp and her husband were too old to keep up their property. Mrs. Duchamp swept incessantly, and when she wasn't sweeping, she washed windows. The two chores were the only ones she could manage, and she did those as if to prove that she could still create a little order where, in actuality, none existed. Mr. Duchamp, crippled with arthritis, did nothing more strenuous than collect rents.

Both the Duchamps could tell stories of better times, times when the Quarter was a safe place, a family place, times when hired help did all the work, and days and nights were filled with slow-paced, gracious living. Neither of them had ever adjusted to a different reality. Instead Mr. Duchamp rocked and told stories to anyone who would listen, and Mrs. Duchamp swept, as if she could sweep away changes she had never asked for.

Krista was waiting in the narrow alleyway leading back to the courtyard when Jess pulled in beside the curb. She investigated the street in both directions before she crossed the sidewalk and got into his car.

"You're afraid of being seen looking respectable?" he asked as he pulled away.

"Respectable and adult."

"How long do you think you'll get away with your act before someone figures it out?"

"Long enough to find my sister." Krista watched Jess drive. He was wearing a crisp, light blue shirt, rolled up at the cuffs, and dark gray denim trousers. His hair was still damp from a recent shower, and his freshly shaved face radiated vitality. Only the bruise on his forehead suggested he might have had better days.

"We'll have privacy where we're going," he said.

"Where's that?"

"Let me surprise you."

They headed toward Lake Pontchartrain, a large, brackish lake at the city limits, and in fifteen minutes' time Jess parked his car at its edge. "A college friend owns a boat house over there." He pointed to their right. "He's in and out of town, and I stayed there when I first arrived. He's gone for the weekend, and he encouraged me to use it again." Jess walked around to the back of the car and unlocked the trunk. Then he handed Krista one of two grocery bags.

The houses, a long line of them, were built over boat slips mooring a variety of crafts. Jess's friend had a sleek fifteen-foot sailboat under his.

The gray cypress boat house itself was no less luxurious. Krista followed Jess up the steps and waited on a deck with a hot tub overlooking the lake, until he unlocked the door. Inside, the three rooms were a silver and green bachelor's pad with walls of mirrors, an artificial jungle, a stereo system with speakers powerful enough to level the Superdome, and a bed that rivaled nearby Texas for size.

Jess looked slightly sheepish when he saw Krista's eyes widen. "I know. It's not my taste, either. But the view from the deck's terrific. It's so warm I thought we could cook out and watch the sunset."

Krista was touched, although she tried not to be. Bringing her to the boat house qualified as buttering her up, but just the fact that Jess had gone out of his way to think of it left an undeniably warm glow inside her.

It had been months since anyone had done anything kind for her. She had given up a job she loved, friends and Scott so that she could look for Rosie. Scott, of course, had been hardest of all to lose. He was a man who believed in spoiling a woman. He had specialized in candlelight dinners, orchids delivered at odd times for odd reasons, and compliments. He had made her feel wonderfully feminine, and she, in turn, had stroked his male ego, an ego—she had painfully discovered—that was more sizable than she had ever suspected.

"Thinking of Rosie?"

Krista realized she had been staring out the window. She didn't know for how long. "In a way." She wasn't sure if it was Jess's kindness or just the memories that made her add, "Actually, I was just thinking about all the changes in my life."

"Because of Rosie."

"She was responsible, I guess. I'll have to thank her for some of them." Krista pushed the past behind her. "What can I do to help?"

Jess wanted to know more, but he realized asking would be suspect. His interest was personal, but he doubted she would believe it. "Let me get you something to drink. Then why don't you come outside with me while I start the grill? If you feel like it, you can help with a salad later."

Outside, Krista sipped her white wine while she watched Jess expertly arrange coals and ignite them. He joined her at the round picnic table a few minutes later. "How long have you been in the city?"

"Since February."

"Have you taken any time to sightsee?"

"I've seen all the sights I care to."

"The last months have been hard," he said sympathetically.

Krista had almost forgotten what sympathy sounded like. "I'm sure they've been even harder on Rosie."

"If you don't step back a little and try to get some perspective on this, you won't be any help to anyone."

The sun had dipped lower in the sky, and, sensing night's approach, geese flew across the horizon. Krista tried to remember the last time she had just sat quietly and enjoyed a sunset. That part of her life seemed so long ago.

"Maybe you're right," she said at last. "God knows, whatever I'm doing now isn't working."

"Sometimes it's easier to gain perspective if someone is helping you."

"Do I detect a return to our conversation of this morning?"

He stood. "Not until after we've eaten."

"Do you always feed your victims before you move in for the kill?" She smiled a little to lighten her words. "How many steaks did it take to get Harold Grimes to tell you about the Pentagon blackmail scandal?"

"You're familiar with my work." Jess was pleased.

"I've even read your latest book. It frightened me to death."

The book—his best-selling work to date—had exposed the dumping of toxic wastes in unmarked sites in several major national forests. It had frightened a lot of people, himself included. "I didn't get that information with food," he assured her. He gave her a slow, thoroughly self-satisfied grin. "I just made a few promises I was determined to keep."

"Threats, you mean."

"I can play hardball if I have to."

Krista stood, too. "I think you mentioned something about a salad."

They ate in twilight. The steaks were pleasantly rare, the California burgundy mellow. Krista struggled to stay on guard, but she found it difficult. In the last months she had been on guard all the time. Now the water lapping against the boat slip and the good meal gave her a sense of lazy satisfaction. She allowed herself to forget, just for a few minutes, why she was there.

"Are you getting cold?"

"A little." The sun had long since vanished. Krista helped Jess clear the table, then followed him inside.

"Make yourself comfortable while I put the coffee on."

"If I make myself too comfortable, I'll be asleep in one minute."

"You're not going out to look for your sister tonight, are you?"

Krista considered. She had planned to. She hadn't missed a night since she'd come to New Orleans. Tonight, though, she was just too tired. She had to stay alert, not only to find Rosie but to keep herself safe. "I'm going home to get a good night's sleep," she said, feeling relieved even as she said it.

"I'm glad."

"Of course, this will be the night Rosie shows up at Tallulah's."

"I'll be there if she does."

Krista knew that Jess had just voiced the best reason for cooperating with him. She could continue searching alone, but if she did, her chances of missing Rosie were excellent. If Jess was searching, too, Rosie had less chance to slip between the cracks and out of Krista's life forever.

"Will she recognize you if she sees you?" Krista asked.

Jess knew that Krista had just given him his answer; they were working together now. "I think she might. I found her very engaging. She seemed to enjoy talking to me."

"What would you do if you saw her?"

Jess considered his answer carefully. "I'd tell her that you're in town trying to find her, and that you're desperate to know if she's all right. Then I'd tell her that no matter what she's done, no matter why she's running from home, I'd be sure she was protected when she went back. I'd reassure her that it's not too late to straighten out her life."

"That would be perfect." Krista leaned her head against the back of the sofa and closed her eyes.

Jess knew better than to press her. He made coffee, as he'd promised, then brought it to her. "Krista?"

She opened her eyes slowly; then she smiled. "Thanks."

"So we're working together?"

She sipped her coffee. It didn't give her the hoped-for lift. She was exhausted, and only sleep could cure that. "All right."

"There's just one thing."

All systems buzzed an alert, but she couldn't summon the energy to prepare. "What's that?"

"I get some say in how we go about this."

"Some."

"The first thing I say is that we've got to find you a safer place to live."

"No."

Jess sat down beside her. "Why not?"

"I can't afford anything safer in the Quarter." She held up her hand to stave off his reply. "I've got to live far enough away from the places where most of the kids crash so that they won't see me coming and going and get suspicious. But I've got to be close enough to be able to search whenever I can. Besides, I'm going to sell my car, so I won't have transportation."

"Can you hang on a few more weeks without doing that?"

She shook her head. "No. I'm still paying rent on my apartment at home, too. Without my job at the store, the car's my only source of income."

"You're not safe living in that place."

Krista shrugged. "I know, but I've developed a sixth sense. I know when I'm being watched. I'm careful."

"If I'd been after you the other night, I could have caught you. Then how would you have protected yourself?"

She shrugged again.

"Maybe you're not worried..." Jess lightly touched her chin, turning her face to his. "But *I* am. If we're going to find your sister, we're going to have to keep you safe while we do it."

"I know I'm taking chances." Krista locked gazes with him. She read only concern in his eyes. "I just don't know what else I can do. This is the only way I know to find Rosie."

"The apartment next to yours is vacant, isn't it?"

"How did you know that?" She shook her head before he could answer. "Never mind."

"I was there yesterday asking questions. I talked to your landlady, and she told me."

"It's much worse than the one I'm living in. I don't see how it would help any if I moved into... Oh, I see."

"I'm staying downtown right now, at the Sheraton. If I was living next door to you, I could keep an eye on things."

"I can't ask you to do that."

"You didn't."

Krista tried to imagine having Jess as her neighbor. "No one could know," she cautioned him.

"No one knows *where* you live, do they?"

"No."

"Then there wouldn't be a problem."

She could think of a number of problems, although none of them had to do with anyone suspecting she wasn't a runaway. With Jess so close, it would be harder and harder not to tell him the whole story, and easier and easier to forget that he was, first and foremost, a reporter. But right now both of those were less important than another potential trouble spot.

She was vulnerable. If she'd had any doubts, tonight had proved that to her. A little sympathy, a good meal and a listening ear had already convinced her to turn over part of her search to Jess.

She had been vulnerable to a man once before, vulnerable to his attentiveness, his compliments. She never wanted to be vulnerable again.

One thing she had learned in her months on the street was to be blunt about her suspicions. "If you move in next door," she said, her eyes not flickering from his, "you *stay* next door."

Jess heard the warning. More intriguing was the feeling behind it. "I imagine you think very little of men after the last few months."

"You imagine right."

"And I imagine that you've lumped all men into a single, undesirable category."

"Right again."

"Then imagine a man who's not interested in pursuing a woman who doesn't want him."

"Just so you understand."

He understood a lot, but the most important thing was that Krista had been hurt. That knowledge took the edge from his voice. "And just so *you* understand, I've never pushed myself on a woman, and I don't intend to start. If things go as planned, I'll stay in my apartment and you'll stay in yours. We'll concentrate on finding your sister. Agreed?"

She smiled, just a little, and nodded.

Chapter 6

Less than twenty-four hours later Jess was attempting to make himself at home in Krista's apartment.

"Sure you're going to be comfortable?" Krista frowned doubtfully at the feet hanging six inches over the end of what passed for her sofa.

"More comfortable than I'd be next door with roaches playing hide-and-seek in my navel."

Krista suppressed a laugh, or rather, she tried.

Jess glared at her. "I'm glad someone finds this funny."

"I'm sorry. But the image was irresistible."

"The roaches weren't."

"Roaches doesn't cover it. Try 'elephants with antennae.'"

Jess closed his eyes. He had stayed in some pretty disreputable places in his search for stories, but nothing had prepared him for the apartment next door. The front windows were the only part of it that had been cleaned in twenty years. He had closed the curtains and convinced himself to live with the dirt for a day. What he hadn't been able to live with were the roaches that had come out as soon as he'd turned off the lights.

The walls were thin between his apartment and Krista's. She had heard the commotion and gone to investigate.

"Why haven't their buddies rented this space?" he asked, twisting to get more comfortable.

"I rearranged their genes the first day I moved in."

"What about your genes?"

"My kids will probably all have two heads."

"Didn't we agree that I'd stay in my apartment and you'd stay in yours?"

Krista stifled the impulse to tuck Jess's blanket around him. He had been up all night haunting the Quarter and watching for Rosie while she slept. Then he had made arrangements with Mrs. Duchamp to rent the apartment and moved his few possessions out of the Sheraton. Now, in the early hours of the afternoon, he was desperate for some sleep.

"I should have known you'd use any excuse to get through my door."

Jess opened his eyes slowly. His eyelids only cooperated to the halfway point. "I'm in no shape for debauchery." He closed his eyes, and in a moment he was asleep.

Krista was wide awake. She watched Jess's breathing deepen. He turned, as if trying to get comfortable, then turned again.

She wished she had offered him her bed, but she hadn't yet showered or changed out of her nightgown and robe when he'd taken refuge. She still hadn't, as a matter of fact.

Half an hour later she was dressed in what had almost become her daylight hours uniform. Faded tight jeans, an oversized T-shirt, Reeboks and dangly silver earrings. She left her face scrubbed clean of makeup but covered her fingers with cheap rings. Her hair perched on top of her head in a careless wavy ponytail.

Until now she had been working or sleeping at this time of day. Right from the beginning her instincts had told her that if she found Rosie, it would be late at night. Now she felt a small thrill of anticipation. Perhaps she had been wrong all along. Perhaps Rosie would be up and out on this beautiful spring day. Today could be the day she found her.

She began her search at the small deli she had passed on the night she had been running from Jess. She had only shopped there twice before, both times with kids she'd met. The store was usually locked up tight in the evenings when she was free to talk to the proprietor.

Mr. Majors was said to be an old man with a soft heart. He never lectured, and he never questioned. He did sell kids day-old doughnuts and milk at cost, although the prices he advertised to the general public were inflated. Today Krista considered telling Mr. Majors who she really was, but she suspected he had a certain loyalty to the kids he fed. She wasn't sure if that loyalty would encourage or prevent his cooperation.

She ate a doughnut and polished off a pint of milk before she began some subtle questioning. "Feels like summer, doesn't it?"

"Always feels like summer this time of year."

"I'm not from here."

"You don't sound like you are, darlin'."

"I came in for Mardi Gras and forgot to leave."

"You wouldn't be the first."

"I came with some other kids." Krista pretended to sort through candy bars. "I lost them somewhere."

He harrumphed in answer. Krista noticed how carefully he was watching her. She realized he was waiting for her to shoplift. She held up a Snickers. "I'll take this." She fished in her battered leather bag for some change. "I've been looking for them, but I guess they took off."

Mr. Majors looked perplexed.

"My friends, not the candy bar," Krista said, forcing a giggle.

He smiled and took her money. "All kinds of kids come in here. They all look alike to me. I watch their hands, not their faces." He squinted. "I've seen you before, though."

Krista was encouraged that he remembered her. If he could just remember Rosie. "I was with this one girl I'd really like to find."

"Oh?"

He didn't sound interested, but he hadn't moved away, probably because he still thought she was going to steal something. Krista sorted through packs of gum. "Yeah. I've got some of her clothes. I keep having to move them around."

"Kids come. Kids go."

"Her name's Rosie."

"I don't ask names."

"She's smaller than me, but some people think we look alike. She's blond, too. Hair's darker than mine, more gold, her eyes are blue-green." Krista looked up. Mr. Majors looked blank. She set a pack of Juicy Fruit on the counter and rummaged in her purse again. "I've got a picture of her somewhere, I think. Some guy we met took it with one of those instant cameras."

Krista knew right where the photograph was, but she pretended to look for it. It was not the one she had showed Jess. Having Rosie's school picture would be hard to explain unless Krista admitted she was a relative. Instead she took out a slightly unfocused Polaroid she had shot herself on one of their last weekends together. It showed a smiling teenager in jeans and a red sweater against a background of green grass and trees. She looked as if she belonged at a high school football game.

Krista set the photograph on the counter next to the gum. "Yeah, here it is," she said casually. "Look familiar?"

The old man leaned over and squinted. "Can't say she does. Looks like a lot of kids, darlin'."

Krista hid her disappointment. "Too bad. I'll find her sometime, I guess. I'll just have to keep lugging her stuff around till I do." Krista took the snapshot back and slipped it in her pocket. Then she turned to leave.

"You forgot your gum."

Krista swept the gum into her purse.

"You say the kid's name is Rosie?"

"Yes. Rosie."

"If I see her, who'll I say is lookin' for her?"

Krista stared at him. If she told him the truth, Rosie would run like a scared rabbit. "Uh, don't worry about it. I'm hard to find myself. I'll just have to keep hoping I find *her*."

He nodded, but he looked suspicious.

Outside, Krista settled on a route. She was gambling that on such a beautiful day Rosie, or at least some of the other kids she had met, would be out soaking up the sunshine.

The sun poured honey-thick heat over everything it touched. Flowers bloomed on balconies and over the walls of quaint courtyards. Shopkeepers had thrown their doors open to entice customers and to share their wealth of aromas. Pralines simmering in cast iron pots scented the air along with incense and perfume. Krista took her time walking from place to place. There was no one she knew on Esplanade Avenue at the Quarter's edge. At Jackson Square she recognized a boy she had met at the party several nights before, but he was helping a magician who was performing in front of the St. Louis Cathedral for tips, so she did nothing more than wave.

She bought *beignets* and café au lait at the Café du Monde and ate them at an outdoor table facing Jackson Square, dragging the meal out as long as she could in case anyone she knew passed by. Once she thought she caught a glimpse of Tate, but before she could be sure, the girl disappeared.

A trip to the Moonwalk and a quick walk through the nearby Jax Brewery, a real brewery that had been converted into sophisticated shops, didn't turn up anyone Krista knew. She steeled herself for the next part of her search.

Bourbon Street never closed. Like a junkyard dog, it breathed easier during daylight hours, leashing its awesome energy for the wider audience it found after nightfall. But almost anything could be found there anytime if one knew where to look.

Krista knew. The knowledge hadn't come painlessly, even though she thought she had completed her education on Times Square. Here, though, every bar she investigated, every "bookstore" or "shop" she perused, seemed intensely, mournfully personal because Rosie might have been there, too. The shows were even worse, because as much as she wanted to find her sister, she didn't want to find her on a Bourbon Street stage.

Krista made her customary tour. She knew some of the regulars along the strip by name, and she stopped to talk to them. Some of those she thought she could trust had heard her fictitious story of why she was looking for Rosie. Several had even seen the same photo she had shown the grocer. Once a barker at one of the shows had asked to see it again, then shaken his head and said that no, that wasn't the girl he'd seen after all.

Today no one had anything useful to tell her, and she finally turned toward home. Disappointment was kissing kin by now. The walk back seemed three times longer.

When she slipped into the alley and entered the courtyard Jess was just coming out of her apartment. He was sleep-rumpled and heavy-lidded, the picture of a man who had tried to cramp his six-foot-two frame to fit a five-foot-six sofa. She couldn't resist calling a greeting.

He sent her half a smile, as if that was all he could manage on two hours' sleep, and came down to join her.

"Any luck?"

Krista shook her head.

"I've got a few local contacts I'm going to try tomorrow."

"I hope they're more help than mine have been." Krista lowered herself to the edge of a low brick wall that had once enclosed a shrine to St. Jude. "At least it was a nice day for a walk."

Jess sat beside her. "I was just about to go put out a contract on the residents of my apartment."

"I meant what I said earlier. You're welcome to stay the night at my place."

"I'll take you up on it. I can clean tomorrow, and I'm having a new mattress delivered in the morning, so tonight should be the only night I'll have to impose."

"Do you have sheets and towels?"

"I'll get some up on Canal Street."

As Krista had covered the French Quarter from one end to the other, she'd had plenty of time to think. A question had formed, one she should have given more consideration to before. Now she put it into words.

"Why are you doing all this?"

Jess waited for her to finish, to explain, but she didn't. He wondered if the question was a verbal inkblot test. Whatever he thought "this" referred to might say more about him than any answer he could give. He pondered the possibilities.

"Well, you could be asking why I'm sitting here talking about killing bugs and buying towels, but I don't think so. Or you could be asking why I'm willing to take the time to help you find your sister. Since I've already answered that, though, probably not. Or maybe you're asking why I'm researching this subject at all."

Krista laughed softly. The laughter felt good. She thought she'd left all her laughter outside the New Orleans city limits, but Jess had made her laugh more than once today.

"What do you want to know?" Jess turned to her, encouraged by her laughter. "What do you *need* to know, Krista? You don't trust me yet, do you?"

She sobered. "I don't know."

"You can."

"Maybe it would help if I believed this story could be that important to you. But I don't. There are millions of stories out there. You know enough about Rosie now to make a good anecdote in your book. Why see it through to its conclusion? Especially if a conclusion may be impossible?"

Jess had a nagging feeling that she was probably right. There was more to his decision to stay and help than just professional curiosity. As he'd tossed and turned on her narrow sofa, he had become more and more aware of one thing. At least part of the reason he was staying was because of Rosie's sister, not Rosie herself.

Now, however, he chose to answer the question differently. "I'm in this over my head. These kids aren't names on posters to me. And they aren't stories in police files. I was involved before I started this project."

"What do you mean?"

"I told you about my nephew yesterday. I didn't tell you that he was a runaway, too. It's not something I enjoy talking about."

Krista saw the pain in his eyes and knew he was telling the truth. "You said yesterday that your nephew had been put in a state school. Was that after they found him?"

"Bobby ran twice and ended up in a state school after the second time. He might have gotten some help if he'd stayed, but he found his way out of there, too. He was on the streets for six months before my brother got the call that he'd been found in Atlantic City. He was seventeen when they found him that time. He never made it to eighteen."

Krista was sitting close enough that Jess could feel a shudder go through her. "I'm sorry," she said.

"I didn't tell you to upset you. You know what can happen out here as well as I do. But you deserved to know why this book is so important to me."

Krista struggled for detachment. "That doesn't explain why my sister is."

"Damn it, I want to see one kid make it back!" Jess ran a hand through his rumpled hair. He realized that he'd just exploded at the wrong person. He started to apologize, but Krista interrupted, detachment forgotten.

"No, please. I understand."

"I try to be objective. I tell myself that writing the book will be enough. But every time I talk to one of these kids, I want to get involved. Somebody should have gotten involved in Bobby's life. Maybe he would have made it."

"No one can get involved if they don't know what's happening." Krista realized they had come full circle. Now she was trying to encourage Jess to finish his book and, probably, to stay and help her find Rosie. And sometime during their conversation she had put her hand on his shoulder in comfort. Now she clasped both hands in her lap. "At least I understand your motives a little better."

Jess stood. He wanted to go somewhere and sort out his feelings. "I'd better go see what cleaning supplies I need so I don't have to make two trips to the store."

"I'll help you clean tomorrow." The words were out of Krista's mouth before she had a chance to consider them. She wasn't sure who was more surprised, Jess or her.

"You don't have to."

"I'm unbelievably talented with a mop and scrub brush."

He smiled, and some of the sadness left his eyes. "That I'd have to see to believe."

She waved him away. "Tomorrow morning first thing. You can buy me lunch when we're done. Buy plenty of disinfectant, now."

Krista watched Jess climb the stairs and unlock the door to his apartment. She was trying to summon up the energy to go upstairs herself when she heard a noise behind her. She turned, just in time to see a flash of blue in the alleyway. In a minute she was up and dashing toward the alley.

Tate stood, unmoving, just at the entrance to the street. As Krista watched she flattened herself against a wall. Krista understood why when she glimpsed a pair of mounted police pass on two handsome chestnut horses.

Krista caught up to Tate before the girl could bolt. "What are you doing here?" she asked softly, clamping a hand on Tate's shoulder. "You didn't tell me you knew where I lived."

"I didn't!" Tate wriggled her shoulder, but Krista held it tight. "Let go of me!"

"Hey, not so fast. Tell me what you're doing here, at least." Krista dropped her hand after Tate stopped trying to free herself.

"I was selling flowers when these two cops on foot saw me. I took off, and I ran faster than they did, but then the mounties started after me. So I hid."

Krista was afraid she understood just what had happened. "You hid here?"

Tate glared contemptuously. "I tried to hide in the courtyard, but it was occupied, you know?"

"And you heard everything that was said."

"I heard enough to know you're a liar. And now you've teamed up with a snitch! What are you going to do? Have all your friends arrested?"

"Apparently you didn't hear enough."

Tate was still bristling. "I heard all I wanted to. You're no runaway. You're looking for your sister."

"That's true. And I'd lie to God himself if I thought it would bring her back."

"And sell your body?"

"I've never done that, Tate." Krista felt a surge of relief as she said the words. She was glad she didn't have to pretend anymore, at least not to this child for whom she had come to have a dangerous fondness.

"What do you mean, you've never done that? I've seen how you dress at night, and I've seen you hanging around Tallulah's."

"I got a tip that my sister had been seen in a French Quarter bar." Krista made herself go on. "And I'm afraid she's had to resort to doing what I've only been pretending to." She saw the blank look on Tate's face, and she sighed. "I'm afraid she's become a working girl, a prostitute. So I've had to dress like one and act like one, at least when I'm in Tallulah's or Maxie's or Shady Pete's, just so no one will be suspicious. I sit there and watch for Rosie. And if I'm forced to leave with a man, I get rid of him right away, before we make it to a hotel room."

"I don't believe you."

Krista sighed. "I don't blame you, honey. I can hardly believe it myself." She leaned against the wall. "Tate, have you ever loved anybody? I mean, really loved them. Enough to give up everything for them?"

"You're saying you have?"

Krista shook her head. "No. I'm saying I *didn't* love Rosie enough. Rosie's my baby sister. She's just a little older than you are. She came to me and said she couldn't live at home anymore. I didn't believe her, and I guess I didn't love her enough then to want to help her. So I sent her back home and told her to be a good girl. She ran that night. That was fifteen months ago."

"So now you feel guilty," Tate said with sarcasm. "Too bad, huh? A nice girl like you having to feel bad about herself and all."

Krista ignored the sarcasm. She knew Tate was disillusioned. That just made Krista want to reach out to her more. "I hope it's not just guilt. I hope it's love, too. Whatever it is, I want her home safe more than I want anything else. I want it enough to pretend I'm something I'm not just so I'll have a better chance to find her."

"You lied to *me*!"

"Honey, believe it or not, that's been the hardest thing I've had to do. I like you, and I want you to be safe, too. I hated pretending I went to hotel rooms with men, but I hated it worst of all when I knew you were watching me, because I never want you to think doing that's okay."

"I'm used to being lied to."

"I'll never lie to you again." Krista stretched out her hand, but Tate backed away.

"It doesn't matter."

Krista dropped her hand. "It matters to me. Look, I'm a lot older than you think. I'm twenty-four, and that's old enough to care about hurting other people. I wouldn't hurt you for anything."

"You'll turn me in, won't you? When you're done pretending."

"No." Krista thought carefully about her next words. She *had* considered turning Tate over to the authorities when she had discovered she was only fourteen, but her own predicament and something more had kept her from doing it. Tate had already been caught twice. Both times she had run again as soon as she'd had the chance. There had to be a better solution to her problems than the streets of New Orleans or the punitive child welfare system in her home state.

"I'm not going to turn you in," Krista said finally. "But, Tate, I'd like to help some way. There's got to be a better life for you. Maybe things were rough at home, but if you went back, couldn't you and your parents get counseling and make a fresh start?"

"Don't even think about it." Tate started out to the street.

"Look," Krista called after her, "my place is plenty big enough for both of us. Come stay with me any time you want. I'm still your friend."

Tate stopped. Krista could see her stiffen proudly. "I don't need a friend," she said, throwing the words over her shoulder. "Just stay away from me."

"I mean it, Tate."

Tate turned back to the street. In a moment she was gone.

Krista leaned against the wall of the house and closed her eyes. Tears squeezed between her eyelids anyway.

She heard footsteps from the direction of the courtyard, and she wiped her eyes with the back of her hand. When she opened them, Jess was standing in front of her. "I heard," he said.

She tried to tell him she was fine, but he saw her distress. In a moment he'd folded his arms around her. "Who is she, Krista?"

"Just a kid." She turned her face into his chest. His arms felt strong enough to hold her forever.

"A kid you care about, obviously."

"A lost kid."

He rubbed her back and thought about how good it felt to hold her. "You should go home. You know that, don't you? Look what you're doing to yourself."

"You think I could just go home and forget?"

Jess sighed and held her tighter. He knew what she meant. "You can't let yourself get so involved."

"And you're not?"

"You can't save them all, Krista. Maybe you can't even save any of them."

"Tate's such a neat kid, a *good* kid. And there's this pimp, Chaz, who's got his eye on her. How long's she going to hold out? We let these kids run away and live out here; then we tell them they're too young to get a job while we shut our eyes to what they're forced to do to survive!"

Jess held her until she was silent. His hand moved higher to stroke her hair. He thought how good it was to feel her so close, to feel the strength of her anger and the depth of her caring. Both of them had been alone in this too long. They needed to share what they'd seen.

"They're all good kids," he said at last.

Krista heard the compassion in Jess's voice. It was for her, but even more, it was for the Rosies and the Tates and the Bobbys. She realized she was standing in the circle of his arms, and she didn't want to move out of them.

She searched his eyes. "I don't know anyone else who would understand that."

"We may come to understand too much about each other. We aren't going to keep our distance, no matter what we've said."

Krista moved away, as if to prove him wrong. "I'm not usually this emotional. I—"

He touched her cheek. "Yes, you are."

"It's better if we're professional about this."

His mouth twisted into a wry smile. "Better? Sure. Possible?" He shrugged.

She stepped farther away, until the wall grazed her back. "I'm going upstairs to make some supper and get some rest. You'll probably want to sleep while I'm out tonight, since you didn't get much this afternoon. Make yourself at home."

"I'm coming with you tonight."

"You can't. You're dead on your feet."

"You're not going out by yourself at night again. We don't have to be seen together, but I'll be around if you need me."

"That's ridiculous. You—"

"That's the way it's going to be." He moved just close enough to keep her from bolting. "You want professional, Krista? Then think of this. What good will you be to me if some nut corners you and doesn't listen to your excuses? This is professional."

He touched her cheek again, then dropped his hand. "And personal." Before she could think of an answer, he was a block away, heading toward Canal Street.

Chapter 7

Krista was fastening a dangling rhinestone earring when she heard a light rapping on her door. She pulled her flannel robe tighter as she went to answer it. Jess stood there, looking not unlike a man who has been deprived of sleep for endless hours. She opened the door wider and motioned him inside. "You're not going anywhere tonight. You're going to stay here and sleep while I go out."

He shook his head. Krista wondered how someone who looked as if he were about to collapse could assert such authority.

"I mean it, Jess," she lectured, closing the door behind him.

"Guess what I found."

"Found?"

"Yeah. At my apartment."

"Rats? Graffiti?"

"A roof."

"Of course you have a roof," she said soothingly. She gauged the distance to the sofa and wondered if he could make it on his own. "We share a roof."

"I realize that," he said testily.

Krista made a sympathetic noise.

"*I* have a rooftop patio. It's in back. You can reach it from what looks like an attic door. There's even a table and chairs that I washed down, and right now there's a sunset."

"So you have a sunset, too."

"The sky has the sunset, I have the view." His brow furrowed in irritation. "Do you want to see it or not?"

She tsk-tsked. "Live next door to someone and the things you learn about his sense of humor."

"Fine. I'll watch it by myself."

"You can't *be* by yourself in that apartment."

"My pets promised they'll be on good behavior if you come through. Besides, they're all hiding. Someone spread the word that I bought a roach bomb." Jess let his gaze drift over Krista. Her robe was more modest than the clothes she would doubtlessly be changing into. Still, there was something about a woman in rhinestones and lavender flannel, especially a woman as curvy as Krista.

He touched her earring. "A bit much with the robe."

"Do you think so?" She realized how strange she must look. And even though the robe exposed nothing more than her ankles and wrists, she felt underdressed.

"You aren't a rhinestone sort of person."

"No?"

He yawned. "Pearls. Sapphires, maybe."

"It doesn't pay to look too classy where I'm going."

"It might, actually."

"What's that mean?"

He yawned again and raked his fingers through his rumpled waves. "Come see the sunset, and I'll tell you."

"I'll have to finish getting dressed."

"I'll leave the door open for you. Just go straight back through the living room." He turned without toppling over and left.

Curiosity piqued, Krista dressed quickly. She had bought only a few outfits when she decided to begin haunting the Quarter bars. All of them were flashier than they were revealing. Now she pulled on a green satin top that exposed more shoulder than chest and a short black skirt with black fishnet stockings. She left the stiletto-heeled pumps in her closet for later and postponed doing her face and hair.

Jess had left his door open. She peered cautiously inside before she entered. She had never gotten a good look at the apartment before; now she got a full view of the shambles it was in. Jess had truly gone the extra mile to live beside her.

She picked her way across a trash-strewn floor, her nose wrinkled at the acrid evidence of years of slovenly tenants. The entrance to the rooftop was in a small alcove at one end of the living room. She saw why Jess had missed it at first. The alcove had no light fixture, and all the French doors lining it were draped in heavy, filthy brocade. Only one was pulled back to let in light. Krista was surprised that the curtain hadn't disintegrated when Jess opened it.

She climbed the unfolded metal stairway and stepped out on the rooftop to join him at an ornate iron table. The view was magnificent. "Amazing," she said, dragging out the syllables.

The rooftops surrounding them were a collage of color and form. Some were steeply peaked, some flat or terraced, some mansarded with jewellike dormer windows. The roofs were tile and slate and shingle, and they glistened in subtle earth tones under the caressing light of sunset. Although Krista couldn't see the horizon, the sky above was a Mardi Gras display of color. From someone's courtyard a mockingbird sang a farewell to the sun.

In this hushed stillness of twilight, the moments before the Quarter burst forth into a raucous explosion of sound and energy, it was easy to imagine another time, the gentler time that the Duchamps would not give up.

"I thought you might like it." Jess came to stand beside her.

"It's even prettier than the sunset at the lake."

"Whatever you're paying for your apartment isn't enough."

"I'm not paying."

She faced him. "What?"

"I made a deal with Mrs. D. I clean the place and buy a new mattress for the bed, and she lets me have it this month for free."

"How did you manage that?"

"I showed her my latest book. Seems there's a history of famous authors coming to live in the French Quarter. She mentioned Tennessee Williams and Faulkner, among others."

Krista fought a smile and lost. "Tomorrow when you're scrubbing floors you may not think you got such a good deal."

"Look at that sky. It's almost enough to keep my eyes open for."

She forgot the sunset and the remnants of gracious living. "You don't have to keep your eyes open. Go over to my place and get some sleep. Use my bed. I'll wake you up when I come back and you can move to the sofa."

"No deal." Jess let his eyes dwell on bare shoulders and the faint hint of cleavage under cheap emerald satin. "You have no idea the trouble you're courting, do you?"

"We've been over this."

"Do you know what you do to men when you're dressed like that?"

She could feel her pale skin heat in embarrassment. She knew that the clothes she was wearing emphasized all the things that made her body as different from society's current fashion standard as a pinup girl from a *Vogue* model.

She prevented her hand from rising to her neckline to yank it still higher. "I know what I'm *supposed* to do to men when I'm dressed like this," she countered. "That's the whole point. If I go into Tallulah's dressed like a nun, I'll be treated like one and ushered right back out again with a fifty-cent contribution to the widows' and orphans' fund. I can't find my sister that way."

"*This* way, you may find yourself in big trouble."

"I've been here almost two months. I've survived."

Jess's mouth was a grim line. "What did the man you were going to marry say about this?"

Krista was taken off guard. She answered without thinking. "He said coming here was out of the question. Then he broke our engagement when I didn't listen. Scott's never been good at taking second place."

"Scott." Jess said the name slowly, carefully. "Scott Newton?"

"You've been snooping!"

Jess shook his head. "No. I haven't. But I'm not stupid. He's your stepfather's top aide, so it wasn't much of a guess. For the record, I like him even less than I like Hayden Barnard."

Krista opened her mouth to defend Scott, then realized what she'd been about to do. Her shoulders sagged. "At least you're half right."

"When were you going to be married?"

"At the end of this month." She laughed a little, pleased when the sound was more amused than bitter. "Scott did everything he could to make me forget this trip. He wheedled, he coaxed. He vacillated between ice-cold sarcasm and white-hot anger. Then he began some not-so-subtle bullying. I think he really believed that if he threatened to cancel the wedding I'd stay and marry him instead."

"Maybe he thought you loved him that much."

"Love had nothing to do with it." Krista watched the fading light of day cast shadows across Jess's face. It was strange, but even when she couldn't see him clearly, she had a strong sense of what he was thinking. With Scott, whom she had known longer and better, she had never really been sure.

"Then you didn't love him?"

"I thought I did. I probably did. But love's no reason to submit to blackmail."

Jess was intrigued with Krista's strength. Scott Newton was a growing force in Washington politics. Handsome and self-assured, he was more than a desirable catch, he was *the* desirable catch, a man destined to succeed. Everyone knew that Newton was being groomed for Hayden Barnard's seat in the senate when Barnard ran for president. It took a strong woman, a woman with solid values, to turn Scott Newton down.

"So you told Newton you wouldn't marry him?" Jess wanted the rest of the story.

"Not exactly. I just picked up the phone in Scott's office, where we were having our little chat, and I called the minister who was doing our wedding. I told *him*. Then I went home, packed up my wedding dress and returned it. I had the boutique send Scott the cleaning bill."

Since Krista looked pleased with herself, Jess allowed himself a chuckle. "That may be the first time in Newton's life that he hasn't had things his own way."

Krista gazed back out at the sunset. "There were so many things I didn't see clearly."

Jess would have liked to comfort her, but instead he used her temporary vulnerability to his advantage. "I'm afraid that's still true. You don't see clearly what can happen to you if you keep pretending you're walking the streets."

"My sister is more important to me than the chances I take to find her."

"So with a guilty conscience as big as the Grand Canyon, you take stupid risks to punish yourself."

Krista's gaze snapped back to his. "Who appointed you as my psychologist?"

"It doesn't take much training to figure out what you're doing." Jess leaned forward until they were only inches apart. "You failed your sister, or at least you think you did. You feel responsible for her, probably always have, from what you've told me. So now you're putting yourself in danger because you think you put her in danger. Well, that's not going to bring Rosie back."

"Cheap analysis!"

"How's it going to be if Rosie goes back to Maryland looking for you and you're in a morgue in Louisiana?"

"Cut it out!"

"Not until you realize the truth. Guilt's not going to bring your sister back. Punishing yourself isn't, either. Good sense might."

"And you, of course, are going to supply the good sense?"

He leaned back satisfied. "Yeah."

"Forget it." Krista stood, but his fingers wrapped tightly around her forearm, stopping her.

"This is probably hard to believe, but I care about you."

"Why? If I'm killed looking for Rosie, think what a great story it will make. You're in this for a story, remember?"

"I'm a sucker for happy endings." Jess dropped his hand. "Your death doesn't qualify."

Krista felt a pang of guilt for getting so angry. She recognized the feeling. Jess was right. Guilt had become an old friend since Rosie had vanished. She walked to the brick wall at the roof's edge and stared into the twilight. "What's your idea? Do you think I should tell the truth?"

"Not yet." Jess came to stand beside her. "But I don't think you should go off with men anymore, either. Why not tell anyone who asks that you've found a man to take care of you and you're not looking for anybody else."

"If that was true, why would I be sitting around Tallulah's or anyplace else? Why wouldn't I be at home making him happy?"

"Because he's a businessman, and he travels a lot. You get bored in the evenings."

The story seemed as full of holes as the curtains in Jess's apartment. But who would care enough to wonder for very long? If she threw a little money around and no one was suspicious of her to begin with...

Jess interpreted Krista's thoughtful expression correctly. "It could work, couldn't it?"

"It could. I could dress a little more conservatively, too, so I didn't look like I was advertising."

"I'm afraid that's not going to stop men from trying to get to know you. And that's why I want you in sight. We can work out a schedule of where you're going to be and when, and I'll stay nearby. When you leave, I won't be far behind."

"And if there was trouble, you'd come in with both guns blazing?"

"People already know my views on what happens to kids on the street. No one would think it was strange if I tried to protect one, although in that getup you hardly look like a kid."

"Neither do the sixteen-year-olds out there selling themselves."

Both of them considered. This was no game they were playing, no lighthearted masquerade. They were looking for a child who needed to be found.

"I'll do it," Krista said at last. "Despite what you think, I'm not in a hurry to be cornered by some crazy man who thinks I'm fair game."

"Good."

"And for the record, I'm working on forgiving myself. Every day I tell myself that guilt won't help Rosie now."

"Good again. But keep working on it. You're not there yet."

She smiled sadly. "I'm afraid I won't be there until I find her."

Wanda flopped down in the chair next to Krista's. Tallulah's was darker and smokier than usual, because the night was cool and Perry was keeping the door closed. Krista could hardly make out Wanda's expression.

"You know, I hear rumors sometimes," Wanda began.

"You hear rumors all the time."

"This one's about you and Chaz."

Krista didn't even like having her name used in the same sentence as the Quarter's most notorious pimp. "I don't have anything to do with Chaz," she said, shaking back her hair.

"Chaz don't like outlaws, and he don't like them talking to his ladies."

An outlaw was a prostitute who worked for herself. Obviously the pimps wouldn't like it; their livelihoods were threatened. "I don't like Chaz," Krista countered.

"He's dangerous, Crystal. You watch out for him."

Krista knew just how dangerous Chaz was. The girls who worked for him showed the effects of being under his "protection." They were often visibly bruised and always fearful of displeasing him. Krista had never understood why they stayed with him.

"I don't understand," she said, groping for the right words. "Why would anyone work for Chaz, or any other man?"

"You really don't know?" Wanda leaned forward. "You're for real?"

"I know what happens to Chaz's ladies. I guess that's all I have to know."

"How old were you when you hit the streets?" Wanda held up her hand as Krista started to answer. "Really. No bull."

"Older than some of these kids."

Wanda nodded. "You're not as young as you've been saying."

Krista shrugged.

"You a cop? A P.I.?"

"No."

"I've heard you aren't as friendly to your johns as you should be. Perry says he's gotten complaints."

"I'm choosy. I keep what I make and don't fork it over to some dude in a Cadillac, so I can afford to be."

"You know what? I think you're lying."

Krista shrugged again, although she was feeling anything but nonchalant. "Think what you want."

"You're educated, and even if you weren't, you're pretty enough to be going to classy hotel rooms instead of hanging around this joint."

Krista saw Jess come into the bar. If the night had been long and agonizing for her, she was sure it must have been intolerable for him. She had made her usual circuit of smoke-filled bars, mentioning casually to the bartender in each one that she wouldn't be looking for johns for a while. She had taken seats in dirty corners and watched customers come and go, scaring off the ones who wanted to be friendly. There had been no sign of Rosie, but Jess had made several appearances. She suspected he had kept her in sight most of the time.

"So if you're not a cop, what are you?" Wanda probed.

Krista was tired of everything. She was tired of searching and losing. She was tired of both hope and disappointment. And she was tired of lies. She would not be able to continue her charade indefinitely. Eventually Wanda, along with everyone else, would find out the truth. But as long as she was still trying to keep her identity secret, she couldn't tell the woman beside her. Wanda was good-hearted and savvy, but she was also an irrepressible gossip. Even with the best intentions, she might break a promise to be silent.

Krista compromised. "I'm a woman. And I'm on the run from something I did, just like half the people in this place. Someday I'll tell you the whole story." She stood. "Right now I'm going to head home and get some sleep."

"You didn't ask what I heard about you and Chaz."

Krista waited.

Wanda sighed. "You don't have a curious bone in your body, do you, sugar?"

"So what's the rumor?"

"Chaz was bragging that he was going to make you one of his wives."

Krista thought that of all the terms for a prostitute, that one had to be the most abhorrent. Even after two months on the street she was still enough of a romantic to think that the word wife had another, very special meaning. "Chaz is full of it," she said. "There's a guy taking care of me now. I'm not looking for business, and I'm sure not looking for a manager."

"I hope your guy's bigger than Chaz. Stay away from him, Crystal. When he comes after you, he won't stop if he don't have to."

"Thanks for telling me."

"Next time, you do the talking."

"Deal."

Jess was on the far side of the room, in conversation with a girl Krista knew as Sally. Most of the kids changed their names to something more exotic when they ran away. Krista suspected that Sally hadn't, which meant that her parents probably weren't looking for her.

Discovering that some parents didn't care if their children were on the streets had been one of Krista's most painful revelations. Some kids were "throwaways," not runaways. They came from homes that were breaking apart or already broken, and their parents were too troubled themselves to care what happened to their children. Some had been such problems that their parents had booted them out. Some had never had much of a home to start with. Some had parents who were homeless themselves.

No matter what the reason, the streets were filled with kids who were making it on their own, or trying to, and no one was looking for them. Krista supposed that made Rosie one of the luckier ones—although that wasn't good for much.

Krista paused at the door and turned, hoping to catch Jess's eye. Through the haze of smoke, she thought he looked up and saw her. Satisfied, she walked out and headed toward the raucous clatter of a Bourbon Street night.

Another night, another failure. Krista wondered if Joy *had* been telling her the truth. Perhaps Rosie had never been in New Orleans. In her heart Krista had been so sure that Joy wasn't lying, but then, what sort of judge was she? She had thought that Scott loved her, too. She had thought that he would stand by her always. She had misjudged Scott, and she had misjudged Rosie.

Krista was so engrossed in her thoughts that she paid little attention to her surroundings. She was nearing Bourbon Street, where there would be enough people to ensure her safety. Then, by the time the crowd thinned and every shadow and alleyway became a threat, Jess would probably catch up with her.

For the first time she admitted that she was lucky Jess had come along. He was right; she was courting disaster. Maybe he was right about something else, too; maybe she *had* been punishing herself. Rosie was in danger, so she had put herself in danger to find her.

Krista was a block from Bourbon when a man stepped in front of her. She realized how serious her preoccupation had been.

"Crystal, baby."

"Chaz." She nodded, unsmiling.

Chaz's smile was big enough for both of them. He was an inch shorter than Krista, with an acne-scarred complexion and straight black hair that he slicked back from his face to reveal one conspicuous hoop in his right earlobe. Chaz was given to wearing peacock-bright muscle shirts and gold chains under softer-colored suits. Tonight his shirt was shocking pink, and so was the carefully folded handkerchief in his pocket. His suit was mint green. He had an assortment of gleaming wooden canes, and he always carried one, although he could move like lightning. The canes were for show, and for punishment.

Krista started around him, but Chaz blocked her path. "Don't rush off."

"I have to meet someone, and I'm already late. If I'm not there in a minute, he's going to come looking for me."

"A john, baby? I can take care of a john like that." He snapped his fingers. "Let me take care of him for you."

"I can take care of myself." Krista started around the other side of Chaz, but he swung his cane in front of her.

"I need you, baby. And you need me. There's some bad old people out here on the street. You need protection."

"Apparently I need protection from you."

Chaz swung his cane so the tip pressed against her diaphragm. Two people passing ignored them. "You've got it wrong. I'd take care of you. Ask any of my girls."

"Some of your *girls* are hardly old enough to form a sentence."

"I just want to take care of you."

She said a word she'd only *heard* before.

Chaz's smile disappeared. "I'm trying to be nice, baby. But there are other ways to get what I want."

"I'm sure you know them all." Krista tried to start forward, but the tip of his cane pressed harder, making it difficult to breathe.

"You're pushing your luck." Chaz pulled his cane away, only to shove it swiftly at her once more.

Krista drew a sharp, painful breath. She searched the street in front of her for help, but they were still too far from Bourbon to be under the watchful eye of the police. She could only hope that Jess wasn't far behind her.

"Do you get my meaning?" Chaz asked pleasantly.

"I get your meaning," she gasped. "Now get mine. I'm not working for you. I've got a man taking care of me now, an important man. He won't take kindly to having me messed with."

He cocked an eyebrow, apparently interested. "Oh?"

Krista grasped the end of his cane and pushed it away. "A man with connections, *baby*."

"Oh, I'm scared, really scared." Chaz laughed.

"That shows good sense."

"You know what I think about your man with connections?"

A voice sounded from somewhere behind Krista. "I don't think the lady's interested."

Krista felt a thrill of alarm. Jess had followed her, as she had hoped, but he was furious. It was in his voice, leashed but dangerous. She moved forward, realizing as she did that she was in the odd position of protecting Chaz to keep Jess safe.

Chaz let his gaze play over the man standing where Krista had been. "I wasn't talking to you," he said at last.

"But I'm talking to you."

"I know who you are. You gonna put me in your book?"

"I wouldn't soil the pages."

"You the man with connections?"

"No, he's not," Krista answered, before Jess could. "But if I don't go meet my man now, he's going to come looking for me."

"Go on, Crystal." Jess kept both eyes on Chaz.

"You know the lady?"

"I know most of the ladies on Bourbon Street, and I know the names of the men who exploit them."

"Exploit. Hey, that's a ten-dollar word."

Krista felt Jess take her arm to move her out of the way, but she stood firm. "Jess, let's go." She covered his hand.

"Go on ahead."

"Not without you."

"He pay you to take care of him that way, baby? What else he pay you to do?"

Krista restrained Jess with difficulty. "You're a creep, Chaz."

"Whoa, I'm hurtin'." Chaz tipped his hat. In a moment he was sauntering down the sidewalk. Two young girls materialized out of a doorway, each positioning herself beside him. They turned the corner and were gone.

Jess exploded. "Damn it, Krista, I thought you were going to let me know when you left Tallulah's!"

She felt shaky with relief. She had been more worried about Jess than about herself. "I thought you saw me go."

"I didn't. I just happened to look over and see that Wanda was sitting alone. If I hadn't, he'd still be manhandling you. Or worse!"

She started to tell him that she could have taken care of Chaz herself, but she realized she would be lying. This wasn't a game, and Chaz wouldn't be a good sport about losing, even if it were. "I really thought you saw me leave," she repeated.

Jess sighed. It seemed as if he'd been holding his breath since he'd seen Krista talking to the pimp. He had been submerged in emotions. Now anger was the only one he let himself feel. "Be sure next time, okay?" he snapped.

"Things are heating up," she admitted meekly. She knew she had to thank him. She touched his arm. "Look, I'm sorry. I'll be more careful. And I appreciate your help tonight. I guess I *can't* handle this alone anymore."

Jess grunted in agreement.

The walk back to the apartment was made in silence. Krista unlocked her door, and Jess followed her inside. He had brought all his things over while he fumigated his apartment, and they were stacked in a neat pile by the sofa. He rummaged silently through them for his new sheets.

Krista watched. She still felt as if she owed him an apology. "Look, you take my bed. I'm shorter than you are. I'll be more comfortable on the sofa."

He didn't look at her. "I could sleep anywhere tonight. If it gets uncomfortable, I'll move down to the floor. I bought a sleeping bag instead of a blanket."

"No, really. I want you to take the bed. It's the least I can do."

Jess didn't know how to tell Krista that sleeping in her bed seemed entirely too intimate. He would smell her fragrance on the sheets, feel the hollows where her body had lain. Just the idea pumped new adrenaline into his exhausted body. "I'm sleeping on the sofa," he said in a don't-argue-with-me tone.

"You put yourself on the line for me, but you won't let me do anything for you."

He was too tired to edit his words. He straightened and ran his hand through his hair. "I don't want to sleep in your bed. Sleeping in your bed is a little too much like sleeping with you, and sleeping with you sounds a little too good to me right now. Got it?"

She blinked. Surprise and humor warred inside her, but humor finally won. She gave him a slow smile. "Never too tired, huh?"

"Go to bed, Krista." Despite himself, he smiled back at her. "I'm glad you're all right."

She knew she was exhausted, too, when she wanted to kiss him for the sweet sincerity in his words. "So am I. And I'm glad you're all right, too."

They stood staring at each other, two bleary-eyed, alto-gether-too-vulnerable people.

"Who uses the bathroom first?" Jess asked finally.

"You do."

He nodded. Then, as if his good sense couldn't hold him back, he stepped forward, cradled her head in his hands and brushed a quick kiss across her lips. He moved away before the impact made him kiss her again. "Good night."

He disappeared into the bathroom, quietly closing the door.

Krista stared after him and realized that she wasn't all right, after all. And neither was Jess. She wasn't sure that either of them would ever really be all right again.

Chapter 8

There was bacon scenting the air. And coffee. Krista lifted her head from the pillow and sniffed. The smells were unfamiliar, or at least unfamiliar outside a restaurant. Her mother had never been much of a cook, and Krista and Rosie had grown up on cold cereal for breakfast. Now she knew what she'd been missing.

Fumbling for her watch, she sniffed again. Her stomach growled, despite the fact that it was only eight o'clock. Normally she couldn't face eating until almost noon, but today was fated to be an exception. It was going to be an exception anyway. The presence of the cook made that true.

She rose and pulled on her robe. It was meant for comfort, not beauty, but Jess had already seen her in it and worse. Anyway, it suited her better than cheap satin and red spangles. She ran a brush through her hair and fluffed it over her shoulders before she went out to greet him.

"That smells heavenly, but where did you get it?" she asked through a yawn.

He turned, and her yawn stopped halfway and ended abruptly. He was wearing the jeans he'd been wearing the night before and the same plain yellow shirt. The shirt was unbuttoned, as if he had thrown it on with little thought, and he was barefoot. His hair was tousled, his chin and cheeks shadowed with a morning beard. He looked thoroughly uncivilized, darkly handsome and one hundred percent male.

"At the deli down the way. I woke up and found you didn't have any coffee," he said accusingly.

"I never drink my own. Pure poison."

"Anyone can make a cup of coffee."

"With one exception." Krista determined not to let the heavy dose of morning sensuality throw her. Jess was a man of considerable appeal, particularly since it was obviously unintentional. But the two of them were just working together.

His lips quirked in a half smile. "I couldn't live with a woman who didn't know how to use a drip pot."

"I don't even *have* a drip pot. And I don't recall asking you to live with me." She walked forward to peek over his shoulder as he turned to flip the bacon. "So that's how it's done."

"Who feeds you?" he asked incredulously.

"Anyone I can get."

"You weren't too bad at salad the other night."

"I can chop vegetables." She watched him drain the bacon grease into a cup. "That's what my coffee looks like."

"You haven't learned to cook because you haven't wanted to."

"Right."

He watched the bacon until it was just crisp enough, then removed it to a paper towel before he answered. "Because you're lazy?"

She laughed. "Probably."

He went to the counter to pour them both coffee. The pot was his; he never left home without it. Krista stayed at the stove, and he was just as glad. She was unimaginably beautiful with her hair a white-gold halo and her unencumbered curves covered in lavender flannel. He'd had the poor sense to kiss her last night, and now he was paying the price.

"Actually, I'm not sure it's laziness," she said, pinching tiny pieces off the end of one bacon strip to let them melt in her mouth.

Jess caught a glimpse of Krista sliding the tiny bits of bacon across her lips to catch them with her tongue. He turned away quickly. "Then what is it?"

"I think cooking was just one more responsibility when I was a kid, and I didn't want it."

She'd already said enough about her childhood for Jess to understand what she meant. "If you had learned to cook, then your mother would have turned it over to you."

"Something like that. She wasn't much in the kitchen herself."

"How about Rosie?"

"She wasn't bad. She used to make these great desserts." Krista realized this was the first time since Rosie had left that she'd talked about her without feeling pain. She supposed mourning for a runaway was like mourning for someone who had died. Someday, the pain had to dull. Otherwise you went crazy.

Krista took the coffee mug Jess offered her and sipped as he made omelets. "You know everything about me," she said as he sprinkled cheese on the eggs. "But you haven't said much about yourself. I don't even know if you're married."

Jess knew where *that* question had come from. It was directly related to his behavior the night before, even if Krista didn't realize it. "I was," he said, folding the end of the omelet over. "It ended about three years ago."

"Do you miss it?"

The question was interesting. Did he miss it, not her. "Yeah, I guess I do, though I never gave it much of a chance. Carol's another matter."

"You don't miss her?"

"I rarely saw her. I had my career. She had hers. She was a travel writer with a syndicated column. We weren't even ships passing in the night, more like jets or rockets. Our divorce probably made the Guiness book, because we could never find each other to negotiate details. I didn't even know it was final for a month because the decree took so long to catch up with me."

Krista got silverware and napkins and set the table while Jess dished up the bacon and omelets. "Apparently she missed some good breakfasts."

He laughed, glad she wasn't going to let him get maudlin. "Actually, I didn't cook back then. I started after Carol and I split. I got tired of hotel food, and I got tired of traveling. Until this idea came up, I had settled in Washington again, and I was doing a lot less out-of-town research."

They sat down, and Jess passed a plate of toast that had been warming in the oven. Krista took two slices. "Until this came up?"

"I've been all over the United States in the last year."

"When you're done here, will you be ready to write?"

He nodded. "Yeah."

She wished she could see into the future and know what his book would contain. Would it show a reunion between sisters, or would it tell the story of a woman who had looked until she realized her search was futile?

They ate in silence, until they were almost done. Jess sat back sipping his second cup of coffee as Krista finished. "I'm going to A Place For Us this afternoon after I clean my apartment. I'll talk to them about Rosie," he said.

Krista knew that A Place For Us was the local runaway shelter. Virtually all the kids she had come in contact with had been there at one time or another, either to spend the night, have a meal or receive medical care. Some of them had decided to stay and receive the long-term help they needed; now they were trying to make it back to a different life.

She hadn't visited A Place, because she was afraid she might be seen by the runaways she knew. But she did call regularly.

"I don't think they know anything," she told Jess, then explained her own contact with them. "They have my address in College Park. When I call, I give them my number there. I check my answering machine daily."

Jess finished his coffee and wished he had fixed more. Five hours of sleep hadn't made up for all the sleep he had missed. "I'll warn you, there's a large staff turnover in the shelters. Burnout's always a problem. But I'll show Rosie's photograph around and talk to everyone there, anyway. Maybe someone will remember some bit of information that didn't make it as far as their files.''

''While you do that, I'll be in Metairie selling my car.''

''You're sure?''

''Absolutely.''

Jess knew it wouldn't do any good to argue. He set his mug on the table. ''I hate to leave you with the dishes, but if I don't get started next door, you might have a guest again tonight.''

She wasn't sure that sounded like such a bad idea, but she wasn't about to tell him so. ''I'll do these, then I'll come help.''

''You don't have to.''

''I know.''

''At least wait until the former residents have had a proper funeral.''

She gave a mock shudder. ''That I'll do.''

Krista showered and changed into jeans and a sweatshirt. She braided her hair and covered it with a scarf, although she knew there was no way to stay clean with the job ahead.

By the time she knocked on Jess's door, he had swept away all signs of varmints. The apartment was just dirty now. Extraordinarily dirty.

''The sad thing is, this was probably charming once,'' Krista said as Jess ushered her inside.

''I don't understand why the Duchamps let it go this way. If they can't take care of it, they should sell so they wouldn't have to worry. The property must be worth a fortune.''

''They're afraid of change, so they pretend nothing has changed. Mrs. D. was downstairs sweeping the patio when I opened my door. I told her you and I were going to clean today, and she said she was glad, that the apartment needed a little tidying.''

Jess snorted. ''It needs a match and some kerosene.''

''How about soap and elbow grease?''

He grinned. He was clean shaven now, evidence that he had already given the bathroom at least a lick and a promise. ''When was the last time you did a job this dirty?''

''Last night when I went to Tallulah's.''

He touched her cheek in sympathy. ''This may seem like fun after all. At least here you'll see some progress.''

Because they needed light to be able to clean, they started with the windows. Curtains came down. Those that were beyond salvation went into trash bags, those that might survive the dry cleaners were piled in a corner.

Sunshine beamed through glistening panes by the time they had finished. The light pointed out how much was still to be done, but at least they'd made a start. After a brief rooftop break, Jess started on the wood floors, using wax stripper and an ancient buffer that Mrs. Duchamp had loaned him. Krista started on the kitchen.

She was cleaning the oven when she felt something brush against her leg. In the millionth of a second before she screamed she had the horrifying vision of a roach that had not only survived the fumigation but thrived on it.

Jess came running from the bedroom. Krista was sitting on the floor, whiter than anything in the apartment. A cat was on her lap, purring contentedly.

"I see Cat found you."

"Why didn't you tell me you had a cat?" she shrieked. "Why do you, anyway? You travel with a cat? Nobody travels with a cat."

He waited to be sure she was finished. "I don't have a cat. I don't like cats, never have."

"What is this, then?" she asked, pointing at the pathetic black beast on her lap.

"That's Cat."

"It's not clear to me yet," she said sarcastically.

"I don't like cats. I'd never have one. That's not mine, and it's not a cat."

"The fumes from the wax stripper getting to you, Cantrell?"

He explained again. Patiently. "That's Cat. Not *a* cat. And he's not mine, although it looks like I might be his." He frowned. "He won't go away."

"If he's not *a* cat, what is he?"

"Cat."

"And what do you feed Cat if he's not a cat?"

His tone was forbearing. "It's not hard, Krista. I go to the store and buy cans marked 'Cat Food.' Apparently it's made just for him, though, of course, it should say 'Cat's Food,' but then, not everyone understands the possessive.''

"Or the possessed."

He lifted an eyebrow in question.

"Never mind. You don't by any chance have Dog here, too, do you?"

He shook his head.

"Or Bird? Mouse? Rat?"

"Just Cat. And he comes and goes."

She laughed, because he had managed, through the entire ridiculous exchange, to look perfectly serious. "He rubbed against my leg and I thought your roach bomb might have created a monster."

The barest hint of a smile formed on his lips. "How's it going in here?"

"We aren't going to finish today. Not with just the two of us. I started with the oven, and I'm only three layers down. I won't get more than the kitchen done, if that."

"I'll probably just get the floors finished."

"That will leave the walls, the furniture and the bathroom," she ticked off, using the fingers of her rubber gloves.

"They'll have to wait. Meanwhile, I'm starving. Let's go out."

"I'm not sure it's wise to be seen together."

"We'll get sandwiches and eat them on the roof, then. The deli at the next corner sells po'boys. We can enter separately, if you want. Or I can choose for you."

"I'm not *that* worried."

"Then wash your hands and let's go."

Outside, wispy clouds played hide-and-seek with the sun, dappling the quaint, narrow streets with kaleidoscopic patterns of light. The mockingbirds were in concert; the pigeons were cooing in harmony, and Krista hummed along. She felt something she had almost forgotten. Contentment.

That realization was followed immediately by guilt. How could she enjoy the day when Rosie couldn't?

Jess had been surprised to hear Krista humming. It had touched him. He had seen occasional bursts of humor, even occasional smiles. What he had never seen was Krista relaxed, satisfied, content. Rosie was always with her, if only in her mind.

When the humming stopped he knew Rosie was there again. She was a ghost draining all pleasure from Krista's life. "Krista," he said gently, still walking. "You're allowed to feel good sometimes."

She thought it was frightening that he understood so much about her. She retaliated. "It'll make a better story this way, won't it? A woman so riddled with guilt that every moment of her life is tormented by it?"

"Screw the story."

A block from the deli Krista apologized by continuing the song until it was finished.

They were at the door when Jess realized what she had been humming. "You make me so very happy," he quoted, pleased. "Well, is it true?"

She hadn't even thought about the words. She covered her embarrassment by snapping at him again. "It might be, if you'd stop analyzing me."

"I listen. I don't analyze. I just hear what you tell me."

"The ego is mightier than the sword . . . or the pen."

He laughed as he opened the door for her. "Just tell me what you want me to stop. Listening? Caring? Putting things you've told me together in my mind so I can help you find Rosie?"

She slipped under his arm and let herself enjoy the brush of his body against hers. "Just stop being right all the time."

"Impossible." Jess wasn't sure, but he thought Krista groaned. He smiled, satisfied.

They were inside, heading toward the counter where they could order po'boys, the local version of a submarine sandwich, when Krista spotted Tate. She was standing in the snack food aisle, counting a pitifully small handful of change. Krista silently debated whether she should try once again to let Tate know she cared. The debate was short.

"Hi, Tate."

Tate whirled, and her eyes narrowed as she recognized Krista. "What are you doing here?"

"The same thing you are, probably. Getting some lunch."

Tate slipped her hand, change and all, back in her pocket. "I'm just looking around."

"How did the roses sell today?"

"I'm not doing that anymore."

Krista counted it as a good sign that Tate hadn't fled yet. "No? What happened?"

"I'm just not, that's all."

"I hope you found something better."

Tate looked torn between honesty and pride. Finally she shrugged. "I've been picking up cans. I met this guy. He gives me money for every bag I get."

Krista frowned. "Where do you go to get them, honey?"

"I'm not your honey."

"No, you're my friend."

"Not anymore."

"I hope that will change."

Tate shrugged again as Jess joined them. "I can order for you if you tell me what you want, Krista." He smiled at Tate. "Hi, I'm Jess Cantrell."

"I know who you are. You're a word pimp."

Jess didn't flinch, and his smile didn't dim. "You've got a way with words yourself."

"This is Tate, Jess," Krista told him.

"I don't want to be in your stupid book!"

"Okay. I'm glad you told me." Jess's face became very serious. Krista watched the way he held Tate's gaze. "I like it when people are honest with me. I'll bet you do, too."

"That's the way pimps talk. Sweet talk, so you'll trust them."

"Pimps are good at pretending. I don't pretend."

"How do I know that?"

He sighed. "You can't, Tate. That's what scares me about kids like you out on the streets. It's really hard to tell who to trust and who not to."

"Did your nephew trust the wrong people?"

Krista touched Jess's shoulder. "Tate heard us talking in the courtyard."

"I know." He was still looking at Tate. "I don't know if Bobby trusted anyone. I do know he was doing things that were guaranteed to land him in the morgue."

"Maybe he didn't care."

"I cared."

Tate shrugged.

"I'm just about to order lunch. Will you let me get you something, too? Krista and I were going to eat on the roof of our apartment building."

Krista watched. Tate had been about to refuse, but Jess's last words had intrigued her. For a moment she seemed like the fourteen-year-old kid she was.

"Roof?"

"Uh-huh. You can see almost to the river."

"I'm not hungry."

"How about if I get you a sandwich, then if you get hungry, you can eat it later?"

"I don't take things from people."

Krista jumped in before Jess could respond. "Then earn it. Jess's apartment is filthy. You won't believe it when you see it. We've spent the morning cleaning, but there's still a lot to do. Help us clean after lunch and we'll pay you."

Tate considered. Krista could tell she wanted to say yes, but her pride and a residue of disillusionment were holding her back. "How much?" she asked at last.

"It's hard work. Twenty dollars and lunch? We'll quit at five o'clock."

"Okay. But if I don't like it, I walk."

"Sounds fair."

"And no mind games."

Krista frowned uncertainly, but Jess understood. "We're not going to tell you what to do. Look, you take the afternoon. Watch us both carefully. If you don't like something we do or say, tell us. We'll do the same. Then, afterward, we can figure out if we can trust each other."

Tate tried to look bored. "I'll take a sausage po'boy, *hot* sausage. And a Coke, a big one. And a bag of potato chips, Cajun spiced."

"Two Cokes, maybe." Jess smiled. "An extra one to put the fire out."

Tate didn't smile, but her lips tightened enough to make Krista think she wanted to.

Lunch went well, although Tate hardly said a word. She wolfed down the po'boy and chips as if she hadn't eaten for days. Jess and Krista struggled to carry on an ordinary conversation, including Tate as much as they were able.

Krista hadn't been sure how hard Tate would work. She was the proudest child Krista had ever known, but she was also sure to know she would be paid, even if she hardly lifted a finger. Her incentives to do a good job were few.

If Tate understood that, she didn't show it. From the moment Krista told her what needed to be done, Tate worked hard. Her thin arms moved with lightning speed, sponging the walls with soapy water, then rinsing them. She did what she could reach, then stood on a chair to finish. When the walls were as clean as they would ever be, she used Mrs. Duchamp's vacuum cleaner to do all the upholstered furniture, taking time with each piece to be sure it was done well.

Krista finished all the kitchen appliances, then went on to the floor and cabinets, completing them in time to do the bathroom, too, while Jess put wood polish on the floors and buffed them.

The apartment was ready by five. Even the new mattress was in place, delivered by a burly man who carried it up the stairs on his back with the nonchalance of a tortoise with its shell.

The three of them took turns washing up in the bathroom, then gathered in the living room to admire their handiwork. Cat came to join them, and Tate scooped him up, cuddling him against her. "Where'd you get this old thing?" she asked Jess.

"He got me, I didn't get him. Thanks for not calling him a cat. Krista will never learn."

Tate looked at Krista, as if to see whether she were angry.

Krista smiled at her. "Jess doesn't like cats, so he pretends Cat isn't *a* cat."

Tate pushed her face into Cat's moth-eaten fur. "I don't like cats, either. This isn't a cat."

Jess nodded. "Smart girl."

"You two are nuts." Without thinking, Krista reached over and ruffled Tate's hair. "You're as bad as he is."

Tate stiffened, and her head snapped up. She glared at Krista, who was sure any progress they had made that afternoon had just been destroyed. She felt sick.

"I'm not your sister!"

"I know that," Krista tried to explain, "but I guess I forgot we weren't friends anymore."

Tate buried her face in Cat's fur again. Jess sent Krista a warmly sympathetic look. She blinked back tears.

"I guess we're friends," Tate said into Cat's fur.

Krista wasn't sure she had heard Tate correctly. "Are we?"

"Yeah." Tate lifted her head. "But don't try to hold on to me, you know? I don't like it when people hold on."

Krista held up her hands. "Hands off," she promised. "Would it be holding on if I asked you to come and see me sometimes when you feel like it?"

"I guess not."

"Are we friends?" Jess asked her.

Tate considered, her huge blue eyes a sea of doubt. "No."

Surprisingly, Jess nodded. "Good."

"Good?"

"Don't make friends out on the street, Tate. Not until you're really sure about someone. Dead sure. Especially men."

Tate didn't seem offended by the advice. "Chaz wants to be my friend."

Krista's face must have given away her reaction, because Tate tried to reassure her. "I don't want to be his," she said. "I know what he really wants."

Despite what Tate said, Krista wondered how long it would be before Tate succumbed to Chaz, or someone like him. She was so young and scared, even if she wouldn't admit it. She was also tired and hungry, and almost out of hope. "Tate, if you ever get that desperate, will you come to me first?" she pleaded.

Tate didn't even need to consider her answer. "Not a chance. You'd send me back. I'll take care of myself."

"No, I wouldn't. I'd help you find something better. I promise."

"Promises are worth this much." Tate snapped her fingers. Cat leaped out of her arms in protest.

"Mine are worth more."

"Yeah? I've heard that before."

"Not from me."

Jess looked at his watch. Krista knew he was going to end this impasse gracefully. She was grateful to him, just as she'd been grateful to him time and time again since she had met him. "I've got to get over to A Place For Us," he said. "They change shifts in an hour. This way I can talk to the staff on duty now, then I can wait and talk to the new staff, too."

"What are you going to talk to them about?" Tate asked suspiciously.

"Rosie, Krista's sister. Want to come with me?"

"I might walk with you, but I'm not going in."

"It's a good place, Tate. A safe place. They won't turn you over to the cops."

"I went there once before." She didn't say more, but it was obvious the experience hadn't been a good one.

"Well, I'd like your company on the walk if you don't have anything else you have to do."

"I'm not telling you anything for your book."

Jess smiled, warmly, gently. Gently enough to melt even the hardest female heart. "You don't have to." He turned his smile to Krista. She realized all her own defenses were down when *her* heart put up not the slightest struggle. "You're heading to Metairie?"

She nodded.

"When will I see you?"

"I'll probably be back sometime after dark. This will take some time."

"Thanks for everything today." Jess turned back to Tate. "And thank you. I wouldn't be able to stay here tonight if it weren't for your help." He leaned over and kissed Krista's cheek. As if he had always done so. As if they were more than simply two people working together. Tate nodded a curt good-bye.

Through suspiciously misty eyes, Krista stood on the balcony and watched Jess and Tate walk together through the courtyard. The teenager and the man made quite a pair. Tate with her dark hair and slender build looked enough like Jess to be mistaken for his daughter.

Even as Krista wondered if Jess realized that himself, she knew the answer. The kids had grown in both their hearts, until their parentage, their backgrounds, made no difference. The kids were part of them now.

Somehow, somewhere, they had all become a family.

Chapter 9

About two blocks from A Place For Us, Tate spoke. "I'm not going any farther."

Jess smiled at the stubborn lift of Tate's chin. She had more spirit per ounce than any teen he had met. Despite that, the life she was leading showed clearly. She was much too pale, and grimy around the edges. Her clothes hung on her thin frame, and her lank black hair looked as if she had chopped it off with a child's blunt scissors. But her face was intriguing, and except for Krista's, her eyes were the clearest blue he had ever seen. Tate just might become a beautiful woman—if she made it to womanhood.

"I'm not asking where you stay," Jess said, trying not to look too concerned, "but I am wondering if you have a place to sleep at night."

"I know some kids. They let me sleep on their floor sometimes."

"And when they don't?"

"I find other places."

"Krista has room in her apartment."

"Krista wants to hold on to me. She says she doesn't, but I've seen it before."

"Before?"

"People try to hold on to you because they think it's good for them, not for you."

"That happened to you?"

"Yeah. Bars on the windows, you know? People in those places hold on to you because, if they don't, something might happen to you, and then they'd feel bad or lose their jobs. They put you in a room with bars on the windows, and then they feel better. You feel like you're going to die."

"I didn't see any bars on Krista's windows."

Tate's eyes snapped. "Don't you get it? First people tell you that they love you, then they send you someplace with bars."

"The streets are just one big room with thicker bars on the windows than you'll find anyplace else," Jess pointed out. "When you're fourteen, you can't get free unless somebody helps you escape."

"I'll take my chances."

Jess slid his hands in his pockets. He wanted to grab Tate and take her somewhere safe, but he knew how useless that would be. She would be gone before the police had finished the necessary paperwork, and whatever flicker of trust she felt for him or Krista would be extinguished forever.

"Just remember where we live," he said when he could sound calm enough. "We're there if you need us."

"Sure." Tate left without another word. One second she had been standing beside him, the next she had vanished between two buildings. Jess walked the rest of the way by himself.

A Place For Us was a large, clumsy-looking brick building off Elysian Fields, just out of the French Quarter. The building housed a health clinic, too, which provided care for the kids who drifted in and out off the streets, as well as other community members. A Place For Us served meals and provided beds for street kids, but its larger mission was to help kids turn their lives around. Staff members claimed no miracles. They liked to think that at least half the kids who came through their doors made it back into society someday. The other half drifted farther away. No one who worked at the Place had any illusions of omnipotence.

Jewel Donaldson was one of those people. She had been at the Place since its inception five years before. She was resident grandmother, a woman who had earned retirement with thirty-five years as a social worker in one of New Orleans's most notorious housing projects. Instead of retiring, she had come to the Place and offered her services as a part-time volunteer. A year later she was on the payroll, despite her protests. A year after that, she moved in permanently.

Jewel's success with the kids hinged on her ability to talk tough and smother with love in the same wheezy breath. She was wider than she was tall; her skin was a remarkably unlined ebony, and her hair a thick silver Afro set off by solid gold hoops in her ears. Jewel was ageless and matchless.

Today, when Jess walked through the door, Jewel was downstairs lecturing a bleary-eyed young man staring at a television set. "No girl's gonna look twice at you, boy," she said, shaking one gnarled finger at him. "Not when she can smell you all the way across the room. Go get some clean clothes and get in that shower. You got looks galore, but who'd know it?"

The boy mumbled something, staggering as he got up from his chair. But Jewel didn't reach out to help him. By the time he got to the stairs, he was steadier. He disappeared as the stairway took a turn.

"Crack," she said, turning to Jess. "It's killing these kids."

Jess knew that crack was just one of the serious problems the Place had to face. Runaways had suffered serious health problems for decades. Now new, more dangerous threats were picking them off, one by one. "Is that kid going to make it?"

Jewel shrugged, but her concerned expression belied it. "If I have anything to do with it, he will. He's a good kid, and he wants to live. That's a start. We've got him in a drug treatment program starting next week. Now we're just staying with him twenty-four hours a day, making sure he doesn't get hold of anything while he's here." She laughed as she saw Jess's eyes flick to the stairway. "There was someone at the top of the stairs waiting for him," she confirmed. "And someone will be outside the bathroom door when he comes out. We aren't taking any chances. He's precious. They're all precious."

"You let them know that. That's why you have so much success."

Jewel shrugged again. She would talk about anything except her own commitment. She didn't consider it important. "So, Jess, what do you need to know today?"

He grinned. Jewel never wasted time. "I've got a girl I'm looking for."

Jewel motioned to the sofa, and he joined her there. From somewhere above them rock music cut into the silence. Seconds later two girls came through from the kitchen, dropping crumbs on the rug from the sandwiches they were taking upstairs. One look at Jewel's face, and they went back, returning with plates. The taller girl stuck her tongue out as she went by. Jewel laughed.

"So?" she asked, when they were alone again.

Jess pulled Rosie's photograph from his wallet. Krista had given him a copy when she agreed to let him help her search. "Does this girl look familiar?"

"Picture does, girl doesn't."

"Then you've seen the picture?"

"Her sister calls here about every week or so. We've got a copy of that picture and another one tacked up on the staff bulletin board, along with her sister's phone number."

"You must have a file on her, too."

"No, that's a funny thing. I went digging through our stuff when her sister called the first time, just to see if we did. There wasn't a thing. Not one blessed thing."

The music upstairs went off suddenly, leaving them in silence again. "How often do you update your files?" Jess asked.

"Not often enough."

"And you keep something on every kid who's reported missing?"

"This whole building would be one big file cabinet if we did that. No, just on the ones we get special information about. Flyers, investigator inquiries, police reports. If someone's looking hard for a kid, we usually have something in our files. If we don't, one of the runaway hot lines might."

Jess put Rosie's picture back in his wallet. "Did you ever check the hot lines for Roseanna?"

Jewel nodded. "I thought it was peculiar we didn't have anything. Her sister said detectives had been hired twice and that Roseanna had been traced to New Orleans. If that's true, we should have had something. When we didn't, I called a couple of other places nearby, and the hot lines, too. None of them had any information."

"Is that unusual?"

"It could be poor record-keeping. We all do the best we can, but kids slip through the cracks sometimes. People put off their filing, things get lost, new people come on board and don't realize they're supposed to keep track of everything that comes across their desks."

Jess knew that could be true, but Rosie wasn't just anybody. She was a senator's stepdaughter.

"What's your interest in this?" Jewel asked.

"I met this kid, before she ran away, and I know her sister."

"The sister sounds very concerned."

"Extremely so. To the point of obsession."

"And the girl's never called her?"

"No. She just vanished."

"Then either the girl's met with trouble or there's probably something wrong at home. Most runaways go back in a day or two, three or four at the most. A lot of those who don't contact their folks some way or other, even if they don't go back."

"But not all of them."

"Not all, but in my experience they usually will, if there's any reason at all to. The ones who don't are afraid of what's waiting for them, or they know they aren't wanted."

"Krista wants Rosie home."

"Did Rosie live with her?"

"She wanted to. Krista said no, and Rosie ran."

"And now she thinks it's her fault." Jewel pondered Jess's answer. "Why did the girl want to live with her sister?"

"She wasn't getting along with her parents. I don't know any of the details."

"If a kid runs, and she's gone a year...Roseanna's been gone at least that long, hasn't she?"

Jess nodded.

"Then," she went on, "whatever's wrong between her and her parents is more than just curfews and how much eyeliner she gets to wear."

"Krista defends her parents. She says that Rosie's always had trouble fitting in."

"Kids like that take a lot of abuse. Not physical, maybe, but emotional, and that's abuse just the same. Do the parents want her back, too? Or just the sister?"

"I've only spoken to the sister, but she says her parents paid a detective to find Rosie."

"If they did, he was lousy, or we'd have records."

From above them, a stream of profanity echoed through the halls and down the stairwell. Jewel didn't even look up. "Our young man just found out that someone's been outside the bathroom door waiting for him to finish his shower. He'd planned to get out, sneak in the bedroom beside the bathroom, crawl out the window, tippytoe along the roof edge and slide down the drainpipe. I've done it myself, just to see how easy it is."

Jess tried to picture seventy-year-old Jewel sliding down the drainpipe. He wished he'd been there to see it. "Why don't you just put bars on the windows?"

"This isn't a prison. We can't keep kids who don't want to be here."

Jess thought about Tate's comments. "That kid sounds like he doesn't want to be kept, Jewel."

"He just sounds that way. You would, too, if your body was screaming from the inside out. But that boy wants us to keep him. He wants to live." She smiled, half warden, half angel. "And we're just the ones to make sure he does."

Krista ran her hand over the smooth white finish of her Buick one last time. "All right, it's yours," she told the salesman at the Metairie Buick dealer.

The young man was obviously pleased. He and Krista both knew who had gotten the better deal. "I'll get the papers ready for you to sign."

Krista followed him inside. In less than half an hour she held a check in her hands, and he held a key chain in his. "You really should have sold this yourself. Taken an ad,'' he said, now that the deed was done.

''I would have, if I'd had the time.'' She mustered a smile to let him know there were no hard feelings. ''Will you do me one last favor? Would you mind calling me a taxi?''

She was halfway to the French Quarter before the impact of what she had done really hit her. The car had been a gift from Hayden and her mother when she had gotten her master's degree. It was a beautiful car, large and showy. Even if it had never really been to her taste, it had been a symbol of their love. Now she felt as if she had somehow broken a covenant.

Yet would she have been forced to sell if her parents had been more supportive of her decision to look for Rosie? They had made no offer to help her financially, although they could well afford to. And when Krista's expenses in New Orleans had been more than she had expected, her mother had insisted that she was too busy with her charity functions to help Krista sublease her Maryland apartment or sell the collection of antique dolls that had been bequeathed to her by a beloved great-aunt.

Krista was an adult, and she didn't expect help. But even emotional support was missing. In fact, both Hayden and her mother had sided with Scott when he'd threatened to break their engagement. Now she felt as if she had broken all ties with them.

She had the taxi driver drop her off about six blocks from her apartment so she could drop her check in the night depository of her bank. Then she started home, taking streets that she hoped would keep her off the path of anyone she knew. She was dressed casually, but her conservative skirt and blouse did not fit the image she tried to project at Tallulah's. People usually saw what they were told to, but if she looked too different from what her Bourbon Street cohorts were used to, they would definitely get suspicious.

The sun had set almost an hour before, and although street lamps and shop windows glowed, the back streets she took were too dark for her taste. She hurried along, her heels clicking against cement sidewalks.

Krista didn't want to admit that part of her hurry was because she wanted to see Jess. She didn't need comfort. She had sold a car, and that was all. Now she had enough money to make it through the next four months. If she got a lead that Rosie had moved to another city, she could follow her.

She picked up her pace. She didn't need comfort, but she could still almost see the sympathy that would be in Jess's dark eyes. He could be tough, and he could be gentle. Both came from a basic concern and compassion. He cared more about people than anyone she had ever known, including an excess of politicians who pretended they lived to serve their constituents.

Jess didn't pretend. After Scott, she had wondered if she would ever be able to tell when a man wasn't playing games. Either she was a bigger fool than she knew, or Jess was sincere. She had seen him with Tate. It had been like watching a man tame a wild fawn. He'd had exquisite patience and timing and an innate understanding of why Tate was so frightened of friendship.

Despite the new empty spot inside her, she smiled a little. She was pretending that the only thing she noticed about Jess was his compassion. Certainly that was the safest thing to notice, but there were other things, too. Dangerous things, like the way his very sensual mouth tightened at the corners just before he smiled, and the deceptively casual way he stood when he was ready for anything. Krista had seen the looks women gave him the few times they had been together in public. He drew smoldering stares and smiles, the kind a woman gives a man when she's issuing an invitation.

Krista wouldn't be issuing invitations herself; her energy was all committed to finding Rosie. She had nothing to offer anyone until she did, and, if she were honest, she wanted nothing from a man, either. Not after Scott. Someday, when all this was a long-ago nightmare, perhaps she could begin to live again. But until then she was a woman alone.

Except that she wasn't alone right now. She stopped and looked behind her. She had the unshakable feeling that there was someone there. She wasn't sure why. She hadn't really heard anything, and now, as she stared down the dimly lit street, she didn't see anything.

She shook her head and started walking again, remembering the night that Jess had trailed her. A shopkeeper locking up for the night nodded as she passed. A Porsche pulled up, and two men got out carrying groceries from Schwegmann's, the local discount supermarket. She passed them, glad for their presence and the reminder that there were plenty of people around.

Except that the rest of the block was empty.

Krista chided herself for being silly. It wasn't that late. People were still coming home from work or going out for dinner. Any minute someone else would appear. She stopped and peered behind her. The two men had gone inside, and the shopkeeper had vanished, too. But as she watched, a shadow lengthened just two doors down from the shop. A man stepped into the lamplight. He wore dark jeans and a familiar plaid shirt.

She turned and fled. Even as she tried to convince herself it couldn't be the gunman from Kwick Korners, her heels rang an alarm through the otherwise silent street.

She was almost home before she slowed enough to risk another look behind her. The man in the plaid shirt was less than a block away, in clear view. When he saw her turn, he stopped running. As she watched, he spread his legs and lifted his arm. Making a gun as a child would do with his thumb and forefinger, he aimed at her and jerked his hand, as if he had just fired. Then, laughing, he turned and sauntered away.

She had seen the same man with a far more deadly weapon.

''Jess!'' Krista pounded on Jess's door. She peered over the balcony to assure herself that she hadn't been followed, then pounded again. ''Jess!''

The door opened as she raised her hand to pound again. ''Jess.'' She was close to sobbing, but not close enough to throw herself in his arms. Not quite, anyway.

Jess took one look at her and remedied that. He pulled her against him and shut his door. ''What on earth is wrong?'' His hand was already in her hair, smoothing it back from her face. ''Did you hear something about Rosie?''

She shook her head. The panic that had carried her this far was overwhelming. She couldn't speak. All she could do was hold on to him.

Jess felt every one of her soft curves press against him. He held her tighter, his hand still sliding through her hair. "You need to sit down," he said at last, sorry he had to speak.

She nodded, or at least that was what it felt like to him. She didn't move away.

"I'll help you." He pulled away, inch by inch, until she was almost standing on her own. Then he guided her to his sofa. "Here, sit down. I'll see what I've got to drink."

"I need to call the police." Krista hadn't been sure her voice would work.

"Why?"

"I saw the man from the convenience store."

"The robber?"

She nodded.

"When?"

"Just a few minutes ago. Out there." She waved weakly toward the door. Jess had crossed the room and was already there.

"Did he see you?" he asked, throwing the door open. His stance was tense, alert. If the gunman had been standing on the balcony, Jess would have been ready to spring.

"Yes. He followed me for a couple of blocks. I ran."

He stepped out on the balcony and searched the courtyard below. "Did he follow you here?"

"I don't think so. No."

Torn between going after the man and comforting Krista, Jess finally came back in and closed the door. He crossed to the sofa. "If he did, he's gone now."

Krista took a deep breath and told him about the gunman's little joke. "He must be crazy, Jess."

"Maybe." Jess put his hands on her shoulders and pushed her back against the sofa cushions. "I'll call. They'll want to come and get your statement, anyway. You sit here and calm down. I'll be back in a minute."

In more like two, he reappeared. Krista's eyes were closed, but she looked as if she might never relax again.

"Drink this." He poured wine into a coffee mug and passed it to her, berating himself for not having something stronger on hand. As tightly strung as Krista was, she would have to drink the whole bottle to feel anything.

She wrapped both hands around the mug to steady it. "Are they coming?"

"The dispatcher said she'd have someone come right over. That means it'll be an hour, if we're lucky. The cops are over-worked and underpaid. And they've seen it all."

"But they won't be able to find him if they don't come quickly!"

Jess hated to be the one to point out the obvious. "They aren't going to find him anyway, Krista. He's long gone by now. That's why I didn't go looking for him myself."

"No!"

"I'm afraid so."

"He was following me!"

"He probably spotted you somewhere along the way and trailed you for a few blocks. That's all."

"But that doesn't make any sense. If that's true, why didn't he follow me all the way? Wouldn't he want to know where I live? And he didn't have to let me see him. He could have fol-lowed me and I would never have known."

"You would have. You're harder to fool than anyone I've ever followed." Jess knew she was feeling stronger when she shot him a dirty look.

"A dubious compliment!"

He grinned. She glared at him over the rim of her mug.

"Want some more?"

"I'd like to be sober when the police get here."

"You will be." Krista held out the mug, and he filled it again, then got up and found a mug for himself, pouring the rest of the wine into his. "Did you sell the car?" he asked.

She nodded. "I didn't get as much as I could have for it, though."

"Enough to keep you going for a while?"

"Just." Krista didn't know if it was the wine, the sympathy, the car or the gunman, but she was suddenly choked with tears and her head felt suspiciously light. She shut her eyes, sealing them tight. She was sure she felt the earth's rotation. "I'm never going to find Rosie."

Jess agreed with her, but he wasn't going to tell her so. She wasn't prepared for failure. "I'm sure it feels like everything's going wrong."

She squeezed her eyelids tighter.

He moved to the sofa, put his arm around her shoulders and wondered what had happened to a hard-bitten investigative reporter named Jess Cantrell. Krista leaned against him. "Go ahead and cry," he said.

But it wasn't tears she wanted or needed. And it wasn't comfort. She needed life, and she needed hope. She needed, just for that moment, to know that something was right and that she didn't carry all the world's burdens on her slender shoulders.

She opened her eyes, and they glistened with tears. Her hand lifted and touched Jess's hair in mute appeal.

His breath stopped, as if he no longer needed it. He felt the soft touch of her fingertips travel through him like electricity. He tasted the tear slowly falling down her cheek before he even lowered his mouth to hers.

In one day's time he had blotted out the memory of the lushness of her lips. He had kissed her so quickly the first time that the memory could have been a mistake. Now he knew it wasn't. Her lips were warm and soft, sweeter than anything he had ever tasted. Her body, pressed against his, was the same.

Desire, a pleasant buzz whenever he was near her, now roared with hurricane force. His hands settled in her hair; his fingers dug into its wealth, and he tilted her face so he could deepen the kiss.

Her surrender was so complete, so immediate, that it blotted all caution from his mind. Her lips parted for the thrust of his tongue, and he forgot about comfort and sympathy.

Krista forgot everything but the heat and the strength of the man holding her. For that moment she gave up her doubts, her fears, her weaknesses. There was only taste and touch and exploding sensation. Desperation, too, because Jess seemed everything fine and good, a man of strength, of fire and elemental integrity. She was desperate to feast on all the good things she had denied herself. In exchange she gave him the woman inside her, the woman who could love and laugh and abandon herself in the right man's arms.

Jess was the right man. For that moment he was the only man in the world. And it was that realization that finally made her pull away before the kiss could become more.

"I shouldn't have—"

Jess put a finger against her lips. They were damp and swollen, and he traced their perfect symmetry before he dropped his hand. "Yes, you should have."

"I'm lonely, confused."

"That wasn't confusion."

"I took advantage of your kindness."

He forced himself to take a deep, calming breath and searched her eyes. They were wide and desperately sincere. He wanted to curse and tried not to laugh. He swallowed hard, but laughter erupted anyway. He knew it was just as well. If he hadn't laughed, he would have grabbed her again, and this time he wouldn't have let her go.

Hurt, Krista sat back, folding her arms. "I'm glad you think this is funny."

"This isn't funny. You're funny. *You* took advantage of *my* kindness?"

"You know what I meant."

He circled her with his arms and pulled her closer. Laughter had ebbed to a warm smile. "Shall I tell you how hard I'm working not to take advantage of you?"

"We shouldn't be having this conversation."

"It's long overdue." He turned her so she met his eyes. "I want you, Krista. I've wanted you since things began to fall into place and I realized you weren't what you seemed."

"Jess, I—"

He silenced her with the same finger. "I know. There's never been a worse situation for falling in love."

"This has nothing to do with love."

"Perhaps not yet." He leaned forward, advising himself not to kiss her even as his lips took hers again. He forced himself to be gentle, to woo, to taste, to prove. She resisted; then she sighed, her warm breath caressing him as she gave in to the claim he was staking.

He let one hand trail down her hair to her shoulder, then farther to lightly caress her breast, farther still to settle reassuringly at her hip. Her arms rested on his shoulders; her fingers stroked his hair. When Jess finally began to pull away, she resisted.

"If not love, then what?" he asked. He held her chin so that she couldn't look away.

"Don't make this into something it's not."

"Advice you might want to take yourself." He wasn't smiling now.

"I want to find my sister. I don't want anything else."

"Do you suppose God is listening, Krista? Do you suppose if you say that enough, He'll hear you and bring Rosie back? If you sacrifice enough, you'll be rewarded?"

"You've got no right—"

A knock at the door interrupted the rest of her speech.

"That's probably the police. I was wrong about their timing." Jess reluctantly dropped his hands.

"We haven't finished this conversation." Krista moved away and smoothed her hair. "You've got no right to tell me what I feel."

"But I'm right, aren't I?"

The knock became a bang.

"Shove it."

He smiled a little and shook his head mockingly. "You've picked up some bad language on the streets, lady."

"Shove it again." She fluffed her hair once more and went to answer the door. If the two broad-shouldered cops standing on the threshold wondered why her cheeks were flushed and her lips moist and swollen, they were too polite to ask.

Chapter 10

The police station serving the French Quarter was red brick and quaint, a relic left from a previous age. The cops staffing it were another matter.

In his years as a reporter, Jess had compiled a list of contacts all over the country. Some were people he knew personally; others were people he knew about. Before Jess had come to New Orleans, Sergeant Mack Hankins had been one of the latter. Now he qualified as a friend. Mack had worked personally with many of the kids who came to the city looking for excitement or escape, and he had been happy to share what he had learned with Jess.

The morning after Krista had seen the gunman, Jess sat at Mack's desk, surrounded by all the attendant noises of a normal day at the police station, finishing up the story for him. "Apparently the guy has a weird sense of humor. He pretended to shoot her."

"And he was gone by the time Crane and Michaels went looking for him?"

"I imagine he was gone before Krista got home to call."

Mack, a balding, middle-aged man with a potbelly and matchstick arms, sat back, drumming a pencil on top of a pile of papers. "You know how many of these guys we catch?"

"Very few."

"The dumb ones, mainly. The ones who brag to somebody and get turned in. Or the ones who get cocky and go back to the same place or operate the same way time after time so we can outguess them."

"I'd like to know if anyone matching his description has been reported in other robberies."

"I'll check into it. Why?"

Jess shrugged. "I'm not sure," he said honestly. "Just a feeling I have."

"Good enough." Mack continued to drum. "Anything else bring you here?"

Jess leaned forward to take out his wallet. "Yeah. I've got a photograph I'd like you to see." He pulled out Rosie's picture. "Does she look familiar?"

Mack dropped his pencil and took the photograph in both hands. He squinted, ignoring the wire-rimmed glasses nearly buried under more papers on his desk. "She's a pretty girl. Who is she?"

"Krista's sister, Roseanna . . . Roseanna Jensen. Krista calls her Rosie."

"This Krista, she someone special?"

Jess thought about the kisses of the night before. He had left Krista's apartment when the police did, and she had promised him she would stay in for the rest of the night. Both of them knew she was too shaken to go out looking for Rosie. Jess had made a tour of the likeliest night spots, but he had come home early, too. Come home to lie awake and think about the woman whose soft, warm body lay sleeping in a room bordering his.

Jess saw a knowing gleam in Mack's eye. "I met her while I was working on my book. We have an agreement. I'm helping her look, and if we find her sister, she's going to let me interview her—if Rosie cooperates, of course."

"I haven't seen the girl." Mack handed the photo back to Jess. "Should I have?"

Jess returned the photo to his wallet. "Krista's been looking for some time. She got a tip in New York that Rosie was here. From a hooker."

"We all know what a reliable source that is."

"Krista's sure the girl wasn't lying."

"Why do you want this story? There must be a thousand stories out there."

"There's a senator involved. Hayden Barnard. Krista and Roseanna are his stepdaughters."

Mack began to drum again. The phone on his desk rang, and he answered, still drumming. Another policeman dropped a new stack of papers on Mack's desk, and two desks away, a woman giving a statement began to cry. Mack hung up the phone and never missed a beat.

"Hayden Barnard, huh?"

"Runaways happen in the best of families."

"Yeah, but not many of even the best of families have his kind of clout." Mack flipped the pencil, and it landed point down in a mug containing several others. "We'll have something on her, I'm sure. It'll take me a while to go through reports. When did she run?"

"Fifteen months ago, give or take."

"Roseanna Jensen? With an *e n*?"

Jess gave the other essential facts to Mack, then stood to leave. "When should I check back?"

"Give me a day or two." Mack hefted himself from his chair to say goodbye. "This Krista, she as pretty as her sister?"

"Rosie's a child. Krista's a woman."

"A pretty woman?"

"No." Jess watched as Mack's theories tumbled, then took pity on him. "A beautiful woman."

"You going after her?"

"Help me find her sister first. Then we'll talk."

Mack laughed. "I'll see what I can do."

With her hair in a frizzy topknot and her curves molded by blue denim, Krista drew more than her share of looks from appreciative teenage boys. It was Saturday, and the French Quarter was crowded with tourists and locals alike. There were scores of teenagers roaming the streets and lying on the grass of Jackson Square. She blended in, as she had intended. If Rosie was nearby, she blended in, too, because Krista had seen no trace of her.

When Rosie had first run away, Krista had played a game, although there had been no fun in it. She had tried to clear her mind completely and become totally receptive so that if somehow, somewhere, Rosie was thinking of her, their minds could touch.

They had played the game together as girls, sometimes with surprising results. Then, of course, they had been in the same room, and the game had been a way to pass the long hours until their mother came home from work. After Rosie's disappearance the game had been a desperate attempt to find clues. Those results had *not* been surprising. Once or twice Krista had experienced a strong sense of desolation, but she hadn't been sure if the feeling had come from inside herself or was being sent by her sister. Each time she had concentrated all her energy, silently pleading with Rosie to call her. Each time the phone had not rung.

Now Krista sat under a cluster of crape myrtle trees in Jackson Square and closed her eyes. She had spent the morning searching in all the usual places. She still had Bourbon Street to check, and she was gathering her energy. She let her mind drift until her thoughts were still. She closed her ears to the birds and the buzz of cars and conversations. She ignored the warm breeze playing along her skin. She continued clearing her mind until she was as receptive as she could make herself.

Time hung suspended. For the first time in months she experienced the deep sadness that had come to her twice before. She could almost see Rosie. She felt the sting of tears and didn't know if they were her own or her sister's. She tried to see more, a place, a clue, but there was nothing. Call me, she silently pleaded, as the vision and feeling faded. But even as she said the words, she knew they hadn't been heard.

She opened her eyes. Jess was sitting beside her.

She wasn't surprised to see him. He always seemed to be there now, especially when she needed him. He had been there last night, and she'd regretted needing him ever since.

Her feelings for Jess Cantrell were proving to be a complication in a life that was already far too complicated. She had no way of knowing that he was thinking the same about his feelings for her.

"Are you all right?"

She didn't even try to smile. She tried to put last night out of her head. "Sometimes I try to talk to Rosie in my mind. Most of the time I don't feel like she's there, but sometimes I pick up this strong feeling . . ." Her voice trailed off.

"What kind of feeling?"

"Sadness. Hopelessness. I'm never sure if it's mine or hers."

Jess stretched out beside her. His knee brushed hers, and both of them were far too aware of it. "Is that what you were doing just now?"

"It was worse today than it's been before. I told her to call me. She didn't hear."

Jess didn't say that sometimes when you wanted something badly enough, pretending you had it could be a substitute. He didn't say that ESP and telepathy were parlor games and could only mislead her. Instead, he coaxed her to talk. "If she did hear you and she called Maryland, you wouldn't be home."

"My answering machine has a special message for her. It tells her to call me collect at my apartment here night or day."

"So anyone who called you in Maryland would know you were here?"

"Anyone who wanted to could trace the area code to New Orleans," she agreed.

"Or anyone who heard your message and knew you weren't home could steal you blind before you got back."

"My building has a security guard. Hayden insisted on it."

Jess tried to reconcile the Hayden Barnard he knew with the solicitous stepfather Krista spoke of. The Barnard Jess knew was solicitous only when it suited his agenda of the moment. He was a ruthless man, warm and considerate only half as often as he was cold and calculating. Never mind that he and Jess were always on opposite ends of the political spectrum, either. Jess's feelings about the Minnesota senator had nothing to do with environmental policy or funding for the Pentagon. They had to do with integrity, and he had been privy to the Capitol Hill rumor mill long enough to doubt Barnard's.

"But Rosie won't call, anyway," Krista said, burying her fingertips in the warm grass. "It's sixteen months today that she's been gone."

Jess was sorry that today was such a sad anniversary. He was also sorry about last night. Not sorry he had kissed Krista—he could never be sorry for that—but sorry that they were both so confused and concerned about it today.

He knew better than to add to the confusion, but he touched her hand anyway. "I'm still working on it, Krista. I've barely started."

The brush of his fingers did strange things to her pulse rate, so she tried to ignore them. "You haven't told me what you found at the Place."

He recapped his visit, but he didn't tell her that the shelter had found no flyers or detective or police inquiries about Rosie in any of their records. Krista didn't need to know that, not until Jess was sure it was important.

"You talked to the staff?"

"I talked to them all. Talked to the kids, too. Rosie didn't look familiar to any of them."

"It's hard to believe she wouldn't have gone there even once if she was here."

"Some kids avoid the shelters. They're afraid they'll be sent back home."

"But Rosie was identified by a shelter worker in New York. So we know she went to one, at least. Maybe she's just never been here."

Jess heard the sadness in Krista's voice. He wished he had more to cheer her with. For a moment he thought about how unfair life was, not just for Rosie and the kids on the streets, but for Krista and him, too. They were a man and a woman like many who had just discovered a mutual attraction. Yet they were caught up in something that made that attraction impossible. They deserved to explore what might be. Instead they were doomed to play sinister detective games in a city made for laughter and love.

But then, when had life ever been fair? His livelihood depended on it not to be.

Krista moved her hand so they were no longer touching. "Did you find out anything today?"

"I talked to a cop I know this morning. He's checking the station records. If there's anything there, he'll find it."

"Maybe I should go back to New York."

"Or Minneapolis, or San Diego, or Detroit, or Memphis—"

She stopped him with a wave of her hand. "I know. She could be anywhere."

The French Quarter was bad enough. Jess couldn't abide the thought of Krista walking the streets of Manhattan again. He knew the odds were against her finding Rosie, even if the teenager spent every night of her young, sad life hustling in plain view.

Jess pushed to his feet. "Let me buy you lunch."

"We shouldn't be seen together so much."

"If anyone comments, tell them you're helping me with my book."

Krista didn't look at him. "I won't be much company."

"Despite what they teach at places like Tallulah's, a man doesn't have to have his ego stroked every second of the day."

"I don't know why you stay around, Jess."

"Don't you?" He held out his hand.

She let him help her up. "I don't want to talk about last night."

He was glad one of them could get to the point. "Right now I'd rather eat than talk, anyway. There's a seafood place on Bourbon where we can get a seat by the window and people-watch. The glass is tinted. We won't be visible from the sidewalk."

"I saw a blond girl today, about Rosie's height. For just a fraction of a second..."

"How often does that happen?"

"Two, three times a day. Sometimes it's the way someone walks, sometimes hair color, sometimes size and build."

Jess tried to imagine what that was like for her. "But you keep right on looking."

"I'll always look. No matter where I am, no matter how old I get to be. I'll always be looking."

"If you're going to be looking, you might as well eat while you do it."

Her eyes met his, and she tried to smile. "I told you once before. You can't be my father."

He put his hand at the small of her back to guide her toward the sidewalk. "I have a tough-guy image to maintain. I can't be anybody's father."

"You don't want kids?"

He was silent for a moment. When he spoke, there was no humor in his voice. "Right now I feel like I've got thousands of them."

Krista knew he meant all the kids on the streets, kids he'd talked to, whose lives he'd touched, if only for a few seconds. "Your book will make a difference."

"Yeah. I tell myself that, just like you tell yourself that if you give up your life for Rosie, she'll come back."

They walked to Bourbon Street without touching or speaking again, as if the reminder of what they were dealing with was enough to quench all their other feelings. It was only when they were seated by a window and their lunch had been ordered that Jess opened a new subject.

"I thought maybe we could drive out Airline Highway later today if you're game. There's a thriving business in human flesh out there, and I thought we could show Rosie's picture around."

Krista had done a minimum of searching there already. Some of the motels along the highway were notorious. One of them had been the site of the downfall of a popular television evangelist. "That takes money. The clerks don't like to talk unless they're paid."

Jess lounged back in his chair and folded his arms. "Funny thing, they always seem to talk to me."

He was the vision of self-satisfaction. Krista couldn't help smiling. "Why?"

"I don't know. Could be because I always tell them I'm going to mention them by name in my book unless they cooperate."

"I wish you would! Every just-crawled-out-of-the-gutter bastard who runs one of those places ought to be mentioned."

"Problem is, not everyone would be sympathetic."

"Not everyone knows how young the girls are who take care of these guys."

"Or, if they're older, how young they were when they started." Jess watched Krista, who had barely taken her eyes off the parade of passersby.

"There are places, aren't there, where the law won't pick up a kid sixteen or over? Where they aren't even considered runaways?"

"Yeah. The kids get their hands slapped if the police pick them up for prostitution, then they get put back on the streets to finish up their night's work," he confirmed.

"Why don't we protect our kids?" Krista turned away from the street. "Does it say somewhere in the constitution that we can't keep kids safe?"

"How do you keep a kid safe who doesn't want to be?"

"There have to be better laws, better protection, more enforcement—"

"Would any of that have kept Rosie at home?"

"No. But she might have been found and brought back."

Jess leaned forward. From the sidewalk, black hair and a slender, lithe body caught his eye. "There's Exhibit A."

Krista turned to see Tate. Krista was on her feet in a flash. "She's with Chaz." She started around the table.

Jess clamped his fingers around her arm. "I'll take care of it. Sit down."

"She knows me better than she knows you."

"Sit down." Jess didn't let go of her until she was in her seat. "I'll be back. Don't eat my crawfish."

He was gone before Krista could respond.

She leaned forward to watch, but Chaz and Tate had already disappeared from sight. Jess stalked by the window. Krista debated whether to follow him, despite his orders. As if to solve her dilemma, the waitress arrived with their salads. She knew that by the time she took care of their bill, the events outside would be over.

She was toying with her lettuce, watching the window, when Jess finally came back. He was walking slowly, and Tate was by his side. They stood outside the window for a minute. Krista could guess what Jess was trying to do. Then, slowly, as if he were leading a wild horse into a corral, he brought Tate through the front door of the restaurant and over to their table.

"I am not your kid," Tate told Krista angrily. "Don't try dragging me around like I am!"

Krista forced a smile and held out her hands, palms up. "No ropes, no handcuffs."

"And I'm not hungry. I just had a steak. A big one. And French fries."

"Did you have dessert?"

"I could have. I didn't want any."

Jess pulled a chair out for Tate as if he were seating Princess Di. "Then may we have the pleasure of your company?" he asked. "While *we* eat?"

"I'll have a Coke, but that's all. And I won't drink that if you hassle me. Got it?"

Jess tapped the side of his head. "Ingrained forever."

Some of the starch went out of Tate. "Good." She sat down, and folded her arms tightly across her chest. "So?"

Krista searched frantically for the right thing to say. She knew that if she said the wrong thing, Tate would be out of there like a shot. "So, what's new?" Her voice squeaked with the effort.

"Don't go messing with my life."

Krista took a sip of water and cleared her throat. "I asked what was new. That was harmless enough, wasn't it?"

Jess signaled their waitress and ordered a Coke. "Are you ready for dessert yet?" he asked Tate, before the woman left. "They're famous for their bread pudding here."

Tate made a face.

"Ice cream? Pecan pie?"

Tate rolled her eyes. "Chocolate ice cream."

Krista breathed a little easier. "So, where'd you have a steak?"

Tate pushed her chair back, as if to leave. "I don't have to answer questions."

Jess answered for Tate. "Chaz bought her lunch across the street."

"We were discussing a business deal," Tate said angrily.

Krista shut her eyes. She was afraid she was going to be sick. "Tate, please don't leave, honey. Just stay here and talk to us. I won't ask any more questions. Okay?"

Tate didn't push her chair in, but she didn't leave, either.

Jess started on his salad. "Eat, Krista."

"You let him tell you what to do?" Tate asked.

"I listen. If it's good advice, I take it." Krista picked up her fork, although she knew she couldn't eat. "If it was bad advice, I'd ignore it. If he *always* gave me bad advice, I wouldn't be eating with him."

"How do you know if it's good advice?"

Krista knew they were talking about a lot more than whether she should have picked up her fork. "First you have to decide if the person giving the advice has anything to gain."

"So what if he does? Everybody's out for themselves, anyway."

"Not always. And then, there are degrees. Sometimes what's good for one person is good for another. Sometimes it's not."

Tate accepted her Coke from the waitress. "How do you tell? I mean, I know how *I* tell, but how do *you* do it?"

Krista thought she understood why the parents of teenagers usually looked as if they needed a long vacation. "First I consider the source. If it's Jess, or someone like him, I know he doesn't get his kicks hurting people. I also know he's mature and responsible."

"How do you know that?"

"Yeah, how do you know that?" Jess looked up from his salad and gave Krista a lecherous wink. She heard the rumble of a chuckle from Tate. Silently she blessed him for knowing how to lighten the tension.

"By watching him," she answered. "He cares about people. He does things for them that don't get him anything in return."

"Maybe he puts that stuff in his book."

"Not the kind of stuff I mean." Krista waited as the waitress set fried oysters in front of her and took away the untouched salad. "Did you ever see Chaz do anything nice for anyone?"

"He bought me lunch."

"He wants you to go to work for him."

"You want me to do what you tell me to. That's why you're buying me this Coke."

"Yeah, but what will Krista get out of it if you do?" Jess interrupted.

Tate considered as she sipped. "She'll feel better about her sister," she said, finally. "She can't find her, so she's trying to save me. Only I don't need saving."

Krista wished she could deny it, but Tate was partly right. "At least I'm not trying to make you sell your body, honey."

Jess intervened as Tate stiffened. "Ever try a crawfish?" he asked quickly, holding one out to Tate.

"Disgusting!" Tate eyed the bright red "mud bug" with intense suspicion.

"Ever have lobster?"

Tate snorted. "We didn't eat lobster where I come from. We didn't even eat fish. My grandmother hated it. She used to say if the good Lord wanted us to eat fish, he would have put it on land where we wouldn't have to get wet catching it."

Krista realized that this was the first time Tate had ever mentioned a family member. "She sounds like a great-aunt of mine."

"She was a funny old lady." Tate set her Coke down to stare out the window. "She died when I was ten. Then I had to go live with my mother."

"What about your dad?"

"What about him?"

Krista knew she had just trespassed again.

Tate was silent for a moment; then, as if she needed to share more than she needed to keep up a pretense, she answered. "I don't know who my father is. My mom says I'm just like him, though." As if she were hearing words she couldn't repeat, she flinched. "I'm *not* like him. I'd never leave a kid of mine. And I'm not like her, either."

"You're like *you*, Tate," Jess said gently. "And maybe like your grandmother?"

"She was a funny old lady." Tate continued to stare out the window.

Krista forced herself to eat. The oyster battled the lump in her throat, but she finally got it down. When she thought her voice would be steady, she spoke. "My great-aunt was always giving me advice. To this day I'm sure I'm going to be hit by a car unless I'm wearing my best slip and panties."

Tate looked appreciative of the attempt at humor.

"Did your grandmother give you advice?" Krista asked.

"All the time."

"What would she want you to do about Chaz?"

"She'd want me to eat!"

"There are other ways," Krista said firmly. "Don't go to work for him, honey. Please. He'll sweet-talk you, but then he'll come after you with his cane the first time you don't bring in what he expects."

"You've got it wrong. I'm not going to be one of his ladies. He wants me to dance in his club. He says I can make a lot of money."

Krista was caught up short, but Jess moved right in. "Have you ever been in his club?" he asked Tate.

"Are you kidding?"

"Do you know what kind of dancing they do in there?"

"I've peeked through the door."

"What you see through the door is just the beginning."

"Chaz says I won't have to do anything I don't want to."

"Chaz is a lying pimp."

"He says I'll just dance. He says if I don't want to make dates with customers for afterward, that's my business."

"If you believe that, you haven't been paying attention to what goes on around here," Krista said. "Look, I know you're desperate, honey. You can't keep living the way you have been. But there are better alternatives. There are places for kids who can't live at home, good places. And there are places where families can go to get counseling so they can live together. The people at the Place can help you. I'll help. Jess will help. Don't go to somebody like Chaz!"

Tate's expression made it clear she had dismissed what Krista said. "I don't want help. I want a job." She stood.

"There's chocolate ice cream coming," Jess reminded her.

"I'm not a baby. You can't bribe me with ice cream or stupid promises. Eat it yourself." Before either Krista or Jess could say another word, Tate was gone.

"She's not a baby, but she thinks Chaz will let her just dance." Jess pushed away his platter of crawfish.

"If she goes to work for Chaz, I'll report her to the cops and have her picked up." Krista didn't even know she was crying until Jess reached across the table and wiped a tear off her cheek.

He didn't know who was breaking his heart more. Tate or Krista. "Krista, don't cry." He wanted to take her in his arms.

"I mean it, Jess." She blinked back the rest of her tears. "I'll have her picked up."

"Chaz's too smart to have her where the cops could find her. Have you ever been to his place?"

"Not inside. I've watched the exits."

Jess forced the picture of Krista, waiting, watching for her sister, out of his mind. "It's a rabbit warren. Room after room. You have to have somebody vouch for you to get up to the second floor." He stopped; he knew he didn't have to go any further. "The cops wouldn't find her. And if they did, Chaz would show an ID saying she was old enough to work for him. He's slicker than a snake."

"Then we have to report her now! Before Chaz gets hold of her."

Jess passed his untouched ice water to Krista and watched her drink. "I talked to one of the supervisors at the Place about Tate. I told her what I knew. She knows Tate, knows where she's from. She says that Tate's in a bad situation there. Her home state has only the most minimal standards for dealing with kids. Since she keeps running, they won't even try to put her in foster care. They'll put her in a locked facility. Most of the kids are hard cases. She wouldn't be safe, much less helped."

"So what do we do?"

"I guess we pray."

Their waitress deposited the dish of chocolate ice cream on the table and left before they could tell her to take it back. Neither Jess nor Krista made a move to touch it.

"I want this to be over with," Krista said.

Jess knew what she meant. She really wished it had never begun. But it *had* begun, and now both of them were ensnared in a net that seemed to be pulling them closer, even as they fought to find an escape.

They had spent months in a world they would never forget. Both of them were changed.

In that instant he saw clearly how easy it would be to stop fighting, to reach out to her and hold her forever, to let the net, which was nothing more than their own humanity, ensnare them forever.

Krista lifted her gaze to his. For that moment they both knew what could be ahead of them. Each of them saw fear in the other's eyes.

Jess pushed his chair back. "Are you all right?"

She nodded, although it was a lie.

"I've got some notes to transcribe this afternoon." He thought how safe, how sheltering, paper and pen could be. Not like a net. Not like his feelings.

"I'll see you tonight."

"Yeah." He picked up the check. Krista was staring out the window. He knew that if he touched her, there would be no escape. "See you then."

"See you." Krista kept her eyes on the sidewalk, where there was a steady stream of people. She didn't see one of them.

Chapter 11

A week later Krista slipped into a shiny black sweater scattered from hem to neckline with dime-store rhinestones. She let her hair fall to her shoulders and fluffed it with her fingers until it looked like cotton candy. Then she outlined her eyes with the heavy hand of a little girl playing with her mother's make-up.

By the time she had finished, she looked sixteen trying to be twenty. She wanted to look especially young, because tonight she was going to abandon caution and mention Rosie to everybody she knew. Rosie, a fellow runaway, a girl she had to return some clothes to.

She rested her face in her hands for a moment. Cat brushed against her leg. He was visiting her, as he often did when Jess was gone. She and Jess shared Cat as they had shared few other things in the last days. Since their confrontation with Tate, their despair and frustration had been kept private.

During the day Jess had gone his way, and she had gone hers. At night he had stayed close, but there had been no more moments of intimacy, no mutual confessions of need or desire. As if they had talked and decided that caring too much would sink them both, they had maintained impersonal facades. For all practical purposes they had been what they truly were. Strangers.

It was better this way. They had shared more than they should have. It was easy, in an emotional situation like this one, to believe that more was possible than really could be. She had no room in her life for a man, not until Rosie was found. And Jess was a self-confessed workaholic who had succumbed to his addiction once more when a good story came his way.

It was better, too, because Krista knew she would be leaving New Orleans in the next week or two.

She lifted her head, checking dispassionately to see if she had smeared her makeup. Then she picked up Cat, who purred like the feline Jess insisted he wasn't. "You'll be sorry to see me go," she whispered. "Who's going to feed you chopped liver?"

Cat purred on, unconcerned.

Krista wondered if Jess would take Cat with him when he left New Orleans. She thought he might. From what he had told her, he had plenty of material to use in his book. He was ready to write, and he'd told her he had a retreat in southwestern Virginia where he might go.

"You'd love all those trees," she crooned. "Squirrels and birds and trees. Cat heaven."

Cat stretched lazily, as if in anticipation.

Krista hadn't yet told Jess that she would be leaving New Orleans before the month's end. Day by day the realization had grown. There had been no sign of Rosie. She hadn't been seen by Krista or Jess nor, apparently, by any of New Orlean's finest—although Jess had yet to pin Mack down long enough to see what he had found, or hadn't. If Rosie had been in the city once, no one that Krista had spoken to so far remembered her. Which was why she planned to talk to everyone who would listen tonight.

She wasn't ready to give up her charade. Not quite, anyway. For months now she had gone to all the places where Rosie might have been, listening, observing, then listening some more.

Rosie had not shown up. Now Krista had to face the fact that Rosie wasn't going to and concentrate on the possibility that she might have been here once, then moved on. The people at Tallulah's and places like it still believed Krista was one of them. They would answer her questions if she posed them correctly and not think twice about her reasons. And even if they grew suspicious now, she had little to risk.

If she was satisfied that no one knew anything about Rosie, she would go back to New York to find Joy. If she got a lead instead, she would follow that. But whichever way her luck went, staying in New Orleans was hopeless. She had only a few more months to look before her money ran out completely; she had to make the best use of her time.

She wasn't hiding her decision from Jess. It was just that she hadn't seen him since she had made it. He hadn't been home when she'd awakened, just past noon. And he hadn't come back. She'd checked several times. Now she frowned at her reflection in the mirror. It was late. She usually liked to start her "tour" of Bourbon Street by eight o'clock, and it was already nine.

She felt a quick thrill of disappointment that intensified into anger. Maybe Jess was as tired of this search as she was. Maybe he was tired of her. That was fine. He didn't owe her anything, did he? Afraid to dwell on her feelings, she didn't analyze them. After all, she and Jess had kept their distance all week. Why should tonight be any different?

Jess looked at his watch and briefly considered calling Krista. But if he went to search for a telephone, he might miss Mack. He had missed him enough times this week that he was determined to avoid it again, at any cost. And he'd been told by a reliable source that Mack was a patron at the Cajun Lounge in the evenings.

"Want another drink?"

Jess looked at the "I'm-oh-so-available" barmaid whose narrow shoulder strap seemed to slip an inch lower every time she came to the table. He hypothesized just what another inch would do to his libido. The answer was easy. Nothing. There was only one woman in New Orleans who could make him burn to touch her. And that wasn't a safe subject to think about.

"I'm fine," he told the barmaid, although it was as far from the truth as he could get.

"Still waitin' for your pal?"

"Still waiting." Jess carefully avoided looking at any part of her except her eyes. They were red-rimmed and watery from all the smoke in the bar.

"I could help you pass the time later, if he doesn't get here. I'm off in an hour."

Tallulah's wasn't the only bar in town where business was conducted, apparently. Jess let his gaze flicker around the room. Half the patrons at the Cajun Lounge were cops. Off duty, obviously, but cops none the less. He wondered if any of them were assigned to vice. "My friend is a cop," he told the woman, watching to see if that made any difference.

She shrugged. "There's no law against you buyin' me a drink, is there?"

He smiled a little and decided he had been researching his book for too long. "No. I've got to go in a few minutes though. Sorry."

"Too bad. I noticed you soon as you came in the door. You've got a sad face. Lady troubles?"

"You could say that."

"She's crazy, then." She winked, then turned and started across the room.

Lady troubles. He almost wanted to laugh. His "lady" wasn't giving him trouble. She wasn't giving him anything. They were staying so far away from each other that the twenty-nine-mile causeway over Lake Pontchartrain wouldn't be long enough to connect them again.

He wasn't even sure why. It had something to do with sharing too much, caring too much about what they'd seen, knowing that if they went into each other's arms the world would never look the same again. Sexual attraction wasn't new to him. There had been other women in his life, including a wife who had been a passionate bed partner. Carol hadn't been passionate about anything else, though. She hadn't cared deeply about anyone or anything, and, in her defense, he hadn't cared deeply about her.

He cared deeply about Krista, though. He wanted her in his bed, true. He wanted to feel her skin against his and her body moving with him. He wanted to pour himself into her and feel her flow through him. But he also wanted more, and he knew there would *be* more. That was why he had spent the last week at a distance.

Wanting more scared both of them to death.

He lifted his gaze from the table and looked toward the door. A gust of warm air fought with the air conditioning. Then Jess saw the familiar body of the man he had been waiting for.

Mack Hankins. Another problem.

Jess left his beer on the table and stepped out into the aisle, just as Mack started by. "Mack," he said with a nod.

In the seconds before he recovered his poise, the policeman had the grace to look ashamed. "What are you doing here, Cantrell?"

"Waiting for you." Jess gestured to his booth. "Join me for a beer?"

"I'm meeting somebody—"

"Yeah. Me."

"You know where I work."

"You know I've been there. You're either away from your desk or in the middle of something important."

Mack grimaced, but he still didn't move toward Jess's table. "Come in tomorrow. I'll be there in the morning."

"You're here now."

Mack grimaced again, but this time he crossed the floor and slid into the seat across from Jess's drink.

"A beer?" Jess slid across from him, looking for the barmaid.

"Nothing. I'll do my drinking later."

"I want to know what you've found.'

"I told you yesterday. These things take time."

"You've had a week."

"Well, I've come up with a big fat zero," Mack said belligerently.

Jess sat back. "Now we're getting somewhere."

"Nowhere, Cantrell. No place. Roseanna Jensen ran away. You know how many kids run away each year?"

Jess waved the question aside. "How many of them are senators' kids?"

"Who cares?" Mack pulled a pack of cigarettes from his pocket and offered it to Jess. Jess shook his head. Mack lit one and smoked for a while before he continued. "Everything was done that should have been. The kid ran. The cops looked. No one found her. If she turns up somewhere, she'll be sent back home."

"Then why have you been avoiding me?"

Mack continued to smoke, staring just past Jess's ear. "I wanted to have more for you," he said finally. "I did what I could."

"More?"

Mack shrugged, but he was obviously tense. "I did what I could."

Jess examined him. Mack was an experienced cop. He didn't get involved in cases. If he had searched the records and there had been nothing useful, he wouldn't look as if he wanted to slug someone. "You're not telling me everything, are you?"

"I'm telling you what I know." Mack started to slide across the seat to leave, but Jess clamped his hand on his wrist.

"The guy who robbed the convenience store where Krista worked. Did you find any other suspects who fit his description?"

"Do you know how many crimes are committed in Orleans Parish every day?"

Jess lifted his hand. "Thanks for all your help," he said sardonically.

"I told you what I know. I did what I could."

"Then why do I get the feeling it wasn't enough?"

Mack dropped his cigarette on the floor and ground it into powder. "Don't come back to the station. Go write another best-seller, Cantrell." He turned and started toward the door. If he'd planned to meet someone, he'd changed his mind.

Jess felt a familiar stab of frustration; it was an old friend, and usually the prelude to something important. Mack wasn't leveling with him. Hayden Barnard's stepdaughter had disappeared without a trace. The police records showed nothing useful. Mack hadn't even indicated that the case was still open.

Jess knew a dead end when he saw it. But there was usually a way around one, taking a shortcut, blazing a new trail, hacking the weeds from an old path.

He stared into his beer and wished he could read its effervescence the way gypsies read tea leaves. He was missing something, and, more than ever now, he suspected it had something to do with Hayden Barnard. He was the factor that made this case interesting. He was the variable that no other runaway story had.

Jess hadn't made a study of the man himself, but he had worked with another reporter who considered getting dirt on prominent politicians his life's mission. Dan Ferris was retired now, counting sea gulls on the coast of Florida somewhere, but if Jess could locate him, talk to him, Dan might just qualify as a trailblazer.

Jess left some cash on the table and went to get his car. He didn't have time for a face-to-face chat with Dan Ferris, but there was always the telephone.

"So you say you came here with this girl at Mardi Gras and lost her?" Wanda peered through Tallulah's darkness in an attempt to read Krista's expression.

Krista let only weariness show. It was real. She had waited for Jess until nine-thirty, then struck out on her own. Tallulah's was her last stop, but Jess had never showed up anywhere along the way. She was going to have to walk home alone, and she wasn't looking forward to it.

She sighed, as if too bored to discuss the subject she had brought up herself. "Yeah. I've still got some of her stuff, and I'm tired of hauling it around."

"How come you never mentioned her before?"

Krista shrugged. "Didn't seem important. I guess I'll just toss out her junk. Too bad, though. Rosie was a nice kid. I hate to do it to her."

"Rosie?"

"That's what she told me to call her."

"And you say she was blond? About five two? Pretty?"

"I've got a picture somewhere. I'll see if I can find it and bring it with me tomorrow." Krista had purposely not brought

Rosie's photograph because she hadn't wanted to look too anxious. Now she cursed her caution. Time was running out.

"I know most of the girls who come through here."

"She sound familiar?"

"Have you talked to Sally?"

Krista was almost too tired to remember. She had talked to anyone who would listen at all of her regular stops. There hadn't been one flicker of interest until now. But then, these weren't people who got excited easily. Life had hollowed most of them out until there wasn't much left inside.

"I don't know if I've asked her or not," she said. "Think she might know something?"

Wanda sat back. "Why are you lying about this girl?"

Adrenaline surged briefly, then died away. "Why do you think I'm lying?"

"Everything you are is a lie. This girl has something to do with it, don't she? I was right before. You're an eye."

Krista weighed the problems with Wanda circulating that story versus Wanda circulating the real one. "Rosie's my sister," she said, finally. "And I've been looking for her for most of a year, full time for the last four months."

"I knew it. I knew you weren't a hooker."

Krista made a wry face. "Thanks. I guess."

"You don't have the look, no matter what you do to yourself. How old are you, anyway?"

"Twenty-four."

"I would have said twenty-one, maybe."

Krista decided to throw herself on Wanda's mercy. "I've got to find Rosie. She's been gone for sixteen months now. Somebody in New York said she was coming here, but I haven't seen her, and my time's running out."

"Why didn't you just tell people who you were, right up front?"

"Would they have helped me?"

Wanda sipped her drink without comment.

"Will you help me?" Krista asked.

"What do you want me to do?"

"Keep this between us, at least for a little longer. If I can't find out anything, I'm going to tell people the truth. But just give me a little time to try it this way."

"I can do more than that."

Krista knew Wanda was dragging this out to make her pay because she hadn't been honest. Wanda was enjoying herself now. Krista stifled her impatience. "What?"

"I might know something."

"What?"

"There's this girl Sally's talked about who might be your sister. Sally might stop back later. Wait, and we'll ask her. You got a picture with you?"

"Not the one I'd show Sally. A school picture." Krista fumbled in her purse and took out the picture. She passed it to Wanda. "Do you think I should show it to her and tell the truth?"

Wanda appeared to consider; then she shook her head. "Sally's a runaway, too. I don't think she'd help if she thought you were looking for your sister." She passed the photograph back to Krista. "She don't look familiar to me."

"Can you see why I haven't been honest with anybody?"

"Anybody? I've seen you walking with Jess Cantrell. Does he know?"

"He followed me and found out the truth." Krista smiled and used a little tact. "You're both great observers. If everyone was as smart as you two, I wouldn't be here right now."

"Just one thing. How did you get rid of the johns who picked you up while you were pretending?"

"I got very good at scaring them to death. There are lots of reasons for johns to be scared these days."

Wanda hooted with laughter as Krista gave her a few examples. By the time Krista finished, she had forgiven her.

Dan Ferris not only had dirt on Hayden Barnard, Jess would have needed a dump truck to haul it all away from the telephone. It had taken him hours to locate Dan's number, then another hour to get through to him. The final hour had been spent, pen in hand, listening and scrawling furiously.

Nothing Dan had said made Jess smile. Their parting words, least of all.

"Why the hell didn't you make any of this public?" Jess had asked.

"Because I couldn't prove a damn thing. I spent years trying. The guy's got some kind of stranglehold on the people who could put him out of office. Everything I've just told you is rumor. And if you quote me, I'll deny it all."

"He get to you, too?"

There had been a short silence on the other end of the line; then Dan had uttered his final statement. "I'm sixty-eight. Healthy, as far as I know, but I could go any day now. When I do, you'll get a package from my attorney. Then you can figure out what to do with it. Maybe you'll risk everything you've got and maybe you won't, Jess. It'll be an interesting test. Too bad I won't be alive to see it."

Then the line had gone dead.

Now Jess stood. The calls had been made from Krista's apartment because he didn't have a phone. He owed her a bundle for them, although she didn't know that yet. She had been gone by the time he got there, but her lock had been easy to pick. He had been irritated at first to find the apartment empty, but he had known it was his own fault. He hadn't called to let her know he would be late, and she had obviously gone off to look for Rosie without him.

Now it was time to find her. She would be leaving Tallulah's or some other place before too long, and he didn't want her alone on the street. In fact, he didn't want her on the street at all. He wanted her in his arms, and he wanted her safe. From everything he had heard tonight, the second might be harder to manage than he'd thought.

Jess locked Krista's door behind him, then took the stairs two at a time. He cursed himself for putting a hunch before her safety. He should have called her; he should have told her to wait. He should have delayed calling Dan. In retrospect, the last sin seemed small. He hadn't known the things Dan would tell him. It was knowing them now that made his gut twist.

Krista hadn't talked about where she had planned to go tonight. There had been no need; she had expected him to be with her. Now Jess tried to second-guess her. She would have gone to Tallulah's, but first or last? How had she done it the last time? She usually tried to go at different times so she could catch different groups of people.

He finally settled on going to Tallulah's first. He debated the best route, then decided on going the back way. He could save time if he stayed away from the crowds on Bourbon Street. It was still early enough that Krista probably wouldn't be on her way home yet. He prayed that his instincts were correct and began to walk quickly through the narrow streets.

"About five two? Blond?" Sally yawned. "She pretty?"

"Yeah." Krista tried not to look excited. "Do you think it might be the same girl?"

"Could be. The girl I know calls herself May Rose."

Rosie's birthday was in May. Krista didn't trust herself to speak.

"Her boyfriend calls her Rosie," Sally finished.

Krista prayed that the "boyfriend" wasn't a pimp. She forced herself to ask a question. "Why haven't I seen her if she's still in town?"

"She's in Houston. Supposed to be coming back any day now, though. She went over there for a couple of months."

Krista knew better than to ask why. Kids drifted back and forth from city to city for a variety of reasons, few of them savory. If May Rose really was Rosie, Krista didn't want to know why she had spent the last two months in Houston. Her first priority—her only priority—had to be finding her sister. Then she could worry about the life she had led.

"Any day now?" Krista inspected a fingernail.

"Yeah, she called last week. Said she'd be back this coming weekend. She's never mentioned knowing anyone named Crystal."

Krista improvised. "She's probably mad. Probably thinks I took off with her stuff. She'll be surprised to see me."

"If she calls, I'll ask her if she knows you."

Wanda intervened. "Don't do that. Crystal here's been looking for her for a while. Let her surprise her."

Sally looked bored.

"I've got this picture a guy took of Rosie with a Polaroid. I'll bring it with me sometime, and you can look at it."

Sally had her eyes on a man in the corner.

Krista felt the way she always did when she was with Sally or any of the other runaways who hung out at Tallulah's. Sally should be at home studying algebra or making plans for prom night. She shouldn't be here, and what was about to happen should be prevented.

Sally stood. "Gotta go."

"It's late." Krista knew she shouldn't say anything. Finding Rosie might depend on her silence, but she couldn't make herself stop. "Can't you quit for the night?"

"Not yet. I shouldn't have been sitting here talking to you. If Chaz finds out—"

"Why do you stay with Chaz if he makes you work so hard?" Krista saw Wanda's warning glare, but she couldn't stop. "What do you get out of it?"

Sally looked surprised. Surprised and very, very worn. "He takes care of me."

"He gives you any trouble for talking to us, you come see me," Wanda said, silencing Krista with another glare.

Sally started across the room.

"You wanna find your sister or what?" Wanda asked, when Sally was out of earshot.

Krista swallowed. Frustration. Tears. Pain. "God, I hate this place."

"You've been hanging around here for months, but you still don't see what goes down with these kids, do you? Why they let Chaz and the other pimps run them into the ground?"

Krista shook her head.

"These kids leave home, and they're all alone. Nobody, nothing. They don't know where to go, what to do to eat, who to trust. So along comes Chaz or somebody like him. He's never somebody their parents would approve of, you know? So they feel daring just talking to him. He buys them a meal, tells them they're beautiful, sexy, special. He tells them with their talents and looks they could make big money. He seduces them, until he's like God."

"You make it sound like some kind of crazy religious cult."

"It's not that different." Wanda leaned forward and patted Krista's arm. "That's another place a lot of runaways end up. The ending's the same, too. After the guy gets a girl under his power, he rules her life. She stays with him because she's afraid to rule it herself. If he beats her, he tells her it's because he loves her. He tells her it's for her own good."

"It's so sick!"

"Yeah. But where's the sickness start? With the pimps? With the guys who want twenty minutes alone with these kids in a dirty room somewhere? With a world where kids who run away don't have choices?"

"I just want my sister back!"

Wanda shook her head sympathetically. "You're way past that. You're trying to tell me you're going to find your sister and go home? You're gonna forget about Sally and the other kids you've gotten to know?"

Krista couldn't answer. She had learned to live one day at a time. The future was a big empty void.

"You won't forget," Wanda answered for her.

"I'm not a social worker. I'm a librarian."

"And I'm an ex-hooker. I've been where these kids are." Wanda patted her arm again. "Go home for now. Bring your sister's picture in tomorrow and see if Sally recognizes it."

Krista stood. It suddenly seemed imperative to get some fresh air. She was walking toward Bourbon Street before she realized that she hadn't even said goodbye to Wanda.

And Jess was nowhere in sight.

Chapter 12

Tonight Chaz's shirt was a vivid chartreuse. His suit was a pale yellow, and his matching wide-brimmed panama had a chartreuse ribbon adorning the crown. Only his expression, a thunderous storm cloud, spoiled the colorful effect.

Krista could feel the flesh of her forearm compress and bruise under Chaz's punishing fingers. She aimed a kick at his knee-cap, but his cane blocked her attempt. He pushed her against the brick wall of the dark alleyway from which he had materialized.

"Where's your bodyguard, Miss Crystal?"

"I don't have a bodyguard!" Krista tired to jerk her arm free, but despite Chaz's slight build, he was strong.

"The man who's 'taking care' of you," he prompted, his voice poisonously cordial.

"He had business tonight," she lied. "But he was going to meet me around the corner in a few minutes. He'll come looking for me if I don't show up."

"And what will he find, baby?" Chaz shook his head sadly, clicking his tongue. "Ah, well. There are lots of lovely ladies of the evening to console him."

"What's your problem, Chaz?" Krista asked, forcing bravado into her voice. "You don't need a troublemaker in your stable. You've got girls falling all over you."

"Oh, I agree." He smiled thinly. "I don't want *you*. Not anymore. But your little friend, now she's a different story."

For a moment Krista thought he meant Sally. Perhaps Sally had reported that Krista had criticized Chaz. But that had only been minutes ago.

"Tate," he said, refreshing her memory.

Krista forgot her own precarious position. "Leave Tate alone. She's fourteen. You try to employ her and I'll report you to the vice squad."

Chaz squeezed her arm tighter. Krista gasped. "So brave," he said. "So much spirit."

"Stay away from Tate!" Tears sprang to her eyes as Chaz squeezed harder. She tried to kick him again, but this time he struck his cane against her legs. She cried out in pain.

"Your little friend's going to work for me," he said. "And you're not going to say a word to anyone. Do you know what a ho's testimony is worth, baby?"

"How about a journalist's?" Jess stepped into the alleyway just as Chaz was raising his cane once more. In a moment the cane was in Jess's hands, then it was pinned firmly against Chaz's throat, and Chaz was spread-eagled against the wall. "Don't even think about it," Jess said as Chaz raised a knee. "I just need one more excuse to finish you off."

"You're a dead man," Chaz gasped.

Krista moved as far away from him as the narrow alleyway would permit. Her leg and her arm throbbed painfully. "Jess, let him go."

"Why should I?"

"You'll end up in jail."

"I don't think so."

Krista wondered. Chaz obviously had powerful friends or he wouldn't be allowed to operate the businesses he did. "You can't kill a man just because he's slime."

Jess seemed to consider. "You're sure?" he asked, still pressing the cane against Chaz's throat.

"Jess!"

Jess sighed. "Search him."

For a moment Krista didn't know what he meant.

"Search him," he repeated. "He's not above shooting us in the back."

With her face screwed up in disgust, Krista ran her hands over Chaz. His wallet was fat, but apparently he considered his cane the only protection he needed.

"Nothing." Krista moved away.

Jess stepped back, still holding the cane. When Chaz jumped forward, Jess merely stepped to one side. Chaz crashed into the wall behind Jess. "I forgot to give you back your cane," he said, as Chaz turned for another try. He whipped the cane against Chaz's legs, much as Chaz had used it against Krista. When Chaz sprawled to the ground, Jess stepped back and slammed the cane against the edge of the doorway behind him, splintering it. Jess tossed the pieces to Chaz. Then, taking Krista's arm, he backed out of the alleyway. Chaz, his panama battered and his suit streaked with mud, watched them go.

"He'll kill you," Krista said. "He'll find you and kill you. Going after one of his kind is like taking on the Mafia."

Jess felt a thrill of exhilaration. Getting his hands on Chaz, even briefly, had been a pleasure. He steered Krista toward Bourbon Street. They would be safer in a crowd.

Krista limped along beside him, not daring to ask him to slow down. She would have visible bruises tomorrow, but nothing was broken. Chaz knew just how to wield his cane.

"I'm sorry," she said, when they were walking down Bourbon.

Jess ignored her apology. "Why the hell did you go off without me tonight? Did you want an instant replay of the last time he came after you?"

"I didn't know where you were. You didn't call. I waited until nine-thirty—"

"You didn't wait long enough."

Anger fused with Krista's gratitude. "You can't expect me to read your mind. I'm here to look for my sister! I can't very well do that in my apartment, can I?"

"You should have waited. You should have known I'd come back."

"How should I have known that?" Krista shook Jess's hand off her arm. "We're supposed to be looking together, but you didn't even call to let me know where you were. You've barely talked to me for the last week."

"There are some things you haven't talked to me about either, lady."

"I don't know what you mean."

"You will." Jess put his hand on the small of Krista's back to hurry her along.

She tried to sound defiant. "It's a good thing I did go out tonight. I might have a lead."

Jess didn't slow his pace; in fact, he urged her to move faster by increasing the pressure of his hand. "What kind of lead?"

She didn't want him to deflate her hopes. She considered not sharing the story of May Rose.

Jess cut into her thoughts. "You don't want to talk about it now? Fine. We'll talk about it when we get to your apartment. When we're done with everything else."

Krista wanted to be angry at Jess. He was acting like a husband. She couldn't be angry, though, because he had put himself on the line for her over and over again. If he hadn't come looking for her tonight, anything might have happened. No matter how he had acted for the last week, he cared enough about her to risk his life.

They were almost home before she got her emotions under control enough to apologize. "I'm sorry. I really am, Jess. At the least I should have left you a note telling you where I was going and when."

"Why didn't you?"

She knew why. She had done it to get back at him, both for not calling and for treating her so distantly all week. It had been silly and childish. Normally, she was neither.

"I was angry and hurt," she admitted.

He didn't have to ask why. His own anger began to burn away, even though he tried to refuel it. He wanted to be angry at her, but his major emotion was relief. He wanted to kiss her until he knew, in every cell, that she was really all right.

"What did Chaz say to you?" he asked gruffly.

"He was angry because I talked to Tate about working for him."

"How did he know?"

Krista considered. "I guess Tate told him I was against it," she said as they started down the alleyway into their courtyard.

"She must have been using you as an excuse."

"She's not working for him yet."

"Have you seen her since last week?"

"No." Krista hesitated, then admitted, "I've been looking for her, though. Tate can't be found if she doesn't want to be."

"Dickens would have had a field day with her."

Cat stood at the bottom of the stairs. Jess didn't even lean over to rub his ears. "We'll talk at my place." Still resting his hand on Krista's back, he guided her up the stairs.

"I'd like to change."

"It's late, and I'd like to get this over with."

She debated whether to insist, then shrugged. She was anxious to know what was going on.

Inside, Jess's apartment was hot and still. One of the details Mrs. Duchamp had failed to mention to him was the idiosyncrasy of the air conditioner. He briskly opened windows, but there was little breeze stirring. "Let's go up to the roof," he suggested, when it was apparent the apartment would take some time to cool down.

Krista was reluctant. She could imagine the roof in the moonlight, and she was just enough of a romantic to want to avoid it. "Let's go to my place. I can fix us something cool to drink."

"I don't want a drink. I want fresh air."

Krista didn't point out that he'd just had a long walk in it. She saved her energy for things to come.

The roof was as she had imagined it. Moonlight touched its surface with silver, caressing the old slate like fairy dust. The darkness beyond them glittered with lights from the surrounding buildings.

Jess wished he hadn't been so insistent. Krista's hair gleamed in the moonlight, a soft, nearly iridescent gold. The rhinestones on her sweater twinkled like fireflies. He was no longer angry, if indeed he ever had been. He was, in fact, in exactly the same place he had been in a week before and a week before that. Much too aware of her.

A breeze that had been too slight to cool the apartment played with Krista's hair. She stood at the brick wall on the roof's edge and gazed out at the city. "I could almost love this place."

Jess thought she was being generous, considering how little of New Orleans's good side she had seen. "It's like everywhere. You find what you look for." He thought about the things he had to ask her, and the things she hadn't told him. "If you don't know what you're looking for, then you find trouble."

Krista knew they weren't talking about the city. She turned back to him. "Why don't you just tell me what's on your mind."

"I can understand why you didn't trust me when we first met."

"I thought we'd been over this before."

"And I can understand why you still wondered if I could be trusted, even after we began working together to find Rosie."

This time she waited for him to go on.

"What I can't understand is why you haven't trusted me since then." There was enough light that he could see her expression, although the finest nuances of it were lost to him. She seemed perplexed. For one moment he wondered if she really hadn't known or even suspected why Rosie had left home.

"I trust you," she said softly.

He stepped closer so he could see her more clearly. "Then why didn't you tell me the truth about the things your sister said when she pleaded with you not to make her go back home?"

Krista turned away. The night seemed suddenly chill. She crossed her arms against it. "I did."

"What did you tell me?"

"I told you she and my parents had fought. She was angry at them. She didn't want to live with them anymore."

"Is that what Rosie told you?" Jess stepped behind her. He was close enough to touch her, but he didn't. He had no comfort to offer.

Krista shuddered and wondered how Jess knew what had been said that day. "That's what she told me."

"She didn't fight with your *parents*, did she, Krista? She fought with Hayden—or rather, she fought him off." He hesitated, then asked softly, "Or did she manage to?"

Krista moaned. She rested her head in her hands. "You weren't there. You're making horrible guesses."

"Correct guesses?"

"I don't want to talk about this."

"But you're going to."

"Why? So you can frame an innocent man?" Krista faced him. "You don't like my stepfather. His politics don't agree with yours. I've read your books! Hayden's light-years away from what you believe. But he's an honorable man!"

Jess knew he should hit her with the truth. He knew she would crumple if he did and tell him everything he wanted to know. This time, though, the woman was more important than the story. He went slowly. "Is he?"

"He is!"

"What did Rosie tell you that night?" His voice had lost its edge. He was seducing the truth from her.

Krista knew what he was doing. "Lies," she said simply.

"What did she say?"

"I've said all I'm going to."

"Did she tell you that Hayden tried to molest her?"

Krista shut her eyes, but it was the wrong thing to do. She saw Rosie, just as she had been that day sixteen months before. Rosie's face was tear-streaked and her hands trembled. She was pleading.

Jess saw that Krista couldn't answer, but she didn't need to. The answer was written clearly on her face. Even in the near darkness.

"God, Krista, why didn't you tell me?" He reached for her, but she twisted away. Before he could stop her, she ran to the metal stairway leading down to his apartment. He followed close behind, down the stairway and through the apartment. He caught her at the front door. His hand closed over hers as she tried to turn the knob.

"Why, Krista?" he repeated.

"Because it's not true! She was lying! Hayden's a good stepfather."

"You're denying what you know!"

"He's treated us both just as if we were his real daughters. He's the one who got Rosie into a school where she could really learn something. He's a warm, affectionate man. Rosie misunderstood, or she lied! I don't know which!"

Jess's stomach turned over. He wished to God that he didn't have to be the one to make her face the truth. But there was no turning back now. "I've spoken to a friend, Krista. A reporter who's retired now. He told me a lot about your stepfather." He released her hand and touched her cheek, but to give which of them courage, he couldn't say. "Hayden Barnard has been accused twice of molesting teenagers. One of the girls was a senate page. Both times it was hushed up and charges were dropped. Both girls swore afterward that they'd lied to get attention. Barnard had enough clout to be sure the story never ran anywhere. It probably never will."

Krista gasped, sucking in lungfuls of guilt and shame. "No."

"I'm sorry."

"Are you?" She pushed him away as he moved closer. "Damn it, are you? You have what you came for, don't you? What a story this will be!" She tried to open the door again, but he stepped in front of her.

"Part of you knew it was true."

"No!"

"And that's why you're here. Because you're so filled with guilt because you didn't believe her—"

"No! No!" She beat her fists against his chest. "I still don't know it's true!"

He held her wrists. "There are two young women who tried to bring charges against your stepfather. Two separate incidents, Krista."

"No." Her fists uncurled, and she stopped fighting him.

"How many lives will you let him ruin?" Jess asked softly. "He's already ruined three that we know of."

She slumped against him. "I didn't believe her." She was crying now. "I didn't."

Jess slipped his arms around her, holding her close. "You didn't want to believe her."

She sobbed against his shirt, all defenses gone. "I...I was angry at her. I didn't want to believe it. You don't know how much better things were for us after my mother married...married Hayden. I didn't want to believe it was all a fairy tale! I wanted us to be a family."

"A family with one rebellious teenager. Like thousands of others." He stroked her hair. It clung to his fingers like the filmiest of cobwebs.

"When Rosie told me, I just...just couldn't accept it. I told her I thought she was lying. She fell apart. She shouted at me. I got angrier. I told her she was a spoiled brat." She sobbed harder.

"And since then?"

"I haven't...I haven't known what to think."

"Then you've suspected." It was important that she face reality, even though he would have preferred to leave her with her illusions.

"Hayden and my mother haven't seemed to care whether Rosie was found or not." Her suspicions, black as the night surrounding them, finally came pouring out. "They said they...they cared. They seemed to do all the right things, but Hayden especially seemed relieved when Rosie wasn't found. I told myself it was because she was so hard to live with."

"What else did you suspect?"

"That...that they didn't want me searching. They haven't helped me at all. They keep demanding that I come home."

Jess wondered if Krista's mother suspected the reason her youngest daughter had run away. Had she chosen her husband over her child? He supposed it was a question he had no right to ask, but the possibility made him sick. "There's more you have to know."

Krista wiped her eyes, but the tears kept falling. "I don't *know* anything, Jess. This is just a suspicion. Those girls dropped the charges against Hayden. They could have been lying."

"Two *separate* incidents, Krista. They were bought off or threatened. Your stepfather's a ruthless bastard, and twisted to boot."

"You can't be sure!"

He put his hands on her shoulders and shook her gently. "Krista, stop this! Do you want to find your sister? Or do you want to live in some kind of fantasy world? There are two young women who tried to nail Hayden Barnard. They were scared away. My contact says he tried to interview them. They ran like rabbits. There's a damn good chance there are more girls out there who didn't have the courage to even try to go after your stepfather!"

"You don't know—"

He gripped her shoulders harder. "Then listen to what I *do* know! Nothing's been done to find your sister. There's been no detective on this case, at least not one who was told to look."

"Yes, there was. I—"

"You took Hayden's word for it. There is nothing on file at any of the runaway shelters about Rosie's disappearance. I checked at the Place. They couldn't find anything, so I've been doing some checking in other shelters. I've checked a dozen of them, Krista, all over the country, and not one of them has anything about Rosie in their files. The national hot lines don't have anything, either."

She was stunned into silence.

"Mack, my contact at the police station, was all set to help me. Now he's as evasive as hell. He's as much as told me his hands are tied. Why, Krista? Who has the power to tie a cop's hands?"

"But *I* hired a detective," she said in a small voice. "I paid for one myself."

"And you told me he picked up a lead right away, didn't you? Then what happened?"

"I . . . I don't know. He said he couldn't find anything—"

"I'll tell you what happened. You told your stepfather about the detective, didn't you? *After* you got that lead. You didn't tell him before because you knew he'd try to convince you that you were wasting money. So you told him after you found out that Rosie had been in New York. Then the leads stopped. And a few weeks later your detective told you he was stumped."

It had happened just that way. Krista tried to think of something, anything, that would explain the events differently. But the facts led inexorably to Hayden Barnard.

"Rosie..." Her eyes widened. Her fears went beyond tears. "She could be—"

Jess was one step ahead of her. "We don't know he's *that* ruthless." His hands went to her hair. "Right now we've got to believe she's still alive and that Barnard just doesn't want her found."

"She could be dead!"

Jess wanted to tell her that wasn't possible. But she would know he was lying. Instead he offered his own theory as comfort. "I think if she were dead, your stepfather wouldn't be trying so hard to keep you from searching. He could have had her killed and fixed it so there wasn't a trace of her. Then he could have made a real public show of searching for her. He could have turned it into a crusade. Now, of course, if he does that and Rosie shows up, she might tell *why* she ran. So he's doing what he can to keep her from reappearing."

"But if she does reappear..."

Jess nodded solemnly. "We've got to find her first."

Krista began to shake with fury. "The bastard! The rotten, filthy bastard!"

"You said something about a lead."

She couldn't speak. She was choking on the ashes of betrayal.

Jess put his arms around her, although he knew what small comfort that was. She was warm and soft, although it was the steel at the core of her that was holding her together. "I'm sorry," he whispered into her hair.

"I didn't want to believe it!" She tried to tell Jess just exactly what Rosie had said about her stepfather, but she couldn't get the words out. "Hayden never... He didn't.... She ran before he could...could—"

"Shhh..." Jess pulled her closer. "I understand. I'm glad."

Krista put her arms around his waist. Forgotten was the distance they had so carefully maintained. She needed to be held, and she needed Jess to be the one holding her. "How could I have been so blind?"

Jess barely heard her. She felt so good in his arms. The last week might as well not even have existed. He had been running as hard and as fast as the kids he'd interviewed. And whatever his reasons, now he realized he had run in a circle.

Krista lifted her face to his. Her eyes were red-rimmed, her makeup streaked. He rubbed his thumb along her cheekbone. "I'm sorry," he said. Since he was sorry for more things than he could name, he didn't explain.

"I should have told you right at the beginning."

"I understand why you didn't."

"I've failed her every step of the way."

"You've done what you thought was right and best. Always."

"But I've been wrong!"

"Krista." He lowered his mouth to hers. If he'd had any illusions that the kiss was for comfort, they changed abruptly.

Her arms slid from his waist up his back, and finally around his neck. She held on to him as if he were the only anchor in a tilting world.

He thought about how short life was, and how precarious. He thought about pain and its temporary cure. And all the while he kissed her.

Jess knew Krista needed him tonight, and he needed her. Whatever obstacles they had put between them were gone. At this moment she was his—and might always be if he took her to bed. She wasn't a woman who gave her loyalties lightly.

She moaned softly and moved provocatively against him. She was caressing him straight through to his soul. He needed her courage, her passion, her devotion.

As if she'd just realized what was happening, Krista tried to draw away. Jess held her tighter. She relaxed again, as if she had just needed proof that he wanted her despite the things she'd kept from him. His hands crept to her bottom, and he pulled her tightly against him to give her all the proof she needed.

When he finally pulled his mouth from hers, she was clinging to him. Her hips were nestled against his, his arousal fully evident to both of them. He knew that if he took her to his bed, she would go willingly.

He also knew it wasn't the right time for either of them. He would always wonder if she had made love to him because she desperately needed assurance and comfort, or because she needed him. Only him. She would wonder the same.

"Krista, you'd better go," he said softly.

She shuddered. She had never felt so alone, so shattered. "I don't want to."

"That's why you should." Jess lifted her arms from his shoulders. They felt as heavy as lead weights.

"Hold me, Jess."

"I can't make everything all right!"

"I know!"

Self-denial only went so far. In the last analysis Jess was only a man. With a groan, he let his arms fall to her shoulders once more. He felt her sigh against his lips, felt the sudden release of tension in her body. This wasn't an answer, but tonight it was as close to one as they had.

Krista was desperate to get closer to him. He was real. He was good. He was all the things that the other men in her life hadn't been. She wanted to touch him, to absorb his heat and vitality through her pores. She wanted to drown all thought in the darkest, deepest essence of him until there was nothing left except the distilled purity of hope and faith and love. Without him, without this, she wasn't sure that she would ever believe in anything good again.

She could feel Jess tensing. His hands slowed; his lips caressed her softly. She knew what he was thinking and what he was trying to do. "Don't be gentle," she said fiercely. "I don't need gentleness. Make me feel something good, Jess. Make me!"

She was swept up in his arms in a moment. Moon and stars bathed the apartment in forgiving celestial light. A breeze stirred, and night jasmine blooming on tangled vines in the courtyard perfumed the air. The bedroom seemed a haven.

At the bedside Jess laid Krista against his new sheets. Before she could even reach for him, he stretched half across her. She slid her hands under his shirt, kneading the sleek warmth of his skin.

"I've tried not to think of you here," he whispered. "I knew I already wanted you too much."

She was flushed with heat at the thought. He had wanted her. And all along, when she had allowed anything except guilt and sorrow to surface, she had wanted him, too. She settled into his kiss, moving against him. She didn't want to think; she only wanted to feel. Not sorrow, but passion. Not the death of hope, but life.

Impatiently they undressed each other. Krista wouldn't let Jess move far enough away to make it easy for either of them. They writhed and struggled, sliding against each other to remove their clothing until there was nothing between them except heat and the slick friction of skin against skin.

Jess knew they should go slower. He hadn't even taken the time to light the shadeless lamp that sat by his bedside. He wanted to see Krista, to explore every lush inch of her, to glory in the softness of her breasts, the curve of her waist, the flare of her hips. He wanted to find what made her moan, what made her cry out in pleasure.

Instead there was no light, and there was an urgent need to possess her. There was no time to analyze pleasure because desperation was too great. They were both too raw, too caught up in the emotion flowing between them, for anything except completion.

Krista arched her back to pull him closer. He was everything good and powerful and strong; he was all the things no one else had ever been for her. In a world where nothing was as it seemed, he was real. She wrapped her legs around him and took him inside her. The room receded. Time receded.

The only thing left was the knowledge that until that moment she had always been alone.

Chapter 13

Moonlight turned to early morning sunshine before Jess awoke. Sometime during the night he had gotten up to pull his sleeping bag over them rather than shut the windows, but other than those few half-slumbering moments, he had slept deeply. So deeply, in fact, that when Krista left he didn't hear her.

Now, with dawn lighting the room, he realized he was alone. The bed—no wider than a child's—seemed too generous. He lay at one edge, his arm thrown over the top of the pillow as if to shelter the woman who was no longer there.

When had Krista gone? And why? He felt the first stirring of regret. No matter how much he had wanted her, last night shouldn't have happened. She was not a woman to give herself casually. For all her passion she had seemed curiously innocent, not like someone who had been engaged to one of Washington's most notorious bachelors.

Perhaps it was the intensity of their lovemaking that had been new to her. It had been new to him. He had lost himself in her. There had been moments with no boundaries between them.

There were boundaries now. She was gone.

Jess sat up slowly. He was tempted to throw on his clothes and go look for her right away. He didn't, though. By leaving she had asked him for time to put the night in perspective. He owed her a little time. But a little was all she was going to get. She had to know that he didn't regret what had happened, that he had wanted her, that he had needed her as much as she had needed him.

But what else would he tell her? There were no promises either of them could risk. Too much stood between them, too much uncertainty, too many barriers. Rosie stood between them. In a strange way so did Tate and the other street kids. He and Krista were no longer the people they had once been. How could he make promises when he wasn't sure who he was anymore, or where his life was going?

He got up and headed for the bathroom. He wouldn't know what to say to her until he saw her. Rehearsing was a waste of time.

He waited less than an hour before he knocked on her door. When she answered she looked as if she had tried to put things into perspective in the shower. Her hair waved damply down her back, and her face had the just-scrubbed shine of a small child's. She was wearing a daffodil-yellow jogging suit.

"Beignets," he said, holding the bag up for her to see. He wondered how she would feel if he kissed her. He decided against it.

"I've got water on for coffee," she said, not quite meeting his eyes. She ushered him inside.

Jess realized that he not only didn't know what to say or whether to kiss her, he no longer knew how to treat her, either. Last night had changed everything. He felt as if they were starting all over again. He tried to sound nonchalant. "These are fresh, so we'd better eat them fast. But skip the instant. I've got a pot brewing next door. I'll be right back."

Krista watched Jess go back the way he had just come. He seemed uncomfortable. Endearingly so. She was glad. She was such a mixture of emotions herself that she would have exploded at casual sophistication from him. Now, even though she still felt as if someone had parked an eighteen wheeler on her chest, she found herself breathing easier. She went to set the table.

She and Jess were eating before either of them said more than "Here's the sugar," or "I'll get the milk."

"Are you all right?" he asked when his first *beignet* was gone.

"What are we talking about?"

He reached across the table and wiped powdered sugar from her chin. It was the first time he had touched her since the night before, and it reassured him. "Whatever you want to."

"I don't want to talk about last night."

Jess knew she meant their lovemaking. He wasn't sure he was ready to talk about it, either, although he knew they would have to, sooner or later. "Then how are you feeling about Rosie?"

"I've got to be all right, don't I? If I just curl up and die, I'll never find her." Krista stirred her coffee for the eighth time.

"It's going to evaporate before you drink it." He covered her hand with his and reached for her spoon. Then he wrapped her hand around the mug. "You need the caffeine."

"I need my sister." And she had needed his touch, although she hadn't admitted it until this moment. She was sorry when he dropped his hand.

"Tell me about your lead."

Krista was filled with turmoil. Through the night and this morning, just as she had been about to give in to despair, she had thought of May Rose, and she had been filled with hope. Then she had remembered all the other dead ends and false leads, and she had panicked that she would never find Rosie. She knew now that her sister would never call her and ask to come home. There was no way that Rosie would subject herself to Hayden's advances again. Whatever sort of life she was leading, she would count herself lucky to be away from her stepfather.

Krista had thought of Jess, too. In fact, she hadn't been able to keep from thinking about him. He was inextricably bound up with Rosie and the search, and with her own feelings of humiliation and betrayal. But now he was also bound to her in the most elemental way. Their lovemaking had been born of desperation, but it had also been almost unearthly in its beauty. They had been part of each other, and she felt about Jess as she had never felt about a man before. But he had said once that there had never been a worse time to fall in love, and he couldn't be more right. In this, too, Hayden Barnard was to blame. How many other lives had the powerful senator ruined?

"Krista?"

"I want my stepfather brought to justice!"

He didn't tell her that this wasn't a rerun of "The Lone Ranger." There was no good guy who could ride in on a white stallion, rope and tie Barnard and cart him off to jail. In the world of the rich and powerful the truth could be bought and sold, and justice was only the title of a department in the federal government.

"What was your lead?" he asked again.

"Do you know Sally?" Krista told Jess about the encounter with Sally and Wanda, and Sally's information about May Rose.

Jess listened carefully. "So you've graduated from just watching to asking questions now."

"I decided I'd watched long enough." She stared into the still-untouched coffee. "I've only got limited resources, Jess. And I can't exactly expect Hayden and my mother to help me out, can I?" she asked bitterly.

He wanted to put his arm around her, but he schooled himself not to touch her. Things were still too confusing between them. "I think you made a good decision."

"You do?" She risked a glance at him.

"I wish you'd talked to me first, but I can't disagree with what you're doing. You haven't seen Rosie in all these months. Now it's time to be more aggressive, or it would have been," he corrected himself, "if you hadn't run into trouble last night."

"What do you mean?"

"I don't want you back at Tallulah's or anyplace near Bourbon Street again. Not after what happened with Chaz. It's too risky."

"I'm not going to let him stop me."

"Chaz may not be the only one after you."

"What are you saying?"

Jess knew it was a mark of her naïveté that she hadn't realized this herself. "We know your stepfather doesn't want Rosie found. He knows you're looking for her."

"So?"

"He may try to stop you."

"He's already tried to stop me. He's told me over and over that I'm wasting my..." Her voice trailed off as Jess's meaning became clear. "You think Hayden might hurt me?"

"I wouldn't put it past him, Krista. The stakes are high."

Her coffee was cold, but she drank half of it without even noticing.

Jess saw that her hand was shaking. He guessed it was more from rage than fear. Krista didn't have enough fear inside her to keep her safe.

She set her cup down with extreme care, as if she were struggling to keep herself from shattering it. "I'm going back to Tallulah's, and I'm going to take the picture of Rosie for Sally to see."

"I could take it."

"Sally would know something was wrong."

"You could give it to Wanda. Wanda could show—"

"*I'm* going to take it myself."

Jess put his hand on her arm. She winced. Frowning, he pulled her sleeve up to reveal a large ugly bruise. His expression grew thunderous. He knew he hadn't made the bruise. "Chaz?"

"He's not a gentle man."

"And you'd risk more of this, or worse?"

"What is Rosie risking?" Krista stood up and walked to the window. She didn't even see the building facing her apartment. Her eyes were unfocused and clouded with tears. "You know what she's risking, and so do I. She could be sick or dead. Her life may be ruined or over by now. Whatever the truth is, though, I have to know! And if she's still alive, I have to find her."

There was nothing Jess could say to that. He supposed that if Krista had reacted differently, he wouldn't feel the way he did about her. "I'll go with you. But this is it, Krista. If this doesn't pan out, you never pose as a hooker again. We'll cover the country together, and you can tell everybody the truth. Then, if you don't come up with any leads, you quit."

"I quit looking here. I start looking in New York again."

He opened his mouth to protest, then realized just how little good it would do. Last night had not bound her to him. Her life was still her life. "Are you going to show Sally the picture tonight?"

"I planned to."

"Then I'm coming with you, and I don't care if it looks odd. I don't want to risk Chaz coming after you again."

"Okay."

Jess joined her at the window. He stood so close he could smell the apple blossom scent of her shampoo. As if hours hadn't intervened, he wanted her again. Still. "Are you going to be all right?" he asked gently.

"I'm going to look for Tate today."

"And what are you going to say to her?"

"I don't know."

"Stay away from Bourbon Street. Chaz probably won't be out in daylight, but don't take chances."

She turned. They were only inches apart. "If you had met me in Washington, Jess, if we had dated, gone to cocktail parties and the zoo together, would last night have happened?"

"Washington cocktail parties and the zoo have a lot in common." She didn't take her eyes from his. The question was still there. He shook his head. "I don't know. What matters is that last night did happen. And it will again."

She didn't smile. "We're both too vulnerable."

"If vulnerable means that all the crap's been stripped away, then I guess you're right."

She sighed, and then, because she couldn't help herself, she touched his cheek and stretched up to kiss him. "I don't know what to do with the way I'm feeling."

"Neither do I."

"Loving Scott was easy."

"Then you never really loved him."

"I hope you're right, because I'd hate to think I was that stupid."

Jess knew if he stayed even a minute longer, he would take Krista in his arms. And that would blow any perspective either of them had gained straight to hell. He turned and started toward the door. "I'm going back to the Place to talk to Jewel. I'm going to tell her what we suspect. She may have some ideas on where to go from here."

"I'll be back after lunch sometime. If I'm not, send out the troops."

"Just stay in plain view and you should be all right." He paused in the doorway. He couldn't think of anything else to say. Not that he could let himself say, anyway. He gave a mock salute and left her staring after him.

Krista and Jess found ways to keep themselves occupied and apart for the rest of the day and the evening. When he finally went back to her apartment, it was to pick her up for the walk to Tallulah's. On the way she told him what she had discovered.

"Tate's living behind a Dumpster. She's lined the area with old cardboard boxes she's flattened. The kid who showed me where she stays was actually jealous." Krista cleared her throat. It was hard to go on. "There's a water faucet on the wall behind the Dumpster, and he turned it on to show me that Tate had running water. He said there wasn't any water where he stayed."

Jess didn't want to tell Krista that he had seen worse. He'd seen kids living *in* Dumpsters. "Tate wasn't there?"

"No." It was almost midnight. Krista had not made her usual rounds tonight. She was through watching and waiting for Rosie to appear. Tonight she would find Sally and show her the snapshot of Rosie. If nothing turned up, then she would visit her usual hangouts and show the same snapshot. Then, if that failed, she would throw herself on the mercy of everyone she knew, tell them the truth, and beg for help. Unfortunately, she suspected that the combined mercy of the bartenders and strip show barkers wouldn't fill a thimble.

"She wouldn't want you to know she was so destitute."

For a moment Krista thought Jess meant her sister. Rosie. Tate. They were becoming mixed up in her head. She had almost forgotten about Rosie when she had been out searching for Tate today. Rosie was a light-year away from her, but Tate was almost in reach.

"Are you going back tomorrow to confront her?" Jess asked.

"I don't know." Krista wished that life was as simple as it had once been. There had actually been a time when she could make a decision and know it was the right one. And if she hadn't known what to do, Scott had been there to tell her.

Jess gave a low whistle. "You should see the look on your face."

Krista realized her thoughts about Scott must have been visible. Maybe things were horribly complicated now, but she would *not* want to go back to a time when Scott had ruled her life. She was not the woman she had been sixteen months ago, and she was glad. And she was also glad that the man walking beside her was Jess Cantrell. "You didn't say if Jewel had anything new to offer when you talked to her this afternoon."

Jess was silent for a moment. Jewel's observations had been startling. He had told her as many of the new developments as he had felt wise. She had looked at him for a long moment, guessing the rest, he imagined. Then she had shrugged. "Sometimes running away and staying away is the best thing that these kids can do. This Roseanna was smart enough to see that. Maybe she'll be smart enough to stay out of trouble on the streets. What wouldn't be smart is if she tried to go home. Maybe her sister better face that now."

Jess couldn't tell Krista that. Not tonight. He was honest, but vague. "She didn't have any new information."

Krista shrugged off disappointment. "I hope Sally's at Tallulah's."

He reassured her about that, as he'd done twice before already. "When I talked to Wanda at the shop this afternoon, she said she'd try to have Sally there around midnight."

"Thank you, Jess."

He wanted to tell her there was very little he wouldn't do for her, but he knew she didn't need to hear that or anything else personal right now. He could imagine how she was feeling.

"When we get to Tallulah's," he said, "you go in first. I'll wait outside for a while, then I'll come in. I've never seen Chaz there, but he probably won't start anything in public, anyway. If he is there, come right back out."

"If May Rose is Rosie..."

He knew what she was thinking. If they found Rosie, and Barnard knew it, would Rosie's life be in even more danger? It was exactly what Jewel had hinted at. "We'll keep her safe," he said with more assurance than he felt. "Right now, let's just worry about one thing at a time."

Krista thought that would be an incredible luxury, but she didn't say anything. Jess was just trying to calm her. She knew he was worried, too.

They walked through the honky-tonk of Bourbon Street. Tourists passed, clutching potent hurricanes in hourglass-shaped glasses, and hard-faced men and women stood on street corners assessing them. Jazz floated through the air, blending with the essence of the warm spring evening and the smell of boiling crawfish. Overhead, at one of the street's more notorious bars, false legs swung gaily out an open second-story window, then disappeared from view again.

They turned off Bourbon a block before they got to Chaz's place, to avoid the risk of running into him. The side streets were darker, but anything was safer than a confrontation.

Two doors down from Tallulah's, Jess stopped and put his hand on Krista's arm to stop her, too. The only thing he could say was completely inadequate. "Good luck."

"Thanks." She took a deep breath and started toward the door.

Jess watched as she went inside. He didn't want to follow too closely because if Sally were there, she might get suspicious. When Krista didn't come back out right away he relaxed a little and leaned against the brick facade of the building behind him. As he waited, he watched the night's activities unfold around him.

Half a block past Tallulah's, another bar was hopping. It was not a bar for women, although tonight its patrons were participating in a Marilyn Monroe look-alike contest. Several men dressed as the buxom blonde wove their way down the street past Jess. One of them wolf-whistled, then broke into shrill, drunken laughter.

Across the street, in the direction he and Krista had come from, a small group of people entered the front door of a hole-in-the-wall café that served mostly French Quarter residents and employees. Jess had eaten there himself and found the food as good as any he'd eaten in the city's best-known restaurants.

The people of New Orleans knew how to eat, and they knew how to party. It was truly the Big Easy, the City That Care Forgot, and if sometimes New Orleans forgot to care about the kids loose on its streets, it was really no different from all the other cities Jess had seen. Northern cities, southern cities, western cities and cities in proper old New England. Runaways flocked to places already embroiled in urban problems. Legislators made laws, cops tried to enforce them, but the problem was bigger than anyone wanted to believe.

Jess's mind wandered to his book. He should have started it by now. He had already collected a whopping advance, and he had a deadline to meet. How did he tell his publisher that he had met a woman and couldn't leave her behind? How did he explain that the book seemed somehow less important than the lives he had studied?

A movement across the street caught his eye. A man in a wide-brimmed panama and white suit was exiting the café. Jess tensed immediately. Even at this distance, he recognized Chaz. He watched as Chaz headed away from Tallulah's, toward his own club, but before Jess could relax, he got a glimpse of Chaz's companion. She was wearing tight shorts, and even if the phrase "hot pants" had gone out of style, it was still appropriate for this occasion. Her halter top barely covered her small breasts, and she lurched down the sidewalk in platform shoes.

Tate.

Jess was following them before he even knew what he was doing. He had covered half a block before he realized that he had left Krista at Tallulah's. But her most immediate threat was strolling down the street, his arm draped around Tate's shoulders. If Krista stayed at Tallulah's until he returned, and Jess was sure she would, she was safe.

Tate wasn't.

Jess didn't analyze his feelings. What detachment he had held on to through the last months was gone. He was fed up with detachment, with the careful bloodless dissection of society's faults. In that moment there was only one girl, one child, who needed someone else to make her decisions.

Jess covered the distance to Chaz's place at a pace that should have gotten him there only seconds after Chaz and Tate. He had lost sight of them in a surge of people rolling off Bourbon Street after a set at one of the jazz clubs had ended.

At the front door he pushed past the barker who was promising all passersby the thrill of a lifetime. Inside he ignored the "host" demanding the club's cover charge. When the man grabbed his arm, Jess shook it off.

"Vice," Jess snarled, sparing the man one glance. "You touch me again and I'll have you downtown so fast, you'll think you've been saddled to a hurricane."

"Where's your badge?" The man, greasy enough to slip through cracks in the sidewalk, thrust his hands in his pockets.

"With my gun. Wanna go for it?"

The man briefly seemed to consider, then stepped back as Jess pushed past him. "Your boss just came through with a kid," Jess continued. "I want her. You tell me where they went or you're an accessory."

If the man wondered what that was, he didn't bother to ask. "I didn't see nuthin'."

"Better think again." Jess turned back to him and grabbed his shirtfront. "Better think hard."

"I told you—"

Jess realized he had the attention of everyone in the room, which was just one of a labyrinth of rooms weaving its way half a block behind him. "Okay, here's the law," he said. He pushed the man up against the bar. "Enticing persons into prostitution, persuading, placing or causing entrance of person under twenty-one into the practice of prostitution by force, threats, promises or any device or scheme is an offense."

"I ain't—"

Jess slapped his hands against the man's chest. "Mistake of age is no defense. That means, stupid, that if you think the girl is twenty-one and she's not, you're still in deep—"

"Okay, okay." The guy held up his hands. "But I ain't seen—"

"Penalty's two to ten years. With or without hard labor."

"I ain't no pimp."

"The law targets everybody. Transporters, maintainers of places, solicitors. Including," he said, looking around the room, "lessors. Know what that means, folks?"

Three men got up and slunk out of the room.

Music started, and a girl dressed in ten spangles away from nothing walked out on a runway behind the bar. She took one look at the commotion below her, turned and fled the way she had come. The music whined to a halt. "How old is she?" Jess asked.

The man gave up. "The girl you want's down the hall. There's a stairway. Go up one flight, go left past three—four rooms, then go left again. There's a couple of steps down, then another right."

"Don't try and follow. My partner's outside, and backup's on the way."

"Hey, I'm gone." The moment Jess let go of the man's shirt, he made good on his words. The room emptied behind him except for the bartender. He was watching Jess with interest. "You're not from vice."

"Want to make a bet?"

The man laughed. The sound was almost human. "Nah. Go on. Got no customers, so I'll just take me a little vacation."

Jess doubted the bartender could be trusted, but he didn't have enough time to worry about it. He took off up the stairs.

The stairwell and corridor smelled worse than his apartment before it was cleaned. They were dark and dingy, and every available space was covered with the filthiest graffiti he had ever seen. Luckily, they were surprisingly empty. Jess covered his nose with his hand and walked as silently as possible, listening at every doorway. He followed the directions he had been given, but he didn't trust them. When he reached the room where he had been sent, he paused, ear to the door.

Surprisingly, he hadn't been lied to.

He threw the door open and leaped back instinctively. Across the room, Tate cowered in the corner, sobbing. When she saw Jess, her eyes widened and she screamed, pointing toward the door. In the same moment Jess saw a cane come crashing down where he should have been standing. In a moment of crisis-born clarity it occurred to him that since he had met Krista, he had resorted to violence more often than he'd ever had to in his whole life.

A split second later he and Chaz were on the floor, rolling over and over. He heard the shrieks of women, mixed with Tate's screams and Chaz's grunts. He saw high heels precariously close to his head; then the heels disappeared out the door.

He and Chaz rolled over again. Jess was disoriented, unsure who was on top, who was pounding who, whose face had received the most blows. He heard the sickening crunch of bones and didn't know whose they were, felt his eyes sting and couldn't tell if it was from sweat or blood.

When the knife appeared there was no question who it belonged to, though. Jess thought calmly that it was funny Chaz had chosen to carry a knife. A gun was so much quicker, so much less personal. A gun could have blown him to kingdom come without Chaz having to grunt.

They rolled again, and Jess felt a sharp pain in his arm. He managed to push the knife away, but he knew he was bleeding. Chaz was a street fighter, and he had the advantage tonight as he hadn't in their encounters before. He had the weapon, he was on his own turf, and he probably had help nearby.

Jess knew he had been a fool to bluff his way this far, and also that he would do it all over again, if he had to.

Chaz grunted, twisting until he was aiming at Jess's throat. Jess struggled to keep the knife at a safe distance, but his arm was injured and his strength ebbing. He gathered what strength he had left to shout to Tate, "Run!" He couldn't see if she had obeyed, and he shouted again. "Tate, get out of here!"

The knife inched closer. Then, as if Chaz's strength had ebbed first, the knife fell harmlessly to the floor. Chaz's head followed its path.

For a moment Jess was disoriented. The sudden slackening of Chaz's body had been dreamlike, a desperate wish fulfilled. He pushed himself up on his elbows and gazed through a red haze. Tate stood over Chaz, tears streaming down her face. The cane was in her hand.

Jess's head cleared, and so did his vision. "We've got to get out of here." He pushed Chaz's limp body off his legs and stumbled to his feet. He put his hand on Tate's arm. "Come on."

She twisted away. Jess wondered if he was going to have to carry her kicking and screaming out the back entrance, but she only leaned forward and snatched the knife from under Chaz's shoulder. Then she straightened. She was still crying. "He told me I'd dance with my clothes on. He even bought me this outfit. Then he brought me here."

Jess took a quick look around. He had seen places like this off Times Square. He was in the dressing room of a peep show. Men paid to sit in tiny cubicles while one dancer performed for them. They fed change into timers rigged to give them brief peeks at the action on the tiny stage behind the dressing room. They *didn't* pay to see fully clothed dancers.

He grabbed Tate again and pulled her toward the door. "We're going to find the back way out, sweetheart. I'll take the knife."

"Is he dead?"

As if to answer, Chaz groaned. One hand clenched and unclenched spasmodically.

"'Fraid not." Jess steered Tate out the door. She was only too willing to go. Out in the hallway, he heard the clatter of feet coming up the stairs behind them. "There's got to be a back door."

"There is. Chaz told me where it is. In case there was a raid."

"I'd give a lot for a raid about now."

Tate took the lead. She navigated the maze of hallways as if she had been born in the squalid building. They passed a man stumbling drunkenly down the hall. He gave a lewd wink and slid to a sitting position, as if he planned to barricade the hall behind them.

Just as Jess was certain Tate didn't know where they were, she opened a door and led him out into the humid night. They were surrounded by overflowing garbage cans. Heaven wouldn't have looked any better. "Come on." Jess took control again, leading her through the back courtyard and out onto a side street. His hand was anchored to her arm, and he didn't intend for that to change. "You're coming with me."

For once Tate didn't put up an argument.

Wanda sipped her drink. Both she and Krista were watching the door. "She should be here any minute."

Krista forced herself not to point out that Wanda had said that three times in the last twenty minutes, and Sally still hadn't shown up. She wondered where Jess was. She had expected him to come in a few minutes after she had, but, as yet, he hadn't appeared. She sipped her club soda.

Tallulah's, or the anxiety of waiting for Sally, had given her a fierce headache. The radio was loud enough to permanently narrow her auditory range, and the smoke was so thick that Sally could have sneaked into the room unseen. Perry had tried to match Krista with a young stud in the corner wearing an obscene T-shirt straight out of the store where Wanda worked. He didn't like the fact that Krista was just hanging around instead of making dates and giving him a cut. She had finally told him that he had missed his calling; he should have been a pimp. He seemed to consider the suggestion.

"She should be here any minute," Wanda said again.

"Stop saying that." Krista put her head in her hands to stop the pounding. "I'm sorry," she apologized immediately.

Wanda patted her hair. "I know how you feel."

Krista believed her. She and Wanda might as well have lived on different planets most of their lives, but in the important ways they were alike. That was one of the things she had learned in the last months. Who you were and where you had come from, even what you had done with your life, weren't nearly as important as what was inside you. Hayden Barnard, U.S. Senator, was an empty shell. Wanda, ex-hooker, was full of grace and spirit.

Krista lifted her head. "It's just that I feel so—"

"She's here. Look sharp." Wanda stood up and motioned for Sally, who had just walked in, to join them.

Krista's headache got suddenly, stabbingly worse. She was scared to death. As if she understood, Wanda pulled a chair up to the table for Sally and signaled Perry to bring her a drink. "Crystal's got a hangover," she told Sally.

Krista smiled wanly. It wasn't really a lie. She *was* hung over, but not from booze. From fear, hope, guilt, shame. They were more potent than pure wood grain alcohol.

"So, you got a picture for me to look at?" Sally asked.

Krista reached inside her handbag. She slid the picture across the table so Sally wouldn't see she was shaking. "She look familiar?"

Sally squinted. Smoke hovered in the inches between her eyes and the photo. She raised it and squinted harder. "It's dark in here."

Wanda pulled out her lighter and held it next to the photo. "Better?"

Sally stared. "Yeah, that's May Rose. Least I think it is. Her hair's curly now. When'd you say you got this?"

Krista couldn't make herself speak. She shrugged.

Sally pushed the photo across the table. "It could be her. I never saw her without false eyelashes before, but I guess it's her."

Krista's headache miraculously disappeared, but she felt as if its departure had left empty space in her brain. She was dizzy, and her stomach was doing jumping jacks. May Rose was her sister. May Rose *was her sister*. She didn't know how long she had waited before she spoke. "Well, good," she managed. "Now I can give her back her stuff."

"She'll be back this weekend. I talked to her pimp."

Krista closed her eyes. The room was spinning, and she was afraid she was going to be sick. She had known all along that Rosie had probably resorted to prostitution. But having it confirmed was still too much to take.

"Is she all right?"

Krista heard Sally's question from far away. Wanda's answer came from farther away still. "I told you, she has a hangover. I'm just going to take her outside for some fresh air."

Krista felt Wanda's fingers on her arm. "Stand up, Crystal. Let's get you outside."

Krista managed to stand. The room was still spinning when she opened her eyes. She tried to joke. "Must be something I ate."

"Or drank." Wanda forced a laugh. "See you this weekend, Sally. Bring your friend here, why don't you? On Saturday?"

Sally shrugged.

Outside, Krista leaned against a street lamp.

"Just take a deep breath," Wanda counseled. "It's just the shock, sugar. You'll be fine. Sounds like you're going to have your sister back."

"What if it's not really her? The picture's not very good, and you can't see your hand in front of your face in there."

"Don't borrow trouble. Sally says it's May Rose, so it probably is May Rose."

Krista nodded. The fresh air was helping. "You're right."

"Feeling better?"

The street lamp no longer seemed to be wiggling down her spine. Krista nodded again. "I'm going to be fine in a minute. Just let me stay here until my head stops spinning."

Wanda looked worried. "I could walk you home."

"Jess is around here somewhere. If he doesn't show up in a few minutes I'll go back inside and wait for him."

"What about Chaz?"

"If I see Chaz I'll come right in, so stop worrying. You've done enough for me tonight already. Go home and get some sleep." Krista leaned over and kissed the other woman's cheek. "I can't thank you enough."

Wanda looked embarrassed. "Yeah? May Rose turns out to be your sister, you can take me out to dinner. Commander's Palace."

"You got it." Krista managed a smile. "Now go."

Krista was alone in a moment. It was late enough that no one was on the street, even though there was still noise from the bars and a café across the way. She was so filled with feelings that she barely noticed.

May Rose was her sister. It had to be true. May Rose was Rosie, and soon she'd be back in New Orleans. With her pimp.

Krista tried to put that part of it out of her mind. Nothing mattered, not what Rosie had done, not what Rosie had become. Nothing mattered except having Rosie by her side again. They could go away together, start a new life. They could change their names, and Krista could support Rosie until she finished high school and college. She would spend the next years making up to her sister for not believing the truth about Hayden. Jess would help.

She was surprised that the last thought had crept in. Jess had made no promises, issued no invitations. They had made love, but his first interest in her had been the story Rosie could tell. And, of course, now there was no question of Rosie telling anything. If she did, no matter how skillfully Jess camouflaged the truth, Rosie's life would be in danger.

So after the weekend, after Jess was sure that she and Rosie were together again and safe plans had been made, Jess would disappear.

Just as he had disappeared this evening.

Krista's head was clear enough now that she began to worry. Where was Jess? She stood straighter and searched the street. There was a couple strolling together on the next block. As she watched they turned and were lost to view. Cars had passed as she had stood by the street lamp, but now the street was empty except for a large, dark American car coming from the east.

Jess had planned to join her inside Tallulah's. What had happened to him? The car came closer, but she paid little attention. She was alert enough to know it didn't belong to Chaz. Chaz drove a lilac limousine that had pimpmobile stamped all over it. This car was sedate, if just as expensive.

She looked toward the door of Tallulah's and debated whether she should go back inside and wait, but the thought of the smoke and noise turned her stomach.

When she gazed back at the street, the car had stopped, just in front of her. The door opened, and the driver slid out.

He was holding a revolver, just as he had been the first time she had seen him. This time the man from the convenience store was wearing a suit.

With his gun he motioned to the back door of the sleek gray Continental, which had been pushed open from the inside by an unseen hand. "Inside, Miss Jensen. And don't give me any trouble."

Chapter 14

After Chaz's club, Tallulah's didn't seem like such a bad place to bring Tate, although Jess knew he could be arrested for corrupting a minor just by walking her over the threshold. He half expected that to happen. It would have been the ultimate irony.

He didn't plan to keep her at Tallulah's long. He wanted to get Krista, then take Tate back to Krista's apartment. He wasn't going to leave Tate outside. Chaz was in no shape to follow them, but he hadn't gotten where he was without making "friends." Tate could end up at the bottom of the Mississippi—and Jess had told her as much.

Tate hadn't yet recovered her bravado. She was silent and shaken, and she had kept up with Jess as if she were glued to his side. At the door to Tallulah's Jess stopped and instructed her. "I'm going in, and you're coming with me. We'll get Krista and get out. Don't talk to anybody. Don't even look at anybody."

He didn't wait for an answer. He shoved the door open and pushed Tate inside. His eyes immediately began to burn, and for a moment he couldn't see anything. Then he began to make out dim shapes. He scanned the room as best he could. "Do you see her?" he asked Tate.

"You told me not to look at anybody," she said, her voice quavering.

"You can look for Krista."

Obediently she did. "She's not here."

Jess had suffered one too many blows to the head. His eyes just wouldn't focus properly. "She's got to be. Look harder."

"Maybe she's in the bathroom."

"Maybe." Jess's arm throbbed, and his head was swimming. The stab wound wasn't bleeding hard anymore, but under his sports coat his shirt sleeve was still soaked with blood.

"Do you know where it is? I can go see," Tate offered.

"Over my dead body. We'll wait." He started looking for a place to sit.

Tate took his good arm. "Over here."

They took a table by the door. Ten minutes later Perry came out from behind the bar to join them. "Looks like somebody worked you over good."

"Looks like it."

"You too beat up to order a drink tonight, Cantrell?"

"I'm waiting for somebody."

"The space here ain't free."

Jess wondered if Perry could read well enough to appreciate the things Jess would be saying about him in his book. "I know this big Cajun cop, a real crusader. He keeps telling me if I'll just report some of the things I've seen, he'll get busy with warrants. Things like bartenders who set up hookers with johns."

"You ain't scarin' me." Nevertheless, Perry stood. "Who you waitin' for?"

"Crystal."

"You're too late. She and Wanda left ten minutes ago."

Jess knew Wanda and Krista had planned to talk to Sally together. "She was going to meet me here."

Perry cackled. "Sally was with 'em too. She said Krista had a hangover. Not on my drinks, that's for sure. You can't get a hangover the way I make 'em." He was still cackling as he walked back behind the bar.

"Damn." Jess rested his head in his hands.

"Where is she?" Tate asked. She sounded like a scared little girl—which wasn't far from the truth.

"I don't know." Jess considered his alternatives. His head roared in protest. "I'm going to take you to Krista's," he said at last. "If she's not there, I'll go out and look for her. You're going to lock yourself in, take a shower and go to bed."

"You're not my father." She said it with no enthusiasm, as if she was only giving lip service to rebellion.

"I am tonight! And you're going to do what I say like I was the one who burped you and changed your diapers. Got it? Tomorrow we'll talk about where you go from here." He lifted his head. "You think about how good you are at making your own decisions, Tate. Do you really believe the girls in that peep show just dance for those men?"

Tears clouded her eyes. She shook her head.

Jess stood. "Come on."

Tate followed him out the door.

"You're looking well, Krista."

"You're looking like a bastard, Scott." Krista shifted on the butter-soft leather cushions of the Lincoln and stared at the man beside her. Not a blond hair was out of place. His Brooks Brothers suit folded in perfect creases at his elbows and knees. He looked wholesome enough to shake hands at a campaign banquet.

He smiled thinly. "Well, since we're being brutally honest, darling, you look like a whore."

"Good."

"What if somebody we know saw you like this?" He rubbed the sleeve of her satin blouse between his fingers. "You're a senator's daughter."

"Stepdaughter, and I'll have to see if there's anything I can do about *that*."

Scott nodded, as if she had answered a question he hadn't yet asked. "We're not going far. I'm staying at a friend's home. We'll talk there."

"Sure we will." Krista reached for the door handle. They were embroiled in French Quarter traffic. Even though it was already tomorrow, there were still enough cars on the narrow streets to keep the Lincoln creeping along.

"The doors are locked."

Krista discovered he was right. The locks were apparently controlled from the front. "Borrow the car from a hit man?"

"Why don't you just sit back and relax? We'll be there soon."

Krista considered smashing her window with her purse, but she knew Scott would stop her. He was a man who always looked charmingly relaxed, but he was rarely caught off guard. "Who's your friend?" she asked, nodding to the man driving the car.

"Carter, introduce yourself to the lady."

"I'm sure Miss Jensen remembers me." Convenience Store Carter made a slow turn onto Canal Street, then picked up speed.

"Yes indeedy. Once a bad guy, always a bad guy." Krista inched as far away from Scott as she could.

Scott laughed. "I'm glad to see you've kept your sense of humor."

"Anytime I start to lose it I think of you."

"You've developed some hard edges, darling. Did they come with the profession?"

"*I'm* not the politician."

"I've missed you."

"I might have missed you if there had been any *you* to miss."

Scott's thin-lipped smile disappeared. "You couldn't leave well enough alone, could you?"

"No."

"I tried to stop you."

"You did, didn't you? You and Carter." Krista looked out the window. She wasn't feeling as cocky as she sounded. In the last months she had learned to make no assumptions. Just because she and Scott had almost married didn't mean that he wouldn't kill her if he thought it was necessary to save Hayden's career. He had already sent Carter as a warning, one she hadn't taken.

She had never questioned Scott's loyalty to her stepfather. Now she knew that loyalty extended to kidnapping. Murder was one step away.

"I never thought you would be so stubborn," Scott said regretfully.

"How can you do Hayden's dirty work for him? Don't you have any pride?"

"We'll talk when we get to the house."

"What's wrong? Don't you want Carter to hear us? Doesn't he know what Hayden is?" Krista leaned forward. "Carter, how do you feel about men who—"

Scott jerked her back against the seat. His fingers dug into her arm, just where Chaz had bruised it. She cried out in pain. "We'll talk when we get to the house!" he repeated.

"Who seduces teenage girls!" she finished. Scott twisted her arm, and she cried out again.

"Carter doesn't care about the lies your sister told, so shut up!"

"They weren't lies!" Krista was desperate. If Carter didn't know, and she could get his sympathy...

"Lies," Scott said firmly. "She's a liar, and she always has been. Hayden did everything for her, and this is the way she repays him!"

Krista tried to pry his fingers loose. "There were other girls, too."

"More lies."

Carter spoke. "I'd sit back and relax if I were you, Miss Jensen. You'll just get hurt if you don't."

"Good advice," Scott warned.

Krista realized that Carter didn't care what her stepfather had done. She rested her head against the seat, and Scott released his grip on her arm.

The rest of the trip passed in silence. When they turned off St. Charles Avenue, Krista recognized the Garden District, a section of expensive, historic homes. They had been built by American entrepreneurs who hadn't been welcome in the Creole-dominated French Quarter during the nineteenth century, and many were elaborate architectural gems.

Carter turned, then turned again. Finally he stopped in front of a Greek-revival style mansion of three stories. The brick walkway was flanked by two towering live oaks. "If you try to scream or run, I'll knock you out," he said.

"Did you get your training from the gestapo or the KGB?"

"Army intelligence. Vietnam." He gave her a toothy grin. "I was one of those guys who'd go up in a chopper with two Cong and come down with one."

Krista shuddered. Whether it was true or not, he had made his point.

The lock on her door clicked. Carter was holding the door open for her before she could move.

With Carter on one side and Scott on the other, Krista was whisked up the walkway. Inside the entry hall, she got the impression of overstated elegance and wealth. She was too busy observing Scott and Carter to notice any details except that they seemed to be alone. The house was silent.

"Miss Jensen and I will talk in the library, Carter."

"I'll be outside the door."

"Afraid Scott can't take care of me himself?" she taunted.

The look in Carter's eyes was almost admiration. "You don't know when to quit, do you?"

"This way, Krista." Scott took her arm in a no-nonsense hold and steered her past drawing rooms and parlors. She had the crazy feeling that she was the beleaguered heroine in a costume drama. Any minute now the ball would begin. Only she might not live to see it.

The library was paneled with mahogany and adorned with English hunting prints and the mounted heads of two boars. The door closed behind them, and Scott headed straight for an ice bucket and cut crystal decanter. "Scotch on the rocks?" he offered.

"I don't drink with people I despise."

"You didn't always despise me."

"I didn't always know my stepfather was more important to you than I was."

Scott took a sip of the drink he had made himself. "What if I told you that wasn't true."

"I wouldn't believe you."

"I have a career, Krista. Right now it depends on Hayden's goodwill, but not forever. I'm making a name for myself. Soon I can go off on my own. Your stepfather's going to run for president. Did you know that?"

She just stared icily at him.

"When Hayden vacates his senate seat, I'll run for it. He'll endorse me. Even if he doesn't get the party's nomination, he'll be vice president. Either way, I'll have his place."

"So you're saying that I wasn't as important as your career."

"I'm saying that I knew I'd have nothing to offer you if Hayden withdrew his support of me. I'd be just another struggling young attorney."

"Instead you're a lying, cheating, pandering gofer!"

Scott went pale. "I don't pimp for your stepfather." He slammed his glass down on the desk behind him. "Your sister lied! Hayden's a good and honorable man!"

For just the tiniest part of a second Krista believed him. Then she saw his gaze drift ever so slightly from hers. Scott knew the truth. She wondered if he had admitted it to himself.

"How do you know what Rosie said to me?" she asked softly. "I know I gave it away in the car, but you knew before that, or you wouldn't have picked me up."

"I guessed. She told your mother the same thing."

It was the second revelation that night to make Krista's stomach turn. "My mother knows." She closed her eyes.

"Your *mother* doesn't believe it."

"My mother doesn't know about the senate page or the other girl, does she?" She forced herself to look at him again. "How many others did Hayden go after?"

"All lies, Krista. Every politician has detractors. There are always deadbeats looking for payoffs, or for lies to print in the scandal sheets."

"If Rosie was lying, you wouldn't be trying so hard to keep her from being found."

He didn't answer right away. When he did, he didn't look at her. He picked up his drink again and swished it back and forth. "If your sister goes to the press with her story, Hayden

Barnard's career will be over. The public doesn't care whether a story is true.''

''I care.'' Krista closed the distance between them. ''Look me in the eye and tell me it's a lie, Scott. Tell me Rosie was just confused, or acting out to get even with Hayden for something. Tell me.''

''It was a lie.'' His eyes proved it wasn't.

''How can you stand living with yourself?''

Scott didn't even protest as he finished his drink. Both of them knew he would be wasting his time trying to persuade her now. ''I live with myself just fine,'' he said at last. ''Hayden Barnard is an important man. He can make a difference in the world. Maybe he has a quirk. Lots of politicians have quirks.''

''Quirk?'' She wanted to laugh; she wanted to scream.

''I'm not going to let anything or anyone stand in Hayden's way. Not you. Not your sister.''

This time she knew he wasn't lying. She played her last, desperate card. ''Do you know Jess Cantrell?''

''Yeah. And I know he's living next door to you and probably sleeping in your bed. I know he's the one that dug up the stories about the two girls.''

She wasn't surprised. She imagined Scott knew everything that had happened to her since she left Maryland. ''Do you know he'll come looking for me, and if he doesn't find me, he'll tear Hayden apart? He's got the credentials and the clout to do it.''

''I know he would—if he could.''

Krista didn't even flinch. She was beyond shock. ''Just what do you mean?''

Scott smiled his thin-lipped smile. ''It's simple, really. There's one sure way to keep you both silent.''

''She's not here.'' Jess came out of Krista's bedroom. Tate was waiting in the living room.

''Where could she have gone?''

Tate had suffered enough for one night. Jess didn't want to worry her any more. Besides, he was worried enough for both of them, and a couple of other people, too. ''If she wasn't feeling well, Wanda probably took her to her place. I know where she lives. I'll check there first.''

"I can help."

"You can help by staying here and staying safe."

Tate sat down on Krista's sofa. Jess suspected her legs just wouldn't hold her anymore. His own were feeling rubbery; he would have to take precious minutes to bandage his arm before he lost any more blood.

Krista's medicine cabinet had everything he needed. He washed his face and put antibiotic ointment on a bad scrape. One eye was almost swollen shut, but other than simple cuts and bruises, he was all right. His arm was a different matter. Objectively he knew that it needed stitches. There was no time now, though. He washed it as best he could and smeared ointment on it. Then, carrying gauze and tape, he went back into the living room. "Tate, you're going to have to wrap this for me. I can't do it myself."

She was already too pale to turn paler. "Yuck!"

"Yeah." He tried to smile. "Can you do it?"

She grimaced, but she took the gauze and began to wrap it around and around his biceps. Then she anchored it with tape. "You should see a doctor," she counseled.

He wanted to laugh at the role reversal, but there was no laughter inside him. "Promise me you'll stay here tonight."

She seemed to consider, but both of them knew it was the only place she'd be safe. "Okay."

"There's probably food and juice in the refrigerator. Make yourself at home." Jess pulled on his blood-soaked shirt for the trip next door to get a fresh one. "I'll be back as soon as I find out something. Keep the door locked."

"Okay."

Jess started toward the door, then turned. Tate looked forlorn. He knew as soon as he left she was going to burst into tears. He went back to her and ruffled her hair. "You're a good kid, honey. Krista and I both care a lot about you."

She sniffed. Jess knew it would be a mistake to stay another second. Tate wouldn't want him to see her cry. He ruffled her hair again, then left.

Hours later he was the one with emotions that were about to explode. After a long search he had located Wanda, who had spent the time after she left Krista with a teenage boy who was a runaway from a small town in Alabama. Wanda had finally persuaded the boy to go to the Place, then taken him there herself. Jess found her there and learned what had happened with Sally and Krista that night. Wanda had been horrified to discover that Krista had disappeared.

Jess and Wanda spent the hours until dawn searching and talking to people who might have seen Krista. No one had.

Now they stood in front of the Café du Monde and watched the street cleaners prepare for a new day.

"I feel awful. I shouldn't have left her. But she promised she'd go back inside in a few minutes. She said if there was trouble—"

Jess cut Wanda off. "It's not your fault."

"I been talking to this kid for a couple of days. I knew I had a chance of getting him over to the shelter if I could find him after Krista and I talked to Sally."

"It's not your fault."

"Jewel wants me to be an outreach worker." Wanda's voice held no pleasure. She was exhausted, and Krista's disappearance had taken all the joy out of Jewel's offer.

"You'll be great." Jess sagged against peach stucco. "You've been doing outreach for years without pay."

"I shouldn't have left Krista."

"Go home and get some sleep."

"Not until we find her."

"I'm going to see a cop I know."

"You're half dead. I don't want to leave you."

"He won't talk to me if you're there." Jess straightened. His arm felt as if Chaz's knife was still in it. "Do me one more favor, though. Call Krista's and see if a miracle's happened."

"Get yourself some coffee while you wait. Please."

Jess grunted his answer, but the suggestion was a good one. While Wanda went to find a pay phone, he went inside and got coffee and *beignets*. They were probably as good as usual, but they tasted like ashes to him.

Had he ever doubted the strength of what he felt for Krista? He wasn't worried about a stranger or even a friend. He was frantic because the woman he loved was missing. Only fear that strong could have kept him on his feet this long.

He was too drained to feel much at the revelation. He loved Krista. He probably had since almost the beginning. Realizing that he loved her changed nothing at all.

Krista was gone without a trace, and all his leads had taken him nowhere. He was supposed to be able to find out anything from anyone, but the stakes had never been this high.

He had only one place to turn, and the possibility of help from that quarter was so slim as to be nonexistent. Yet Mack Hankins was his only chance.

When Wanda came back, he didn't even have to ask her if Krista was home. She looked exhausted and as worried as he felt.

"No answer?"

She shook her head. "Wouldn't Tate answer the phone?"

"She hasn't been. I guess she's afraid to."

"Are you going back there and check?"

"After I see a cop." Jess pushed himself away from the table. "Go home, Wanda. I'll call you as soon as I find out something."

"I'm heading back to Bourbon. I might find someone we haven't talked to yet."

Jess knew he couldn't talk her out of going. She walked him to his car, which was parked illegally and had been ticketed twice that night already. He was just glad it hadn't been booted or towed.

The drive to the station took only minutes. It was early for Mack to be there, but Jess had learned that sometimes he worked this shift.

Mack wasn't there, but he was expected in half an hour. Jess steeled himself to weather the delay and drank bad coffee from the station pot. From the taste of it, it was yesterday's bad coffee.

Mack was fifteen minutes late. When he finally arrived Jess was ready to wrap his fingers around his throat and squeeze help out of him.

Mack's first words weren't encouraging. "I thought I told you to stay away from the station."

"I'm here to report a missing person. Try telling me I don't have the rights of any U.S. citizen."

Mack grunted. His next act gave him away. He searched for a private room to conduct their business. He finally ushered Jess into an interrogation room that smelled like the upstairs hallway of Chaz's club. "I've told you everything I can," he said with no preamble. "There's nothing I can do to help you find Hayden Barnard's kid, damn it! Can't you get that through your thick head?"

"Hayden Barnard's other kid is missing." Jess sat down at the small table where plenty of others had sat before him. Only this time, the cop standing beside him was the one being interrogated.

Mack just stared at him.

"Krista disappeared last night. I've searched everywhere I know for her."

"When was this?"

"Late. After midnight."

"How do you know she's missing?"

"I was supposed to meet her at Tallulah's." Jess saw Mack grimace. "I know. Not my idea of a fun place, either. She went there last night because she thought she might have a lead on her sister."

"Lead pan out?"

"Maybe. Someone recognized the photo. I wasn't there. I got caught up in a little brawl at a place off Bourbon."

"You don't look so good."

"The other guy looks worse."

Mack gave a half smile. "The other guy wouldn't be Chaz Martinez, would he?"

"Friend of yours?"

"We got called last night. I saw the report on my way in. Seems like ole Chaz got dumped out a window."

"That wasn't me," Jess said. "But it would have been if I'd thought of it."

Mack laughed. "We know who it was. Two of the girls who work for him. Said they found him unconscious and took advantage of the situation. He'll be in Charity for a while. Vice closed him down, by the way. Investigating his assault was the ticket they needed to get inside and look around."

"And he'll be out on the streets running his club and his girls again as soon as he's up and around."

Mack shrugged.

Jess didn't have the time to gloat about what had happened to Chaz. "After Krista had the photo of her sister confirmed at Tallulah's, she went outside with another woman. She told the other woman she'd wait for me there or inside. The other woman left. When I got there a little while later, Krista was gone, and no one's seen her since."

"That doesn't constitute a missing persons complaint."

"Damn it, we both know what might have happened to her and who was probably behind it!"

Mack was silent. He finally took the chair across from Jess, but he didn't say a word.

"So, what are you going to do?" Jess demanded.

"I'm under orders not to do a damn thing," Mack said softly. "I don't know how far up the line they go, but I can tell you this, I've never had orders like them before."

"Are you talking about Rosie or Krista?"

"Rosie. I haven't heard anything about Krista. I'd tell you if I had."

Jess believed him. Mack was obviously a man caught in a situation he despised. He was a good cop, a decent cop. Someone in the chain of command, someone who could fire him, wasn't. "What do you know about Rosie?"

Mack shrugged. "I wasn't lying when I told you I didn't know anything. But there's something fishy. There aren't any records. Everywhere I looked my hand was slapped. My supervisor started talking about insubordination, about bonuses I might not get if I didn't play the game...."

"You think it's Barnard?"

"Either he's paying people off or making this look like a national security issue."

Jess frowned. The movement caused his face to throb. "National security?"

"Senator's stepdaughter. Kidnapping. Enemy agents."

"Come on!"

"I didn't say I believed it."

"I'll tell you what happened." Jess told Mack what he'd learned about Hayden.

Mack had heard and seen everything, but he was obviously not hardened to all feeling. He put a few labels on Hayden's behavior before he fell silent.

All Jess's own suspicions had been confirmed. Now he knew that Barnard had closed down the search for his stepdaughter before it had even begun. "He's all those things," he agreed, "but he may be even more."

"I don't follow you."

"A man like that wouldn't balk at murder," Jess answered. "He may have already killed one of the Jensen girls. Are you going to help me find Krista before she's next?"

Chapter 15

"Take these." The doctor handed Jess two white tablets and a glass of water. "Antibiotics," he said before Jess could ask.

Jess swallowed them reluctantly. "I thought you already shot me full of penicillin."

"Would you stop arguing with the man, Cantrell?" Mack stood in the doorway of the doctor's house, arms folded across his chest. He had brought Jess to a friend rather than to an emergency room where a report would have to be filed.

Jess grimaced. His arm had been numbed and stitched, and he'd had injections for tetanus and infection.

"Bed rest," the doctor continued. "For twenty-four hours." He tore a slip off his prescription pad. "And take these until they're gone. Do you want something to help you sleep?"

Jess didn't bother telling him that he wasn't going to sleep until Krista was found. "No." He pushed himself out of the chair and tried not to wince. The anesthetic was wearing off, and his arm felt as if it were on fire. "Thanks."

"You won't thank me when you get my bill. I charge double for house calls, triple if it's my house."

"I'll drive you home," Mack said, leading the way out.

"No thanks. I'll need my car to look for Krista."

"You heard what the doctor said—"

"Come on, Mack." Jess's tone made it clear that arguing was futile.

"Then give me till noon to look into this. I'll pick you up then, and we'll come get your car."

Jess considered. He had been running on nothing but adrenaline for hours. He was in danger of collapse if he didn't get some rest. And until Mack had a chance to investigate, there was very little Jess could do. "Noon."

"You hear anything before then, call the station and leave me a message. I'll have someone reliable call it in to me."

Jess slept on the drive back to the Quarter from the doctor's office. Mack had to shake him awake when they arrived. Jess suspected the so-called antibiotics the doctor had given him had really been painkillers.

"I need a number where I can reach you," Mack said.

Jess groggily scribbled Krista's number on a card and handed it to Mack. Then he got out of the car. "Noon," he warned.

"Noon."

Jess contemplated the distance between the sidewalk and Krista's apartment. It had never seemed longer. As he walked through the alleyway and courtyard, he thought about Tate. He hadn't thought much about her in the last long hours. She was safe here, but somewhere else, Krista was in danger.

Tate would still be upset, but if she had gotten any sleep, she would probably have regained some of her bravado. He hoped he didn't have to fight with her. She was two parts pride to one part good sense. With Chaz temporarily off the streets, Jess knew he no longer had the ammunition to persuade her to stay at Krista's until they could help her plan her future. They. Krista might never help Tate plan anything. Krista might not have a future herself.

The thought was like a knife in his gut. He cursed the body that was rapidly losing strength with each step he took. He cursed the ignorance that tied his hands. If he only knew where to look, he could force himself to go on. Each moment that went by without finding Krista made the search harder and the outcome more uncertain.

There was nothing he wouldn't do to find her, but there was nothing he *could* do. He had never felt so helpless or so desperate.

He climbed the stairs and paused at Krista's door, then knocked, hoping Tate would open it.

There was no answer. He pounded louder and shouted, "Tate, open up! It's Jess." Just as he was leaving to find something to pick the lock, he heard the knob turn. Then the door was open, and Krista was in his arms.

"Jess! I thought . . . I was afraid—"

Exhaustion vanished. He silenced her with a kiss that left no doubt they were both alive. He framed her face in his hands, assuring himself that she was all right. Then he exploded. "Where the hell have you been?"

She burst into tears. He pulled her against his chest and shakily stroked her hair. It was wet, as if she had just stepped out of the shower, and she was wearing a robe. She felt like life, like hope. "I've been so worried," he said, then repeated it. "I thought you were dead."

They held each other tighter. Krista burrowed against him, as if she could never get close enough no matter how hard she tried.

Finally Jess regained some of his good sense. He pulled her inside and locked the door behind them. Then he kissed her again. Her lips were salt-tinged and so soft they melted against his as if the heat of their kiss had destroyed all boundaries. He inhaled the clean fragrance of her hair, felt the warmth of her skin under flannel, tasted gratitude and the pulsing of desire.

At the end of the kiss he remembered Tate. He threaded his fingers through Krista's hair; then, reluctantly, he wrenched his mouth from hers. "Where's Tate?" He scanned the room. She wasn't there.

"I've only been here a little while. She wasn't here when I got home, but she left a note."

"She's gone?" Too much had happened in the last hours. Jess struggled to make sense of Krista's words.

Krista touched his cheek and traced the bandages. "She left the note by the telephone, under a pile of change. It just says she's fine and not to worry about her. She said she hoped you found me, and that she was sorry for everything.''

Jess cursed softly.

"Jess? What happened to you? What did Tate mean?"

Jess led her to the sofa. He sat and pulled her down so she was half across him. "First I've got to know where you've been. Are you really all right?"

Krista started to cry again. She didn't want to, but tears had eluded her until now. For the first time in too many hours she felt safe enough to cry. Between sobs she told him what had occurred outside Tallulah's and in the car. Jess held her close, kissing away her tears. "I don't know how Scott found out that you know about the other girls, but he did," she finished.

Jess thought he'd trade his professional reputation for five minutes alone with Scott Newton. Chaz was a saint in comparison. At least he was honest about who he was and what he did for a living. "I made the call to my reporter friend from your telephone," he told Krista, omitting his other thoughts. "It must be tapped."

"My phone?" She took a deep breath to try and calm herself.

"Don't make any more calls from here. I'll have to call Mack from Mrs. Duchamp's."

"Mack?"

"He's out looking for you right now."

"They took me to a house in the Garden District." Krista took another deep breath. "I thought they were going to kill me."

Jess's arms tightened spasmodically around her. "What did he say, Krista? Think hard."

"I don't have to." She sat back a little and wiped her cheeks with trembling hands. "Scott knows where Rosie is. He says he's known all along. He's had people watching her since she ran away, and he says that if anything about Rosie or Hayden appears in your book or the papers, he'll have her killed! He says if I keep *looking* for her, he'll have her killed!"

This time Jess told her in no uncertain terms what he thought of Newton. And Hayden Barnard.

Strangely, Krista's tears had dried. This went beyond tears and far beyond fear. If Scott was telling the truth, Rosie was dead to her now as surely as if she *had* been murdered. "He means what he says, Jess. After he told me, I promised him I wouldn't tell anyone about Hayden. I begged him to tell me where Rosie was so I could find her and persuade her not to talk, either. I promised that we'd start a new life somewhere and never, never mention Hayden to anyone."

He knew the answer. "And he said no."

"There has to be something we can do!"

Jess heard her despair. He was afraid to offer hope and afraid not to. "Did he have any proof he knew where Rosie was?"

"Nothing he showed me."

"Then we can't rule out the possibility that he doesn't really know. He may be bluffing."

Krista put her head in her hands.

Jess drew her back into his arms. "He hasn't won yet," he whispered into her hair. "Don't give up now, lady. You've come this far. Don't give up."

"Jess." Krista put her arms around his neck and searched his eyes. She saw a reflection of what was surely in her own. Through her long ordeal she had wondered if she would ever see him or touch him again.

He stroked her hair away from her cheek, and his fingers trembled. "Did he drive you back here?"

"After he told me about Rosie, he locked me in the library. Then he left. I waited for him to come back, but he didn't. Finally, about an hour before dawn, Carter came in. He took my purse, but he left the library door unlocked. A while after he left, I did, too."

"They let you escape."

"I guess. I didn't have any money to call here or get a bus or streetcar. And the way I was dressed no cop or respectable person would have stopped to help me. So I hid in somebody's yard until it was light enough to see, then I walked."

He imagined the trip in heels, through neighborhoods where joggers in the fleetest footwear were afraid to go. He was sur-

prised she had made it back alive. He imagined Newton had
hoped she wouldn't.

"I covered the Quarter backward and forward," he told her.
"So did Wanda. But nobody thought about looking in the
Garden District."

"Did you get these looking for me?" She touched his cheek,
his eyelid.

Briefly he told her about Chaz and Tate.

"So that's why you weren't at Tallulah's."

"Wanda told me Sally identified Rosie's photograph."

"Who do I believe, Jess? What do I do?"

Jess had no answers. It was enough, just then, that they were
both alive. Later, when the shock of the last hours receded and
information began to fall into place, there would be time to
think. For now he could only tell her one thing. "Believe in
yourself," he said softly, guiding her face to his until it was only
inches away. "Whatever the truth is, Newton wants you so
scared that you doubt every breath you take."

Krista thought Scott had almost accomplished what he intended. There was just one thing she was certain of. "I believe
in you."

"I don't have answers for you," he said reluctantly. He
wanted to have answers; he wanted to slay dragons, but his
hands were tied until he knew more.

"I'm not talking about answers." She leaned forward and
placed her lips lightly against his, rubbing them back and forth
in a caress, not a kiss. She moved away before he could respond. She silenced him by rubbing her finger where her lips
had been. "Let me believe in you, Jess," she pleaded.

He knew it would be so easy to let fear and sorrow drive them
into each other's arms again. But this time that wouldn't be
enough. Krista was caught in an emotional whirlpool, and she
hoped he could save her from drowning. In the last hours he
had learned that he was no knight. His armor was tarnished. He
had done nothing to bring her back to him, and he wasn't sure
he could do anything to help her now.

As if she had read the thoughts reflected in his eyes, Krista
made a low sound of protest. "No. I don't think you'll make a

miracle happen. You *are* a miracle. You're a man who cares more about people than power. And I need a miracle, Jess.''

"I'm just a man." The most intimate parts of his body were making that absolutely clear. He wanted to smother all thought, all doubt, in her soft heat.

"I know who you are." Urgently, Krista tried to kiss away his doubts. "I promised myself we'd make love again if I lived to see you."

"You thought of me?"

"How could I not?" Her voice caught, and he heard her need.

He had told her he was just a man; he had tried to make her see that this could be wrong for them. Now the thinnest traces of reason vanished. She was his for the moment. After the worst night of his life, he knew how precious the moment could be.

There was no more need for words. Nothing either of them could say could change the uncertainty of their future. Krista stood on trembling legs and held out her hand. Jess took it, and she led him quickly to her bedroom. Sunlight streamed through hand-rolled glass, dancing in rainbow prisms across the white comforter. Outside, on the narrow cast-iron balcony, a pigeon cooed softly.

At the bedside, Krista put her hands on his chest, drawing her fingers together to unbutton his shirt. She stroked his bare skin and felt him shudder. "You want me, too," she said softly.

"Did you doubt it?" He dug his fingers into her hair and tilted her face to his. Her need for reassurance was in her eyes. "I want you in a way that's so new to me, I don't even understand it," he told her.

She drew in a deep breath, and her eyes were unguarded. Jess had a glimpse of the woman she had been before her world had fallen apart. He wanted to give her that world again. He hadn't realized how much until that moment. And his hands were tied.

"I want to make everything all right for you," he whispered, trailing kisses along her forehead, her cheeks. "And I can't."

"*This* is right." Krista slid her hands up his chest and under his shirt. "I know it is!" As he kissed her, she pulled his shirt off his shoulders and over his arms. Her fingers touched the bandage covering the knife wound. "Jess?"

"Another little present from Chaz."

She looked stricken. "What happened?"

"He had a knife. Don't worry, I saw a doctor this morning."

"You should be in bed!"

"I intend to be." Jess reached for the sash tying her robe. The knot was simple to release. His fingers brushed satin-soft flesh. She was wearing nothing under the robe.

Krista saw his surprise and his obvious pleasure. Heat flushed through her. "You're in no shape for suspense," she said.

"I would have made it through cast iron if I'd had to." He lifted the robe and let it fall to the floor. He couldn't think of the words to tell her how beautiful she was. Her breasts were full and round, her waist narrow, her hips a lush promise. Her skin was smooth and opalescent. "Newton is a fool."

"I was the fool."

Jess dropped to the edge of the bed, catching Krista and pulling her to his lap before she could lie down. Then he fell back with her on top of him.

"You weren't a fool." His hands journeyed down her back as her soft breasts pressed into his chest. His mouth found hers and claimed it. Reassurance was gone, comfort a thing of the past. Passion rushed in to fill their places, the passion of a man and woman who were seizing this chance for love because it might not come again.

"You weren't a fool because you trusted," he insisted.

"Because of who I trusted." She took a deep, shuddering breath. Jess knew what she must be feeling.

He vowed not to let her feel anything except need as his lips captured hers again. He rolled her to her back and covered her breasts with hands so hot he was afraid he would melt her skin. He felt her immediate response as she moved wildly against him. Her nipples hardened like precious pearls against his palms; her lips grew soft and moist, and her moan was a Siren's call.

Sunlight stroked her breasts as he did. Jess followed each beam with his lips, tasting sunlight's path and the sweetness of her flesh. She moaned again, offering the fullness of her breasts to him, and he took each into his mouth until she was writhing against him. She found his belt buckle and pulled it loose, found the snap on his jeans and the zipper. He finished undressing and settled against her again in only seconds.

Krista drew a kiss from him, yielding her tongue to his in a rhythm as old as time. The kiss grew and filled her, radiating through her body in a hot surge of passion until all she knew was the taste of him and the poignancy of need.

She moved her hips in rhythm to his tongue and felt his arousal, hot and hard against her. She cried out as his hands cupped her breasts once more, then moved over her to explore each intimate curve. His lips discovered places that had never been sensitive before and made her cry out again.

She felt a rush of warmth as his fingers found the very center of her sensuality. He stroked her perfectly, effortlessly, as if he, too, could feel the wildly building pleasure. She gasped, suffused with such sensation that she could not control her response. Her palms glided down his back and his hips, and she took him in her hands to try to give him a little of the ecstasy he was giving her.

Jess groaned. Her hands were delicate instruments of torture. As if she knew what he was feeling, she stroked and caressed until he was dizzy, crazy with need for her. He shut his eyes as waves of light crashed behind his eyelids. Desire had taken him this far, but it could take him no farther. Blood loss, pain and exhaustion claimed him. He felt her arms encircle him, and he let her turn him over. He was drenched in sweat, too aroused to stop, too dizzy to go on.

He felt the sweetness of her weight on him, the softness of her breasts against his chest. Then he felt her slide against him until she had swallowed him in the hot folds of her body. He opened his eyes and saw that she understood he had no more strength to give her. He wasn't a knight; he couldn't be endlessly strong for her. Instead, they were truly partners.

Truly lovers. Krista moved slowly against him until passion flamed out of control once more. He reached for her breasts, stretching his long fingers around them. Then, as the first convulsion shook him, he let her take him as he had never let a woman take him before. He gave himself up to her pleasure, and in doing so he found a pleasure like none he had ever known.

Except for a sliver of light under the door, the bedroom was dark when Jess awoke. He could hear Krista moving around in the other room, and he wondered how long she had been awake. The absence of sunshine behind the thin curtains told him it was early evening—at least. He still felt as if he needed another full day of sleep.

He rose and showered. The face staring back at him from the bathroom mirror belonged to someone else, a derelict or a down-and-out prizefighter. He splashed water on it and discovered even that hurt. Shaving would have to wait until tomorrow.

Back in the bedroom, wearing a towel slung low around his hips, he found clean clothes neatly folded on the bed. And Krista sitting beside them.

"I thought you'd probably want to change."

He noted that she was dressed, but not to go out. She was in her daffodil-yellow sweats. "Did you get any sleep?" he asked. She looked rested and incredibly lovely, but he knew that her bruises, unlike his, were on the inside.

"A little. I went out to call Mack from Mrs. Duchamp's after you feel asleep."

"Jeez. I forgot." He sat down beside her and took her into his arms. He thought how different this was from the usual affair. Their moments together were stolen amid turmoil. They woke after lovemaking and talked about cops. They shouldn't have to talk at all. They should be able to fall back into each other's arms.

"You had other things on your mind." She snuggled against him. "Mack didn't get my message in time. He came by at noon. He brought your car. He said to tell you it took him thirty seconds to hot-wire it and you'd better get a security system."

"Did he have anything else to say?"

"Nothing we didn't know. He says there's no trail back to Hayden. I told him what had happened to me, and he said without witnesses there's no way I can prosecute Scott for last night.''

Jess heard resignation in her voice. She was learning to play the game, and its name was "Don't beat your head against a brick wall." "Is he going to continue to check into this, or didn't he say?"

"He said that was up to us."

Jess rested his cheek against her hair. "The decision has to be yours."

"I've made a decision." Krista kissed him between bruises, then stood. "Come get something to eat and I'll tell you."

"You cooked?"

"I warmed."

Jess watched her go. She had changed in the short time he had known her. She had always had more courage than she had a right to, but now there was a new maturity to go with it, a sad awareness that neither courage nor being right was enough. He wished the world really was the place she had once believed it to be, or that he could make it that way for her.

He dressed quickly, wincing as he slipped his arm through the sleeve of the shirt. Krista had obviously used his keys to find clean clothes next door, and he was touched by her thoughtfulness. Again he thought how different their relationship was from any he'd known before, how few opportunities they'd had just to perform simple acts of kindness for each other, or talk about casual things. He knew little about Krista's surface and everything about her innermost thoughts and fears.

She had set the table for two by the time he came out of the bedroom. There was a magnolia blossom floating in a bowl between their plates, a bit of romance in the midst of so much uncertainty.

"How do you like your frozen dinner?" Krista's heart twinged at the sight of Jess buttoning his shirt as he walked across the room. "Medium or well-done?"

He smiled, and even surrounded by bruises, the smile made her heart twinge again. "However you're having yours."

"Medium, then." She went back into the kitchen. He was standing in the doorway when she turned, two aluminum foil trays in her hands.

"After this morning, I should be taking you out to Antoine's for dinner and champagne. We should stroll through the Quarter, maybe take a buggy ride, and end up in some wonderful little smoky bar with soft jazz and a dance floor."

"It's never been like that for us, has it? Except for the smoky bar," she added with a little smile.

"I wasn't thinking of Tallulah's." He reached for a dish towel and took one of the trays. Then, before she could pass, he leaned down to kiss her. She didn't pull away, and the kiss went on until the tray began to heat his fingers and he had to set it on the counter. "I wish we could start over that way."

She considered, then shook her head. "I don't need that, Jess. Do you?"

"Need? No. Want?" He shrugged. "I'd like to be able to give you time without worries."

"You did. This morning." She kissed him again.

"Days," he said, wrapping his arms around her waist. He hesitated, then added, "Years."

She was startled. Both of them had been careful not to talk about the future. There was so little they could say, because there was so little they knew.

She had hardly let herself think about a future with Jess. In the brief moments when she had, she had been filled with a longing so fierce she couldn't bear it. What would she do when he was no longer there? Now that she knew how perfectly their bodies and their minds could mesh, how could she leave him? Now that she knew that she loved him . . .

She hugged him harder, then stepped away. There was nothing she could say. Love had come, not dressed in fairy garb and moonbeams, but in the improbable costume of a clown. Falling in love with Jess was another irony, and like all the other ironies of the last months, it would end in soul-crushing defeat. Selfishly, she had demanded he make love to her, but there was nothing else she could take from him. Even if he loved her in return, there were too many questions, too many dangers.

At the table, Krista poured wine. She held up her glass, a dime-store tumbler, in a toast. She couldn't think of anything to say that wouldn't make her cry.

"To a brave and beautiful lady," Jess said. He saw her eyes sparkle with tears. "And to the decision she's made."

Krista nodded and drank, forcing tears away. She watched Jess peel back the foil on his dinner and wondered if she would be able to eat. "I'm going to Tallulah's on Saturday," she said. "I'm going to see if May Rose is my sister. I have to."

Jess reached across the table and opened her dinner, crumpling the foil and tossing it neatly in the wastebasket where he'd thrown his. "Then that's your decision?"

She nodded.

"I'm glad."

She raised her eyes to his and saw that he meant it. "You think I'm doing the right thing?"

"I think it's the only thing you can do."

"If Scott—"

"It's a chance you have to take. He didn't show any proof that he knows where Rosie is. And this girl could be your sister. You're too close to trust Newton now."

The decision was one she'd had to make alone. But now she was immeasurably relieved that he agreed with her. "Sally's going to bring her to Tallulah's on Saturday night. Until then, I'm going to stay inside, in case he's having me watched."

"He'll be watching," Jess affirmed. "Instead of staying here until then, I think we should leave now."

"Leave?"

"The boat house." He thought about how perfect it would be. They would be close by, and the trip to Tallulah's would be simple. But they would be out of the Quarter and away from the constant strain of knowing they were being watched. Jess had faith in his own ability to give anyone the slip. Newton and his sleazeball sidekick wouldn't find them. And he and Krista would have three days to be together.

Krista thought about three days on the lake with Jess. Three days with nothing to do except eat and sleep and make love. Three days before the next decision had to be made. "What about Tate?"

"I'll look for her before I go and see if I can persuade her to go to the Place."

"If May Rose isn't my sister . . ."

"If she isn't, you can decide what to do then."

Three days. For a moment she wondered if she dared. Three days would bind her to Jess so that leaving him would be unthinkable, unbearable. But three days would also give her memories. Could she wade through the pain to reach for them? Krista picked up her fork. "Will your friend let you use it?"

"If I twist his arm."

Krista looked up from her plate. His smile almost tore her in two. She knew the pain was nothing compared to what would come, but suddenly she didn't care. She would face it when she had to, just as she had faced everything else. "If I recall, there was only one bed."

He smiled. "It's a very big bed, Krista. Big enough for you and me." He paused. "And Cat."

Chapter 16

On Saturday at sunset, Cat brushed back and forth against Krista's ankles to assure her he wouldn't mind more of the fish she had just fed him. Absentmindedly she lifted him and held him against her chest. She was standing on the front deck of the boathouse, looking over the water. Just below, a cabin cruiser made waves on the otherwise calm channel. A cool breeze lifted fine strands of her hair and bounced them against her cheeks.

"Saying goodbye?"

She turned and saw Jess standing in the doorway. He was wearing shorts and nothing else except a small bandage on his arm. Her gaze traveled over him. If she was saying goodbye, it wasn't to a place. She lifted a hand in invitation, and he came to stand beside her.

"You can hide out with me anytime, lady," he said.

She leaned against him, and he circled her with his arm.

She thought about the last three days. In a strange way time had been suspended. There had been nothing they could do about Rosie, or even Tate, who had disappeared so expertly into the Quarter that Jess hadn't been able to find her. He and Krista had lived the three days accordingly. They hadn't spoken about Tate or Krista's problems or his book. When they had talked it had been about all the little things they hadn't yet learned about each other.

When they hadn't talked, they had still communicated. Now Krista knew Jess as she had never hoped to know anyone. Their lovemaking had grown even more exquisite. They had learned to please each other so thoroughly that they had clung together for hours afterward, adrift in satisfaction. Now, when she left him, it would be like leaving part of herself behind.

She couldn't tell him that, but she told him part of the truth. "I was thinking about Rosie."

Jess stroked her hair in comfort. "You're frightened. I don't blame you."

"If May Rose is Rosie, where will we go?"

"We'll bring her back here, for starters."

"The same way you brought me here Wednesday night?"

"You didn't like the scenic route?"

"It was fifty-eight marshes out of the way."

"But nobody followed us."

"Okay. But then what?" Cat struggled to get down, and Krista bent to set him on the deck. "We can't stay here."

Jess didn't want to tell her that worrying was futile until they were sure May Rose was her sister. She was frightened enough. "Look, we'll tackle that later."

"I can't take her back home. Her life would be in danger."

"One thing at a time, Krista."

"I'm scared."

He turned her to face him. He wanted to reassure her, but she would know he was lying. "I'll be there with you." It was the only thing he could say.

She wrapped her arms around his waist and pillowed her head against his chest. "That means so much. Everything you've done has meant so much. I don't even know how to say thank you."

"We're not saying goodbye, Krista." He cupped her face and lifted it to his. "No thanks, okay? I don't like the sound of it."

"If May Rose is my sister, then it *will* be goodbye. I'll have to take her somewhere and go into hiding."

"One thing at a time." Jess knew he was avoiding both making a commitment to Krista and admitting that he wasn't ready to. He didn't know what to say. Their lives—the situation—were so confused.

And his feelings? They were as clear as Krista's blue eyes, only he had no idea what to do with them.

"I just wanted you to know what you've meant to me," she said.

"Meant to you?"

Her cheeks flushed with color. "Mean to me," she whispered.

He kissed her hard, lifting her against him. "I'm not part of your past yet," he said afterward. "Maybe I never will be."

She smiled sadly. It was time one of them said the truth out loud. "I can't ask you to be part of this mess anymore. You have a life. You have a book to write."

"One thing at a time." He put a finger under her chin and lifted it until their eyes met. "Okay?"

"Okay."

He didn't release her. "We have a couple of hours before we have to head to the Quarter."

"I know."

"I know how I'd like to spend them."

"So do I."

Cat watched as they went back into the house. In a moment he was the only one on the deck to enjoy the sunset.

After three days of sunshine and fresh air, Tallulah's seemed like a rathole. Krista hated to go inside, not only because of the smoke and noise, but because of what might be waiting. She forced herself to enter when she felt Jess's reassuring nudge.

The bar was crowded. Friday night was always busy. The regulars were joined by barhopping locals who liked Tallulah's ambience in small doses. Jess followed Krista to a corner table that another couple was just vacating.

She saw several heads turn. She was dressed as herself, not Crystal. She had decided there was no point in continuing her charade. May Rose was coming tonight, no matter how Krista was dressed. If May Rose was her sister, she wouldn't understand green satin and rhinestones or what they meant.

Perry was the first to come over. "Ain't this cute. You two a pair now?"

Krista ignored his leer and reached in her purse. She flipped Rosie's school picture onto the table. "Have you ever seen this girl, Perry?"

Perry squinted. "Why?"

"Because she's my sister."

He looked up at Krista, then down at the picture. "Looks kind of like you, doesn't she?"

"Does she look familiar?" Jess asked.

"Can't say." He grinned his gap-toothed grin. "Funny thing, but I just ain't good at makin' identifications. You know?"

"There's a girl who used to come in here called May Rose. Is this her?"

Perry shrugged. "Maybe. Maybe not."

Krista glanced at Jess, afraid what he might do. His jaw looked as rigid as if it had been wired shut. "Two club sodas," she said. "And get someone else to bring them over."

Perry cackled as he left. Krista put her hand on Jess's arm so he wouldn't follow. "We couldn't trust anything he told us, anyway," she said.

"I'm sick of the Perrys of the world."

"I've sort of reached my saturation point, too."

"You probably reached your saturation point the first night you walked in here. But you kept right on coming."

"Do you know what it must be like to be a kid coming into a place like this?"

"I have a book's worth of ideas." And a gut full of feelings about them, but Jess didn't add that. That was part of his personal turmoil, and Krista didn't need more burdens. He was sick of the dirt and the leers and the smell of smoke, though. He was sick of warm club soda and the faked warmth of women who wanted to love him for money.

He thought of his house in the Blue Ridge Mountains of Virginia. He had over a hundred acres on a mountaintop plateau so green it defined the word. His apple trees would be just finished blooming now. There were forty of them, some so old that they shouldn't even be living, much less bearing. But last year, after purchasing the property, he had walked through the orchard and twisted fruit off the oldest of the trees. Firm, perfect fruit, although the orchard hadn't been tended for years.

Anything could thrive there. The air was lung-tauntingly fresh, the water so clear he could command a fortune if he bottled it. The rocky red clay was difficult to cultivate, but so full of nutrients it was worth the trouble.

Anyone could thrive there. When he left New Orleans he would retreat to Virginia to write his book. The land could heal him—if the wounds weren't too great.

"There's Wanda." Krista stood and signaled the woman standing in the doorway.

Jess saw the sheen of nervous anticipation in Krista's eyes. Her cheeks were flushed from more than smoke. He ached to be able to make this easier for her, but he knew it was impossible.

"You're a little early," Wanda said as she took a chair beside Krista's.

"We were afraid we might miss her." Krista accepted the club sodas from a blank-faced barmaid and ordered a beer for Wanda.

"You're not pretending to be on the stroll anymore?" Wanda's gaze traveled over Krista's white pants and blouse.

"The only thing *that* got me was too many narrow escapes." Krista was staring at the door. "I don't know if I can stand waiting!"

Wanda and Jess traded sympathetic looks. "Did you decide to take the job at the Place?" Jess asked.

"I start next Monday."

Jess smiled his approval. "Do you know if a kid named Tate has shown up over there in the last couple of days?"

"I know Tate. She wouldn't go there."

Krista didn't take her eyes off the door. "Have you seen her anywhere else?"

"She was by yesterday to sell me flowers."

"So she's doing that again." Krista realized that staring at the door was akin to willing a pot to boil. With great effort she turned back to the table. "What's going to happen to her when Chaz gets out of the hospital?"

Wanda patted her hand sympathetically. "One kid at a time, okay?"

Krista looked at the hand consoling her. She raised her head and saw empathy in both Wanda and Jess's eyes. Everything came together for her in that second, spurred by Wanda's words and their unspoken understanding. Like a revelation she knew what she had been unable to see until then.

"One kid will never be enough." Krista grasped Wanda's hand. "I'll never be able to forget what I've seen. Tate, Sally and the others." She looked stricken.

Wanda sighed. "Welcome to the club, sugar. You've been a member for a long time already, you just didn't know it. And Jess here, he's the president."

"So what do I do?"

"You sit here and wait for May Rose," Jess said firmly. "The world's problems get solved one by one."

Krista heard his firmness, but she saw his doubts. They had both been changed by what they had seen. He was struggling, too. It was another thing they shared.

"I see Sally." Wanda squeezed Krista's hand and dropped it. "I'll go ask her about May Rose. You stay here."

Krista searched the crowd that had just surged through the door. Sally was almost lost in the middle of it. "What's Sally doing now that Chaz is in jail?" she asked Jess. "How is she supporting herself?"

"One kid at a time," he cautioned.

"There are thousands of kids out there, Jess."

"Steady, lady." He lifted her hand and kissed it.

Sally and Wanda made their way over to the table. Sally was dressed for business, but her heart didn't seem to be in it. She didn't even glance around for available men. She slid onto the last chair.

"Sally says May Rose will be here sometime," Wanda said, before Krista or Jess could ask.

"Are you doing all right?" Krista asked Sally. "You look tired."

Sally shrugged.

"She's thinking about going to the Place," Wanda said, with a touch of pride. It was obvious she had been doing some hard talking.

Krista leaned forward. "Do you have a family, Sally?"

Sally looked at her for the first time. "Who are you, anyway?"

Krista sensed this was no time for games. "My name is Krista Jensen. I've been out on the street for months now looking for my sister."

"May Rose?"

"I hope so."

"So you've been lying."

"I'd do anything to find her."

"Why?"

"I love her."

Sally stared, then gave a humorless laugh. "Then why's she out on the streets?"

"Because I didn't realize how much I loved her until she was gone."

"You gonna have her arrested?"

"No!" Krista sat back.

"What if she doesn't want to come with you?"

Krista had never considered that possibility. She shrugged helplessly. "What should I do if that happens?"

"You're asking me?"

"Wouldn't you know better than anybody?"

"Know? Me?" Sally gave the same disbelieving laugh. "Hey, nobody's ever gonna come looking for me."

Something twisted in Krista's chest. "Then your family is crazy," she said. "You're worth looking for, honey. Just like my sister is."

Something flickered behind Sally's cold stare. "You think so? You know what I did?"

Krista shook her head.

"I was so much trouble at home, my folks split up 'cause they couldn't stand living with me. Then neither of them wanted me. My dad went to California, and my mom moved to Texas with her boyfriend. Chaz found me and gave me a place to stay. Now he's gone, too."

Krista heard a child's pain, no matter how Sally was dressed. "You were just a kid," she said, trying not to let pity overwhelm her. "A kid can't cause those kinds of problems."

Wanda interrupted. "Sally and I have had some long talks about that. There's nothing she can do about her parents' problems, but she can get her own life on the right track."

"After what I've done?" Sally laughed again. The sound was as empty as her parents' hearts.

"If May Rose is my sister, then she's been out on the streets, too," Krista said. "Do you think I love her any less?"

"I don't know." Sally looked her straight in the eye. "Do you?"

"No." Krista knew it was true as she said it. "And I don't think any less of *you*, either."

"Then you're crazy."

"Maybe. But I don't think so."

Jess watched Krista with Sally. She was warm and concerned without being pushy. He knew what she must be feeling, but talking to Sally was helping her deal with her fears for Rosie. He looked up as the bar door slammed shut with a new wave of customers. A blond girl stood in the doorway, looking through the thick smoke as if she expected to find someone she knew.

Krista and Sally were still deep in conversation. Jess caught Wanda's eye, and Wanda nodded, as if she, too, was thinking that this could be May Rose. The girl was dressed much as Sally was. She had on gold spandex pants and a white halter top. Her hair was a mass of permed curls hiding her cheeks and forehead, and her lipstick was a slash of come-hither red. As Jess watched, a man approached her, but she waved him away.

Then she started toward their table.

Jess watched every step of her approach. She was young, no older than seventeen, and thin. She walked with a swagger, even though her heels were three inches high. She looked bored, as if life wasn't worth taking a chance on. Jess knew how many emotions that bored expression could shield. He also knew that even the most accomplished actress wouldn't have managed to hide shock. If this girl was May Rose, she hadn't noticed Krista, whose head was turned slightly, or she had noticed her and dismissed her. If the latter was true, May Rose was not Rosie.

Sally and Krista were staring at each other, an impasse reached. Jess leaned over and touched Sally's arm. When she looked at him, he pointed.

Sally looked up. "Well, if May Rose is your sister," she told Krista, "you're gonna have a chance to see how you really feel."

Krista's head snapped up. She turned and stared at the girl walking slowly toward them.

The bar was dark, the air nearly congealed with smoke. Silently she begged her eyes to find a clue that this girl was her sister. May Rose came closer, then closer still. The resemblance was there.

Krista understood why Sally had identified the snapshot as May Rose, but as May Rose came to a halt at their table, Krista tried to swallow the despair rising in her throat. She stood, pushing past Jess, who was standing, too. "Excuse me," she pleaded. "I've got to get some fresh air."

Jess looked at Wanda. Her eyes were filling with tears, and she was shaking her head. Even Sally looked upset. "I wanted May Rose to be her sister," Sally said. "Crystal's okay."

Jess put his hand on her shoulder. "Thanks for trying." He squeezed her shoulder, then started into the night.

Krista hadn't gone far. She was staring in the window of a tearoom where fortunes were told. The irony wasn't lost on Jess. She didn't turn when he came up behind her. "They all have Rosie's face," she said.

"But she wasn't Rosie."

She shook her head. "No."

He kneaded her shoulders. "I don't know what to say."

"May Rose." She said the name like an epitaph. "Someone else's lost sister or daughter, someone else's little hell-raiser or abused child. Someone else's throwaway or runaway. But not mine."

"Let's go home."

"Where do I go from here, Jess? What do I do?"

He couldn't answer that. "Right now we go home," he said, turning her to face him. There were tears on her cheeks. "It's late. You can't decide anything tonight."

"I know." She went into his arms, and he held her close until her tears were spent.

Jess's car was parked in a lot off of Bourbon, and they walked there in silence. The drive back to their apartment building was silent, too. Before the trip to Tallulah's, they had only been home long enough to drop off Cat and their suitcases in Jess's apartment. Now, with moonlight silvering the courtyard, the dilapidated building seemed almost welcoming.

"Will you stay with me tonight?" Krista asked.

"You didn't have to ask."

They climbed the stairs to her apartment quietly. Jess paused at his own door. "Let me get your suitcase."

"I'll wait for you at my place."

Jess realized she was too exhausted to stand by while he unpacked his razor and toothbrush. "Let me check your apartment first."

Krista nodded. Too many things had happened to her to dismiss the possibility that more were waiting. She opened her door, and Jess walked through the apartment, turning on lights and checking closets. Then, when it was obvious they were alone, he kissed the top of her head and left.

Krista collapsed on her sofa. The night had taken everything from her. Tears, hope, possibilities. She was drained. She stared blankly at the ancient glass-topped coffee table.

May Rose wasn't Rosie. Rosie was gone, probably forever. If she searched for her, Scott would send Carter to kill her. If Scott really knew where she was.

The "ifs" were enough to make her lose her mind. *If* she had believed Rosie in the first place. *If* she hadn't believed in Hayden. *If* she hadn't trusted the private investigator. *If* she had never loved Scott. *If* she searched. *If* Scott knew...

She was wrong about one more thing. Her tears hadn't drained away. Her eyes clouded with them, and she reached for a tissue in a box on the table.

Her hand touched an envelope sitting on the box. For a moment its presence there rang no warning bells. She hadn't been home in three days. The envelope was probably a bill.

Except that she never left mail sitting around because it was too easy to lose.

She lifted the envelope and turned it over in her hands. There was no address, no stamp or postmark. Only the words "Krista Jensen. Personal."

Next door, Jess took his time gathering things together. He sensed that Krista needed a few minutes by herself. There was so little he could do, but at least he could manage that much. He knew the questions she would be asking herself, and he knew that he had no answers. He had plenty of feelings, though, and he was afraid he would overwhelm her with them tonight. She needed time to grieve before they could talk about the future.

He waited as long as he could; then, locking his door behind him, he went to her door and knocked. When she didn't answer, he turned the knob and stepped inside. "Krista?"

He found her in the living room. What color had been left in her cheeks was gone. Her eyes were blue pools of anguish. He crossed to the sofa and dropped down beside her. "What is it?" He touched her cheek, frightened by the absence of a response. "Krista?"

She looked at him, almost as if for the first time. She seemed to struggle to form a word. "Proof," she said at last. She lifted a small pile of photographs from her lap. Her hands stopped in midair.

Jess took the photographs. The top one showed a girl dressed in jeans and a dark sweatshirt. She was standing on a street corner, a backpack slung over one shoulder. The photo was grainy, as if it had been shot from a distance and blown up to its present size. He knew the girl was Rosie.

He cursed as he looked at the second photograph. The girl was with several other teenagers. She was standing outside a store window. The store could have been anywhere; the teenagers could have been anyone's. Rosie was wearing a battered navy pea jacket. There was no snow to place the photograph up north, no identifying landmarks. The girl looked cold, but even Miami could be cold in the wintertime.

The third photograph was the one that had drained the color from Krista's cheeks. Rosie was alone, leaning against a tree. Her eyes were closed, as if she were defeated, exhausted . . . he could read anything he wanted into the pose, and he knew that had been the photographer's intention.

The intention of the man who had drawn the cross hairs of a rifle scope over Rosie's heart had been clear, too.

Rosie was an easy target. The words at the bottom of the photograph underscored the message. "You decide if we pull the trigger."

Chapter 17

Krista was still sleeping when Jess got up the next morning. Her hair was a sleep-tumbled mane, and her face was pressed to the pillow, hiding last night's despair. He doubted she would have an appetite when she joined him, but he went to the kitchen and set out anything that looked edible, hoping to tempt her anyway. It was a simple task compared to the one ahead, tempting her to go on fighting.

He was setting fruit salad on the table when he realized she was standing in the doorway of the bedroom, watching him.

"There's coffee ready."

Her smile was a pale imitation of the real thing. "Pour it right into my veins, will you?"

He thought that courage was a woman trying not to burden a man. He abandoned the salad and took her in his arms.

He felt her slight resistance. This morning she was trying to stand alone, as if she knew she would be standing alone for the rest of her days. "You don't have to be strong," he whispered into her hair.

"Don't tempt me to lean on you." She pulled away.

He thought of all the things he hadn't been able to do for her. "Are you angry with me?"

"Never." She couldn't add that she had to learn to live without him. Like a million other things she wanted to say, it wouldn't pass the lump in her throat—a lump that seemed a permanent part of her anatomy now.

She was keeping her face carefully blank to hide what she was feeling. Jess wondered if she was practicing for all the days to come. "We're going to have to talk about this," he said, touching her cheek tenderly.

"What is there to say?" She moved past him to the kitchen to get coffee. She poured a cup, then stood staring into it, as if it held the answers to questions she no longer had the courage to ask.

"We'll talk after breakfast." Jess took the coffee from her hand and set it on the counter. "But while we're eating, lady, you think about a few things."

"What things?"

"For starters, you decide if you're going to lie down and die or keep fighting."

Her head snapped up, and he saw the first trace of emotion she had shown that morning. "That option's been taken away from me!"

"Think so? Then you're not the woman I hoped you were." He poured warm milk in her coffee and handed it back to her. "We'll talk after breakfast."

Krista knew that if she argued or refused to eat, she would sound like a child. Silently, angrily, she followed him to the table.

Jess saw the first hint of color in her cheeks. He hated baiting her, but it was working. "Start on the fruit, and I'll get the rest."

She was halfway through when he returned, as if she were eating just to show him she could. He set toast and cartons of yogurt on the table between them before he sat down.

Krista's spoon clanked against her empty bowl as she pushed it away to reach for a slice of toast. "I don't know how you can expect me to keep fighting when my sister could die if I do."

"You're thinking like Newton wants you to."

"How else am I supposed to think?"

Jess shrugged and started on his yogurt.

"Don't go playing God with my sister's life!"

"Why not? Everybody else is."

"What are you trying to do to me?"

He almost gave in and told her he was trying to make her want to go on. The emotion in her eyes stopped him. His behavior might be unforgivable, but it was working. "We'll talk after breakfast."

"I'm sick of men making the rules for me!" Krista balled up her napkin and threw it on the table. "Hayden, Scott, Chaz. Now you!"

"You want to talk now? Fine. Go ahead. But I'd like to eat."

She pushed her chair back with a loud scrape and stood, glaring at him with tear-filled eyes. "Are you just like all the others?"

"What do you think?"

Krista stared at him and saw the man she had come to love. He saw the world for what it was, but he had never let that change him. He cared with an almost superhuman passion. And he had never underestimated her, as every other man she had ever known had. He wasn't underestimating her even now, although for a while she had underestimated herself.

Last night she had believed that everything was over. This morning she had believed the same. Now she saw that perhaps it was just beginning.

She sat down and picked up her napkin. "Pass the yogurt."

Jess released a breath he hadn't known he held. "Blueberry or peach?"

"Do you think I care?" she snapped.

He would have bet that after everything that had happened, he wouldn't smile for months. "*I* think you care so damn much you're in danger of doing something stupid." He handed her the peach yogurt and watched her tear off the top as if it were Scott Newton's head. Or his.

"Like what?"

"Like changing your life. Like not going back to being a yuppie librarian with a comfortable job."

"I don't know what I'm going to do."

"But you know what you're *not* going to do."

"We'll talk after breakfast."

He almost choked. "Good idea."

Sunlight was pouring through the windows by the time they finished eating. There was nothing gray or dismal about a New Orleans spring, and today the weather was underlining the lessons both of them had learned in the past weeks: Life went on. Day followed day. It was the only sure thing to count on.

Jess had spent long hours the previous night watching one day become another. Somewhere just before dawn he had charted the pattern of the rest of his days. He wondered why it had taken him so long to see it.

Krista chose a chair in the living room for their discussion. Jess knew she was avoiding the sofa to avoid him. He hoped he knew why. He sat across from her.

"I didn't get much sleep last night," she began.

"I know."

"I'm sorry if I kept you awake."

"You didn't."

"This has all been so unfair to you. You got a lot more than you bargained for, didn't you?"

His eyes gleamed. "A lot more."

"Jess, I know what kind of man you are. You're good and decent and—"

"You're describing somebody else."

Krista shook her head. "There's nothing else you can do for me. You signed on for a story, not a death threat. You stay nearby and it will be *your* picture with an *X* over the heart."

He folded his arms behind his head, sprawling casually like a man who hadn't just been told goodbye. "Then I should pack and go? That's what you're saying, isn't it?"

She swallowed, and for just the tiniest portion of a second, vulnerability shone in her eyes. "I'm going to go back to Maryland and pack my things. Then I'm going to disappear."

"What about Rosie?"

"I can't take the chance that she'll be killed because I'm looking for her."

"What about me?" His gaze didn't flicker.

"Don't you see what I'm getting at? I won't let you be involved anymore! You're a good man. You'd charge windmills if you thought it would help, but it won't! I'm not going to be responsible for ruining anyone else's life.''

He leaned forward. "You haven't ruined anyone's life. This situation has never been under your control. What do you suppose would have happened to you and your sister if you'd believed her and confronted your stepfather right at the beginning?''

She shook her head, bewildered. "I could have saved Rosie from running—''

He waved away her words. "Barnard would have denied everything, and then, before you could have taken a breath, someone on his staff would have arranged a convenient little accident for the two Jensen sisters. Think of the sympathy he would have gotten! Grieving stepfather vows to strengthen seat belt laws, or demands tougher handgun legislation so street hoodlums can't gun down innocent young women—''

"Stop it!" Krista put her hands over her ears.

"No, you stop it!" In one fluid motion Jess reached for her, pulling her hands away from her ears and tugging her to the sofa beside him. "Stop taking the world on your slender shoulders, Krista. Rosie ran away. It probably saved her life, and maybe yours. For now, she's probably safer on the streets than she would be anywhere else. She was tough enough and smart enough to run. And you've been tough enough and smart enough to get so close that Barnard's making threats.''

"Real threats!''

"Maybe." He sat back, giving her the freedom to move away if she wanted. She didn't.

"What do you mean, maybe?''

"We don't know how old the photographs are, but she's dressed for warmth in all of them. It's May now. I doubt the photos are recent. Maybe they were taken this winter, maybe last.''

Krista shook her head, not understanding what he meant.

He explained. "If he had more recent photos, he would have left them.''

"You think they've lost track of her?''

"I think it's possible. Kids learn how to disappear on the streets. Unless someone was following her every minute, they could lose her like that." He snapped his fingers.

Krista wanted to believe him, but she knew Rosie's life was hanging in the balance. "I can't take a chance. Don't you see? They'll be following *me* now. Even if they don't know where Rosie is, if I find her, they'll know."

"That's why we have to approach this differently."

Krista had avoided looking at Jess. Now she couldn't. "I can't accept any more help from you." She let herself touch him, let herself trace the remnants of the worst bruise Chaz had given him. "Stop being a good guy, Jess. Go home. Have a life. Write your book. You've done everything humanly possible here."

He was surprised she had used the word that best described him. Human. Only human. He caught her hand and raised it to his lips. "I have a life now," he said. "And you're in it."

"I can't be."

"I'm going home, and I'm going to write my book. You're going to come with me."

For a moment she wasn't sure she had heard him right. "Home? With you?"

"Yeah."

"The last place I can go is Washington, D.C.!"

"Home to the Virginia mountains. My house there is on a mountaintop. You can see forever, and everything you see is green and lush and clean. The house is large enough for both of us." He laughed a little. "Actually, it's large enough for a football team. It's an old stagecoach inn."

"I can't go with you. I'll put you in danger."

"Newton hasn't threatened you. Has that occurred to you?"

"Maybe he still has some feelings for me. But that won't last. He's ruthless. He'll kill me if he thinks I'm going to do Hayden any harm."

"I wouldn't doubt that he has some feelings for you." Jess stroked her hair back from her cheek. He saw color tinge her pale complexion and knew his touch pleased her. The hard knot of doubt inside him began to ease. "And I wouldn't doubt he would kill you . . . if he could."

"If he could?" Without realizing what she was doing, Krista leaned into his touch.

"Think about it, lady. He can threaten Rosie, because he knows that nothing could ever tie him to the murder of a runaway. He could have her killed, and since no one knows her whereabouts, no one would ever know she was dead. But you're a different story. If you were killed, I know enough and my reputation is good enough to have an investigation opened, just on my say-so."

"Your reputation against Hayden's power?"

He smiled. "I don't have any delusions of grandeur. But there are people who are beyond corruption. I know who they are."

"You couldn't start an investigation if you weren't alive."

"But my attorney and my editor could . . . and will."

"Attorney? Editor? How—"

"Notes on everything that's happened so far are already in their hands."

"Scott won't know that. Hayden won't know that unless you tell them."

"Both of them know me. They know how I work."

He had thought of everything. Krista realized how much she owed him. "Then we're protected?"

"Unless your stepfather gets desperate enough to take chances."

"But Rosie isn't safe."

He wished he could tell her otherwise. "If we had found Rosie, she would have been safe. Now, if we keep looking for her, we're gambling that they don't really know where she is anymore, and that we can find her before they do."

"I can't take a gamble like that."

Jess pulled her close. She was stiff in his arms, but he didn't know if it was resistance or anguish. "You don't have to take gambles alone, lady. I'll take them with you."

"Why?"

He was glad she had finally asked and sorry he couldn't tell her the most important reason. He couldn't confuse her now, though. A declaration of his feelings would have to come later.

Maybe much later. "Because I can't stand by and watch this happen. Somewhere along the way this became my fight, too."

Krista realized she had hoped for a different answer. She knew better than to think Jess loved her as she had come to love him. Her own realization was so new and so fragile. Love had blossomed at the most improbable time and place. Had it been any less deep or abiding, she wouldn't have recognized it.

"There are a lot of fights, Jess." She tried to pull away, but he wouldn't let her. "Pick one you can win, not one that's already over."

He ignored her. "Come to Virginia and help me write my book. I'll hire you as my researcher. You need a job."

"I already told you—"

"Help me pin your stepfather to the wall."

She stopped struggling. "What do you mean?"

"There's always more than one way to solve a problem. If there wasn't, I'd still be writing filler."

She felt a tiny flutter of hope and realized the lessons of the last weeks hadn't really taken. She was a fool. But she was a fool who couldn't keep from asking, "What do you mean?"

"Continuing the search for Rosie is too dangerous, so we'll go at it a different way. I'll use the contacts I have to launch a full-fledged campaign against Hayden Barnard. I'll dig for dirt everywhere I can find it. When I have enough proof, we'll face him down. My information for Rosie's life. Then Barnard can find her for us."

She stared at him, her mind whirling with possibilities. "Could it work?"

"Could it? Yes. Will it?" He sighed, and he let her see the truth in his eyes. "I can't make any promises. It won't fail for lack of trying. I *can* promise you that."

"But your career. You're talking about spending all your time on something you may never be able to write about."

He smiled. "There was a young man living here once." He tapped his chest. "Exposing the world in print was all that mattered to him. There's an older, wiser man here now. He lives for more than seeing his name on a book jacket."

"You would do this for me?"

He ached to say yes, but he was afraid if he did she wouldn't understand. "I'm doing it for you and Rosie, and maybe for all the other kids out there who've gotten a rotten deal." He shrugged. "Do we have to analyze it? Come with me. I'm offering you a job and a place to live. I'm offering you a chance to help your sister."

He had taken her from despair to hope. She couldn't say no; she didn't want to. Jess wanted her with him, even though he had said nothing of love. Time could do more than heal, it could change fallow ground into an abundant harvest. With time, with the peace of quiet days and the fulfillment of passionate nights, maybe it could even turn what he felt for her into something lasting. She was nodding before she answered. "When do we start?"

Jess hadn't realized how tense he'd been until she gave her answer. Now he felt like a condemned man given a reprieve. They would have time together. Not uncluttered, happy hours, but time just the same. After everything Krista had been through and still had to go through, time was all he could ask for. He would give her time and love and patience. And they would come out the other side of all this. Together.

"We pack today. We leave tomorrow. There's no reason to stay here any longer." He paused, then decided to be honest. "And besides, the sooner we get to work on my house, the better."

She was so deep in thought that for a moment she missed what he'd said. Then it penetrated. "Work on your house?"

"I've seen you clean. You're a natural."

"Tell me it doesn't look like your apartment did."

"Bigger. Much bigger."

"Roaches?"

"Mice."

She put her head on his chest, and she wasn't sure if her laughter was real or just a way to release the tears she couldn't seem to cry. "We'll take Cat." Her voice caught on the last word, and the tears came.

He sifted her hair through his fingers. "It's going to be all right, Krista."

"I hope so. God, I hope so."

He held her tight and dared God or anyone else to hurt her again. At that moment there was no one on heaven or earth he wouldn't have fought for her.

Packing was simple. They boxed what they had accumulated and made arrangements with Mrs. Duchamp to have the boxes shipped to Virginia. She stood on the second floor gallery, sweeping and telling stories about New Orleans as Jess carried all his boxes to Krista's apartment. She would miss them, she said. Not many of her tenants appreciated her efforts to keep the place cleaned up.

It was dinnertime when they finally finished. Wanda had come by to say her farewells, and they had told her they were going to spend their last evening searching for Tate. Wanda had promised to help if she could, but neither Jess nor Krista was optimistic that Tate would let herself be found.

"If we do find her, what do we say?" Krista asked after dinner.

Jess watched her brush her hair. It gleamed a pale gold in the lamplight. She didn't look like a woman who had almost been down for the count. He had given her hope. He wondered if he had given her anything else. Was he a fool to wonder if she was coming with him because she might love him?

She turned. "What do we say to her?" she repeated, her eyes wide and vulnerable.

"We try to get her to go back home. Wanda says she'll make the arrangements through the Place."

"And if she won't be found?"

"Don't do this to yourself. Okay?" His hand hovered over her hair, then descended. He tilted her head to his and kissed her. The kiss was meant to be reassuring. It verged on something else and then moved swiftly a mile over the line. Krista welcomed him with every soft curve of her body.

Finally Jess pulled away. "I didn't mean to start anything."

She wanted to point out that the "anything" he referred to had started days before, but she was afraid of his answer. "Let's go find Tate."

The night was warm and the breeze perfumed with magnolia. It was a night meant for laughter, and there *was* laughter from residents stargazing from front stoops and tourists reveling in the semitropical air. Jess and Krista walked the length and width of the Quarter. Silently they said their goodbyes to places that would haunt them both forever.

All of the spots where Krista knew Tate sometimes stayed were unoccupied.

It was almost midnight before they turned to go home. Krista was quiet all the way to the alleyway into the courtyard. "I wanted to find her," she said. The words were so inadequate for what she was feeling.

Jess wished he could have protected her from another disappointment. "Wanda's going to watch out for her."

"I love her, Jess." She said the words as if she was making a confession.

He loved Krista more because of that, although he couldn't tell her so. "She's quite a kid," he said as they entered the courtyard.

"What's going to happen to her?"

He didn't have to tell her. Tate had years to go before she could legally hold a job or rent an apartment, years when she would have to fight for the most meager existence. "I don't know," he said, putting his hand on the small of her back in comfort. "But Wanda's going to do the best she can. Maybe she'll talk Tate into going home."

A thin wraith rose from the edge of the crumbling fountain. "I'm not going home."

Krista and Jess stopped. Then, with a cry, Krista sprinted across the courtyard to grab Tate for a bear hug. "Where have you been?" She shook her, then grabbed her for another hug. "We covered every inch of the Quarter tonight looking for you!"

Tate pulled away and dusted herself off, although Krista could have pointed out that she was the considerably cleaner one. "Here and there."

"Why didn't you let us know you were all right?"

"I'm always all right." Tate didn't quite look at Krista as she added, "I was worried about you, though."

The small part of Krista's heart that had been left intact broke. "I'm fine. Really."

"I know. I just wanted to make sure." She put her hands behind her back as if she wasn't sure what to do with them.

"Will you come upstairs and talk for a while?"

"I'm staying with some kids. I told them I'd be back by midnight."

"Please, Tate?"

Tate shrugged, but she followed Krista when she started toward the stairs. Jess trailed behind.

At her door, Krista silently pleaded with her eyes as she invited him in, too. He nodded and followed them inside.

Tate looked at all the boxes. "Wanda said you were leaving. Where are you going?"

"Virginia. I'm going to work for Jess."

"What about your sister?"

"It's a long story. I'll be looking for her in a different way."

"Well, I'm glad you're okay." Tate started toward the door. Krista reached it before she did.

"Don't go. Look, please listen to me. Okay? Just for a few minutes?" She hurried on before Tate could answer. "Tate, I can't stand the thought of you out on these streets. I know what can happen. Look what almost did. Won't you think about going home? Maybe things aren't great there, but you and your mom can get help. Somebody will help, I just know it. Can't you stick it out there until you're old enough to leave on your own?"

Jess signaled her to stop, but Krista couldn't. "Tate, please? Won't you think about it?"

Tate looked as if she wanted to bolt, but Krista was between her and the door. "My mom doesn't want me," she mumbled.

"She must, Tate. Maybe she doesn't know how to say it."

"She told me she didn't."

"People say things when they're mad. Call her now. How long has it been since you talked to her?"

Tate started around her, but Krista flattened herself against the door. "How long?" she insisted.

Tate slammed her fist against the door frame in anguish. "I called her the night I stayed here. I left money by the phone. Didn't you see it?"

Krista stared at her. "Not everybody's like you," Tate said, her voice breaking. "My mom told me not to call her again. The only person who ever wanted me was my grandmother, and she's dead!"

Krista wrapped her arms around Tate and pulled her close, although Tate resisted. She felt like a child. She was a child. She was Tate, not Rosie, but in that moment Krista knew Tate belonged to her as surely as if blood bonded them. "I want you," Krista said fiercely. "I love you! Don't think for a minute that I'm going to let you stay out here by yourself. Come live with me. I need you and you need me."

"You're crazy. Let go of me."

"You're going to come with me, and you're going to finish school. You're going to grow up to be a hardheaded, tough lady, and I'm going to watch it all happen. You don't even have to decide. I'll decide for you!"

Tate succeeded in wrestling free. "You're crazy! What would you want with me? You can't find your sister, so you settle for the first kid who comes your way? There something wrong with you?"

"There's something *right* with me," Krista said calmly. "You." She looked past Tate to Jess. In that moment she knew what she might have done. Jess was under no obligation to take Tate into his life, too. He had never told her that he loved her; she had never told him that she loved him. Now she was asking him to shelter a bratty street kid who would kick and scream every step of the way back into a real life. Krista was torn between them, and for a moment she was afraid she would be forced to choose.

"I have this house in Virginia that needs cleaning," Jess said, looking at Krista, not Tate. "Know anyone who might help? The deal includes room and board. I prefer dark hair and blue eyes," he added, before Krista could answer. "And a sassy mouth."

"I'm getting out of here," Tate said. She didn't move.

Jess turned his gaze to her. "You haven't seen much love," he said, moving until they were all three in touching distance. "Let me tell you a little bit about it. Love makes no sense. It doesn't happen when it's supposed to, sometimes. Mothers are supposed to love their kids, only sometimes they can't love anybody. Other times love grows in strange places. One day you look up and see somebody you've known for just a little while, and you realize you love them.''

Tate cleared her throat.

Jess went on. ''Sometimes love happens between a man and a woman old enough to know they want each other.'' He looked at Krista and saw that her eyes were shining. He wanted to grab her and kiss her, and he would have if Tate hadn't been standing there. He wondered why the impossible now seemed so gloriously simple. ''Sometimes a man or a woman realizes they love a child and want that child to grow up with them. That's what's happening here.''

Tate cleared her throat again. ''You're crazy.''

Jess gave her a slow, heartbreaking grin. ''You can say that again.''

''You don't love me. You feel sorry for me because you think I need somebody. But I don't!''

''You're going to be hell to live with, aren't you, honey?'' Krista touched Tate's cheek. ''Look, I promise you can be hell to live with tomorrow and every other day of your life. But right now, could you just tell me you're coming along to Virginia? Please? I need to hear you say it.''

''I'm not going anywhere with anybody!'' Tate pushed past Krista and opened the door. ''You really are crazy. Why would you want me?''

''Because you're infinitely wantable.'' Krista clasped her hands in front of her. She couldn't physically restrain Tate no matter how much she wanted to. ''There's room for everything you've got in the car. Be here at eight if you want breakfast. We're leaving as soon as we're finished eating. It's a long drive.''

''Why would I want to go to Virginia?''

''Because we're going to be there.''

''Crazy!'' Tate slammed the door behind her.

Krista's confidence disappeared right along with Tate. ''Will she come?''

''We'll find her and kidnap her if she doesn't.'' Jess stifled the urge to gather Krista into his arms. He waited.

Krista stood with her back to the door. She had a new understanding of Tate's feelings. Suddenly running away seemed like the easiest choice. "Jess, the things you said to Tate . . ."

He folded his arms to keep from grabbing her. "About cleaning the house?"

She knew he was baiting her. "About love."

"Did you like that?"

She nodded. "The part about love growing in the strangest places. I liked that."

"How about the part about a man and a woman old enough to choose who they'll love? Did you like that, too?"

"I liked it. Yes."

"How much?"

She kept her back rigidly pressed to the door, like the victim of a firing squad. She felt like a victim. She was making herself vulnerable again. She would never learn, but she couldn't stop herself. "I love you. I have for a while. I don't know how you feel, but if I can tell Tate, I can tell you. If this changes anything, just let me know."

"Yeah, it changes things. It changes how fast we can make this arrangement legal." Jess pinned her to the door and kissed her until they had to stop for breath. "I love you, too," he said, kissing her face, her hair. "But you've been through so much I didn't think I could ask you for anything right now."

"There's nothing I wouldn't give you. Nothing!"

In the remaining hours of the night, she proved it over and over again.

Chapter 18

Krista woke in Jess's arms. She knew she would have to get up in a few minutes, but she wanted some time just to lie quietly and think about the days ahead.

She had come to New Orleans to find her sister, and she had failed. Rosie was still living on the streets somewhere, out of her reach. Perhaps they would never be reunited; perhaps someday a miracle would occur. Whatever fate brought her, though, Krista knew she could no longer live as if finding her sister were her only purpose. She would never forget Rosie; she would never stop working to find her, but now Jess and Tate were her family, too.

Jess pulled her closer, as if in his dreams he sensed she was thinking of him. She stroked her palm up his arm to rest on his shoulder. A door had been closed temporarily, but another had been opened. Without Jess she would have lost all her faith in people. Now she had faith and love. And hope. Jess had kept hope alive for her.

"You look like a lady with big thoughts."

Krista smiled sadly and lifted her face for a good morning kiss. "The biggest."

Jess didn't ask what they were. He knew what and whom she would be thinking of every day. "Does leaving New Orleans seem like a defeat?"

"No. Virginia just seems like the next step."

"I like that." He kissed her again and wished they had more time.

She couldn't bear to talk about Rosie. "Do you think Tate will come back this morning?"

"I don't know. If she doesn't, we'll go looking for her."

"We can't really drag her off the street, can we?"

"No."

"There's something wrong when she can live behind a Dumpster while her mother refuses to take her back, but *we're* the ones who can get in trouble if we force her off the streets."

"Even if she comes willingly, we can get in trouble."

"You're not serious?"

"Contributing to the alienation of affection of a child. Operating a foster home without a license. Transporting her across state lines. Maybe even kidnapping."

"You knew all this and you still wanted her to come with us?"

"The laws are supposed to protect kids. I've always believed more in the spirit than the technicalities." He kissed her again and then, reluctantly, pushed himself upright. His back was turned when he spoke. He wasn't sure he was ready to see her expression when he dropped his bombshell. "Besides, I think we should probably comply with the law once we get to Virginia and get a license to operate a foster home, anyway."

Krista sat up. "Foster home?"

"Sally's going to need a place to live."

There was a long silence. Finally Jess could no longer stand the suspense. He turned. Krista was frowning. "How big is this house?"

He held up his hands. "I really didn't have anything like this in mind when I bought it."

"How big?"

"Eight bedrooms. But some of them are small. Very small." He hesitated. "As small as this apartment."

"Were you going to start a commune? A hotel?"

"I bought the property. The house was just there."

"Sally's not·from Virginia and neither is Tate."

"There are arrangements we can make with the child welfare systems in their states. The Place will do the groundwork for us."

"You've been looking into this, haven't you?"

"Just as part of my research for the book." He had the grace to lower his gaze when he saw she didn't believe him.

Krista stood and wrapped her arms around him. "You're a journalist, Jess. And I'm a librarian. What do we know about kids with problems?"

"More than anyone else I know."

He was right. In the last months they had both gotten their degrees on the streets. Whatever idealism they had left was tempered with a gargantuan dose of reality.

"We'll take it one step at a time," he promised.

"One Step. I like it. It'll look good over the front door."

"I want you more than I want anyone or anything else." He buried his face in her hair. "We'll go slow."

"Liar."

And since he couldn't let that go without proving he'd meant what he said, it was after eight before breakfast was on the table.

By nine, it was obvious that Tate wasn't coming. Jess loaded his car, and Krista did a last-minute cleanup and check of their apartments. Both of them went slowly, marking time. By nine-thirty there was nothing left to do.

"We won't find her if she doesn't want to be found," Krista said sadly.

"Go stand by the car and look like you're going to cry."

She thought that would be easy. "Why?"

"Because I had the feeling I was being watched the whole time I was packing."

"You think she's nearby?"

"Yeah."

Krista had done plenty of worse things to try to find Rosie. She had become a consummate actress. She walked slowly to the car, then leaned against the hood and buried her face in her hands. Although she had felt close to tears, now she was too interested in seeing if Tate would come out of hiding to really cry.

She stood there for several minutes. Just as she was about to give up she heard a noise from the road.

Tate was leaning on the other side of the car hood when Krista looked up.

"They eat grits in Virginia?" Tate asked.

"Do you like grits?"

Tate made a face.

"Then no, they don't eat grits in Virginia," Krista lied.

"I like it here. I can make it on my own."

"They eat grits here. They even put gravy on them."

"I'm not your kid. And I'm not your sister."

"Friends, then."

"I don't like people telling me what to do."

"We'll have rules, Tate. Whenever people live together they have to have rules. But we'll make them together. And you'll have your own room. You can do anything you want with it and you can go back to school."

"They'll make me start eighth grade all over again."

"I can help you with schoolwork until you catch up. You're smart. You'll do well."

Tate lifted a ragged canvas pack off the ground. It had been hidden by the car. She watched as Jess joined Krista.

"I might as well come," she said. "But if I don't like it, I don't stay."

"We believe you," Jess said, turning the full force of his smile on her. "But give us a chance. Okay? Don't run because you don't want to do the dishes or because you didn't get an *A* on a science test."

Tate gave a grunt of disgust, as if he were the child and she the adult.

Krista laughed. She wanted to hug Tate, but she decided to save affection until they were safely past the city limits and Tate couldn't retreat as easily. She hugged Jess instead.

"Ready?" he asked, releasing her.

She nodded, her throat thick with emotion.

Jess settled Tate in the back seat with his Walkman and her pack. Cat, who had been napping on the car floor, crawled

onto her lap for company. Krista stood by the car door and
took one last look around. She had come for her sister and she
was leaving with Jess and Tate. "Goodbye, Rosie," she said
softly. "Stay safe. Wherever you are, I love you."

She was in her seat and ready when Jess started the car.

Because he understood what leaving meant to both Tate and
Krista, Jess drove slowly through the French Quarter streets,
giving them time to move from the past into the future. Krista
watched the old buildings go by, a car window slide show of
history.

Jess turned, and they were on the street that she had hurried
down the night he had followed her home. They passed the
boarded-up house where she knew runaways sometimes stayed,
and the deli where she had shown the old man Rosie's photograph. She watched the buildings grow more charming until
they were almost to Canal Street.

A glint of sunstruck gold caught her eye. A girl was walking
down the opposite side of the street. They had passed her before Krista had a chance to see her face. But there was something about the way she walked, something about the way she
carried herself.

Krista didn't even know she had grabbed Jess's arm until he
asked, "What's wrong?"

"There was a girl back there. I just saw her from the
back...." Krista's voice trailed off. There would always be a girl
back there or over there or there, somewhere. Every time Krista
saw red-gold hair or a certain walk, every time she saw a girl
the right age or the right build, she would see Rosie. Every kid had
Rosie's face. And it would always be so.

"Let's go back." Jess looked for a place to turn around.

"No." Krista looked straight ahead. "I don't want to go
back."

"You're sure?"

She touched his arm again, but this time in reassurance. "I'm
ready to go home."

Mr. Majors was tired. Instead of stocking nearly empty
shelves, he was sitting behind the deli counter like a man of
leisure. The deli had belonged to his father before him, and he

had worked its counter since he was old enough to see over it. Now, at sixty, he was looking forward to the day when he could hang a "Closed" sign on the door for good.

Nothing tired him more than the kids. For the most part they were good kids, but they read him like an open book. They didn't know that he'd run away once himself when he was thirteen, or that hunger had driven him back to a home that had never known any love. All they knew was that he'd fill their stomachs for next to nothing, even if all he could spare was milk and day-old doughnuts.

They stole from him sometimes, although rarely more than a candy bar or pack of gum. Sometimes they hung around just to talk. He didn't know why. Maybe it was because he listened—he didn't know why nobody else did. They were good kids. For the most part.

He was sneaking a look at the newspaper when the first runaway of the morning came in. The kids could never fool him. They were easy to spot. Dirty hair, dirty clothes, something to carry their stuff in. There was a particular expression they kept on their faces, a blank stare that hid anything they were feeling. He knew what they were feeling. He remembered.

This girl looked familiar, although he wasn't sure why. She was blond and pretty. She was also noticeably pregnant. That was one of the saddest things he ever saw, almost as bad as the sick kids, or the ones who were obviously using drugs. Her eyes were unusual, almost turquoise in color, but they stared right through him.

"Someone told me you'll sell doughnuts and milk cheap to kids."

He thought of the baby. The poor little thing didn't have a chance. "Milk, yeah. I'm out of doughnuts today, darlin'," he lied. "How about a sandwich? I can make you a roast beef po'boy for the same price."

Something flickered across her face. "Why?"

He knew better than to lie again or tell the truth. This one was proud. "Because."

"It's your store."

He hoped not for long. "Dressed?"

She laughed humorlessly. "Or undressed? What's that mean?"

"That means do you want tomato and lettuce on it? You're not from here, are you?" He turned and got out the French bread, but he didn't keep his back to her long. He understood the kids, but he didn't trust them.

"I'm not from here," she agreed. "I was here once for a few days, but I've been away."

"Back to stay?"

"Passing through." The girl turned his newspaper around and started leafing through it. He thought that was unusual. Most of the kids who came in were more interested in trying to pocket something than in reading. He slapped mayonnaise on the French bread and stacked it high with roast beef dripping with gravy. He added more tomatoes and lettuce than he normally did. He wondered when she had last eaten a vegetable.

He was wrapping the sandwich in white butcher paper when he noticed her staring at something on the front page. She was staring. Not reading. "Paper's full of bad news," he said conversationally.

The girl laughed. The sound chilled him to the core.

He peeked over the counter at the paper. There didn't seem to be anything unusual there. All the normal news. It hadn't even been a very bad week. The headlines were about Senator Hayden Barnard, who had just announced his campaign for president. It wasn't exactly a surprise.

"Don't see too many kids your age paying attention to the paper," he said.

The girl looked at him. Her eyes gave nothing away. "Do you believe I used to know him?" she asked. Her hand dropped to the headlines.

Mr. Majors had heard everything in his sixty years. Most everything he had heard was lies. "Hard to believe," he said— and meant that he didn't.

The girl laughed her bitter laugh. She fished in her pocket for change and laid it on the counter. "He's a bastard," she said.

"Maybe you did know him."

She took her sandwich, stuffing it in a bag she was carrying. "Maybe I did," she said. She nodded and was gone.

He wondered about her for the rest of the day. He always wondered about the kids.

That night he called a realtor and asked her to list the deli for sale.

* * * * *

◖ *Diamond Jubilee Collection*

It's our 10th Anniversary...
and *you* get a present!

This collection of early Silhouette
Romances features novels written
by three of your favorite authors:

ANN MAJOR—*Wild Lady*
ANNETTE BROADRICK—*Circumstantial Evidence*
DIXIE BROWNING—*Island on the Hill*

* These Silhouette Romance titles were first published in the early 1980s
  and have not been available since!

* Beautiful Collector's Edition bound in antique green simulated leather to
  last a lifetime!

* Embossed in gold on the cover and spine!

This special collection will not be sold in retail stores and is only available
through this exclusive offer.
Look for details in all Silhouette series published in June, July and August.